The GYRE

ADVANCE PRAISE

"Stacy Carlson has written an enthralling story of flawed, fragile humanity and the uncanny redemptive power of nature at its most brutal. *The Gyre* is a journey through a stark, glittering wilderness, an unforgettable landscape both terrible and holy in equal measure."

—Lynn Coady, Giller Prize-winning author of *Hellgoing*

"Mythic journeys, fairy tales of ice and snow, sailors' vodka-addled and lusty dreams, a monk's poetic yearnings—*The Gyre* has it all! As we follow Arkady Afanasyev on his journey into the farthest reaches of the Arctic in search of his teacher and himself, we encounter story upon story strung together, like pearls, showing us how we are connected to the water, the ice, the ground, the light, and each other. *The Gyre* pulls you in and in and into its profoundly beautiful spiral of a story."

—Kathryn Nuernberger, author of *Held: Essays in Belonging*

"This is an absolutely astonishing saga, packed at every turn with innumerable tangential sagas of survival, magic, incomprehensible courage and persistence, and—always—the great, turning, harsh natural world. It zooms the reader to a long ago and far away universe of struggle, quest, agony, and enchantment. Fearlessly imagined and capably written, Stacy Carlson has created a particular, complex, and searingly unforgettable mythology."

—Joan Frank, author of *Juniper Street: A Novel* and *Late Work: A Literary Autobiography of Love, Loss, and What I Was Reading*

"A gripping novel—both a rip-roaring yarn and a deep inquiry into what makes us human. Like a Caspar David Friedrich painting, Carlson's *The Gyre* places the human against the immense backdrop of an unforgiving landscape—here, the high-Arctic archipelago of Svalbard—with dazzling results."

—Colin Dickey, author of *Ghostland: An American History in Haunted Places* and *Afterlives of the Saints*

The GYRE

A Novel

Stacy Carlson

Alternating Current Press
Boulder, Colorado

Library of Congress Control Number: 2026941071
ISBN-13 (paperback): 978-1-946580-62-7
ISBN-10 (paperback): 1-946580-62-7
ISBN-13 (hardcover): 978-1-946580-65-8
ISBN-13 (ebook): 978-1-946580-66-5

Cover artwork: Petra Pezibear and Leah Angstman © 2026
Author photo: Djuna Swecker © 2026

Printed in the United States of America

10 9 8 7 6 5 4 3 2 1

Also by Stacy Carlson:

Among the Wonderful

For my beloved parents,
Stanley and Susan Carlson

The farthest reaches of the north are a
configuration of the imagination.
—Aritha van Herk

CHAPTER 1

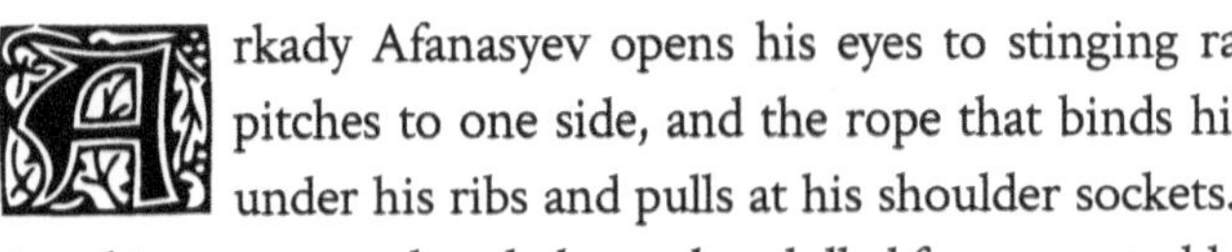

1860

The White Sea

rkady Afanasyev opens his eyes to stinging rain. He pitches to one side, and the rope that binds him digs under his ribs and pulls at his shoulder sockets. In the time his eyes were closed, the sea has dulled from gray to black and the morning light, however wan, has died. Beyond the icy rivulets streaming down his face, the lights of Solovetsky Monastery recede as if the known world were rolling off the horizon on a mechanical spool that, in its place, spits forth a widening void.

"You, who are always becoming and becoming, who can never be fixed at a single point, anchor me now, or I'll spin away forever," Arkady whispers into the gale. "The wave that wrecks the worthiest ship has only a teacup of your strength."

The voices of men rise from below deck, singing some infernal shanty. In the back of his throat, Arkady tastes his last meal from the monastery kitchen: salt cod and cooked grain, eaten from a bowl at the kitchen hearth. The memory soothes him until the waves jerk the lodja, his equilibrium jumps to starboard, and he vomits. His resolve also loosens, but it is too late to go back. It is far too late for that.

"I desire nothing but to walk the path you have set before me," Arkady shouts. "Only by giving up the filth within and without do I truly become yours!"

He smiles through slick fluid on his chin. Behind him, a hatch flies open.

"Ah! The priest." The voice rumbles like two rough stones knocking together. If this creature falls overboard, he'll sink straight to hell. "What are you screaming about? Enjoying some sweet salt air?" the voice roars. "You're a sea dog, why didn't you say so? Won't you come below? Evgeny's got his drum, and we're sailing across worlds, little priest. We're sailing on Starostin's wings."

Standing at the rail, the man lists badly to port, but he's counterbalanced by the heavy cut-glass bottle in his hand. It's an old Pomor, born on the White Sea and raised to pursue exactly this frightful journey north. He's a great tangle of leather, silver hair, buckles, and grime.

"*Vsyó propalo bez vesti!* We're all lost, aren't we?" the Pomor confronts the sea. "Spitsbergen's cursing us back to the forests. We're fucked!" The man raises the bottle above his mangy head. "But not yet! I'll not yet be imprisoned. The island will bear enough hides for one more season."

He addresses a place in the sky where, if they were still at Solovetsky, sunlight would be illuminating the island's many stones: lichen-scarred faces set into walls, quartz-threaded boulders scattered in wild meadows between the lakes, and farthest away from the monks where they can be most easily ignored, stones arranged in spirals long ago by pagan hands.

"I'll not cut trees for some mainland cunt!" cries the Pomor. "I'm free, and I always will be, even if the world is not. *Poshol ty k chortu.* Go straight to the devil."

He drinks. He turns from the rail and leans against the mast, directly above where Arkady sits. Arkady trembles with distaste.

"One last time we ride the sea to Spitsbergen. I have yet one more chance to walk upon her beaches, to lay my cheek against her mossy tits." The sailor's voice softens. "To stay for a winter on

Spitsbergen, like the great ones have before me, to face the Dog one last time."

A jolt from the sea brings the Pomor to his knees. He lays his forehead on Arkady's shoulder, and a vapor of spirits sterilizes the air between them.

"But those are just words," the Pomor whispers. "The truth is I am afraid of the long night. I am afraid of the wind's howling and the winter's unending darkness."

"You're spilling liquor on my leg," hisses Arkady, trying to shrug him away, but the old man's head turns to stone on Arkady's shoulder; he has gone senseless. For the hundredth time, Arkady tries to wriggle out of the ropes and fails.

A pattern of riffles materializes across the surface of the deep and then spirals away, replaced by tiny whitecaps rolling opposite. Arkady watches these traces of much larger, invisible forces moving in a dance that encompasses everything all at once: all lodjas sailing north, all men aboard ships crafted by the hands of their grandfathers from felled trees of the boreal forest, and ahead of them, all ancestors of the sea beasts that will be hunted down.

"This is your way, oh Lord, for those with eyes to see," Arkady murmurs. "I am on the path you set before me. I see your divine hand. I feel it pushing me forward."

His legs ache, and he can't feel his arms, twisted as they are behind him, and yet his fear ebbs. After all, today is Saint Basil's Day. Basil, the fool-for-God who traveled bareheaded, barefoot, and in rags. Basil bore many hardships, including storms at sea, and he ventured in faith to the cluttered wilderness.

Arkady has been tied to the mast because of a belief among the Pomors that a man on his first voyage out of the White Sea is in grave danger. At the prospect of the vast northern ocean and perilous hunting grounds beyond, the untested man's soul is so frightened that it abandons the body, returns to the mainland, and leaves the Pomors with one less hunter for the season. But wouldn't Arkady's soul be just as able to leave him if he were below deck? The truth is he is tied there for the amusement of the men, and in turn forced to see God in wind patterns. *And what better vocation is there on earth*, he thinks.

Suddenly, the old Pomor jumps up, listening. "Feel that? Feel the pull, little priest? We've reached the straits."

Arkady feels nothing. "I am not a priest."

"We're onto the straits at last!" The Pomor grins like a child and swerves astern to embrace the helmsman. Then he goes below, dragging his fate behind him.

CHAPTER 2

ventually, the Pomors carry Arkady below. They dry his face and put him on the bench beside them. They jostle him with their elbows, pull a rough woolen sweater over his head, and make no reference to his chafed wrists and sore shoulders. He drinks bitter tea and sweet fish broth, then the Pomors tuck him away on a narrow pallet built against the lodja's hull. They pull woolen socks over his feet and cover him in sheepskins.

My flesh is weak, but my heart is sure: I cast off my tether to the world and am adrift in your grace. I will chase your holy shadow into the wilds until the end of time. Arkady's prayer is a constant, unwinding thread in his mind.

In the pocket of his wool overcoat, he finds his knotted prayer rope and slips it on his wrist. In the other pocket, he runs his fingers over a bundle of letters tied with string. Even without looking, he knows the slanted, hurried words written across those pages: *Arkady, you must join me in Uncreated Light, which illuminates all things. Come quickly.*

His hope surges, and his vision clears. The hull sheltering him is made from bands of dark and gold wood grain, a curved whale belly staved by beveled ribs. Arkady prays continuously for this whale to spit him onto the shores of his divine path, just as that other great fish released Jonah. Even the trip up to the railing to toss his piss bucket and retch into the foam is his liturgy. But the path before him unfurls wave by wave and disappears just as quickly.

During the voyage, the Pomors sleep half the day and spend the rest knitting socks and hunting vermin among the food stores. They drink ale upon waking and honey wine after breakfast. Their leader, Evgeny, sings at his post by the iron stove while the rest of the men work above deck at the sails or just stand watch with their heads into the wind. There is one with black hair tied up in a braid. Next to him is many-buckled Pasha, the one who visited Arkady at the mast.

Arkady apologizes to God for the Pomors' depravity by praying for their salvation between Prime and Terce, the hours of Adam's fall from the garden. When Caiaphas appears, Arkady prays more fervently that the Pomors will rise from their faithlessness even as he knows they will not. By the time the dove flutters into view at Sext, he is exhausted and hates the Pomors anew for their earthly fixations on pelts, drinking, and foul language, and most of all, their stories.

Every evening the men drink vodka under the stinking oil lamp, and each one is grandfather and child in turn. This time it's Evgeny, trimming his beard at the porthole, who eventually clears his throat and speaks. Arkady watches the others sink into dumb rapture at the sound of Evgeny's godless incantation.

"The evening is long, and our journey is only just begun. I can tell you a story to help the time pass. Do you remember the Spitsbergen Dog's cave, way out beyond the Citadel Range, east of the inland glacier fields?"

And a chorus of voices rises: "Yes, Evgeny! We remember," and, "Go on, we have nothing but time."

At first Arkady disappears from the filth of their stories. He inhabits his prayer instead of the creaking galley. But as the voyage spins on, without the monastery's bells and services and stone-lined paths to guide him, he loses track of the ever-unfurling, ever-renewing liturgy. And as the evenings grow longer—not yet because of a waning sun but because the Pomors are more and more taken with their tale-telling—the men go below earlier and earlier. And most of all because their stories begin to sound familiar, Arkady in his weakness listens to the lies of the world.

"Well, the Spitsbergen Dog lives away from any place the Pomors would ever go since we can hunt what we need at the coast. Why would we ever cross the shifting backs of glaciers?" Evgeny wipes his razor on a rag, puts it away, and takes his place at the head of the table. "Somewhere north of Mount Vivien, the Dog lives in a great ice cavern with carved steps spiraling down into the rocky heart of the island, where a spring from deep, deep below flows with water hot enough to scald. Here the Dog makes his lair. From here he lies in wait and perceives the moment when a Pomor lodja approaches the south cape. Just as the helmsman changes course to follow the coast, the Dog's ears prick up.

"The Dog wants men, but he cannot take them outright. He follows each lodja, slinking along shore and swimming across fjords as the ship navigates the bays to Horn Sound. If the Pomors do not make an offering there, the Dog takes them along the sunken rocks. If they do not leave gifts at Bell Mountain, he takes them. If they do not thank him properly for the bounties of meat, hides, oil, and eiderdown, he takes them. If the men are foolish, if they go into Spitsbergen unprepared, he takes them all for his army.

"Yes, the Dog is a knight of this land, but his commander is the Twelfth Sister, and she takes men in her own way. It is she, not the Dog, who arouses real terror."

At this, the Pomors roar and smash their cups together. Arkady withdraws as far as he can into his berth, but his ears still can't hear the liturgy.

"The Dog would take you, but he lives by a code. He only takes men who make mistakes. But the Twelfth Sister's motives are borne of her own twisted soul and cannot be understood in the world of men. Dark and virulent, she would have you from the inside out and keep you alive for her own amusement.

"During the long night of winter, she dwells in the Dog's hot springs, in the company of her eleven Sisters. They move slowly in the froth, with pink skin and long hair fanning out in the water. When the moon is full, the Twelfth Sister gets out of the water, and mist rises from her body. Her nipples are pink and hard as bottlenecks! She emerges from the cave ripe with desire for humans and takes up her fur cloak. Trailing steam, she creeps into the dreams of Pomors asleep in their winter camps, and she slithers in next to them. Their weakness is her portal."

The stories needle Arkady's flesh. He trembles, and his prayers fly away without touching his heart. Is he weaker than a jellied insect? He flails against the Pomor's words. *Guide me out of this dark story into your clear, uncreated light, which sin can never touch. Take me away from these men into the realms of light, where you are the only word. The Pomors are dead husks. Chaff blown north in the wind of your breath. I am not with them.*

The men talk unceasingly of Spitsbergen. Seasons of abundance, when reindeer make pacts with hunters and the thick-skinned walruses willingly bare their necks. In hushed voices, they speak of ships so loaded with fur and oil that they barely make it back to Arkhangelsk. But when they arrive on the mainland, the Pomors are richer than rich. With equal amazement, the men describe the fine liquor they pour down their throats back home and waking the next morning in terrible pain, their mothers leaning over them as if they were children again, which in Arkady's view they are.

Those who'd spent a winter on Spitsbergen speak softly of the long night: barrels of scurvy grass, cloudberry milk, and the strength required to hack a way out of snowbound huts. Evenings during which all of human history past, present, and future was revealed in a single game of chess. Talking fires and ice bears as big as minke whales rearing out of nightblack water to snatch men from their oarboats.

Finally, Arkady weakens and surrenders. He listens because, in truth, the stories carry him straight back through time to his grandfather Nikolai's low voice as the old man rocked Arkady's bed with one foot and told him about the white foxes' weddings, talking reindeer, and the great bird way—that milky path in the sky where the souls of the dead travel on clear winter nights. As Arkady hovers near sleep, rocking now with the lodja far out at sea, Nikolai is before him, braiding rope and telling tales, his eyes roving here and there. His grandfather gleaned stories from everywhere and saw fabulous creatures wherever he looked. "Just open your eyes, little one, and you will see them, too." Arkady had inherited his grandfather's skittering gaze and restless heart, but unlike Nikolai's wondrous visions, Arkady sees nothing.

A metal cup clatters to the floor, and Arkady jerks back to the lodja and to the single, truest fact: Yes, he is going to Spitsbergen but not to become a Pomor. *Never! I abandon you and all Pomors forever. So my own flesh and blood wouldn't raise me? So you abandoned me? Well, I have no ties to any flesh and blood at all. I abandon you.*

Once the lodja reaches the south cape of Spitsbergen and turns north along the coast, the men speak of Starostin, always Starostin. It's as if the Pomor chieftain were still alive and watching over them, even though the truth is Starostin's long dead, and none of these men ever even knew him. Starostin, who could pilot a lodja through any storm. Who laughed at the ice bears baring their teeth on the floes. Starostin, who lived on Spitsbergen for decades and refused to go back to the mainland, even to die. The long night was nothing to him, the Pomors marvel. Bergs the size of mountains were nothing. The great Starostin: patron saint of the Pomors.

Once the lodja passes the mouth of Horn Sound, it scuds quickly north, and the sailors spend all day at the rail, even though fog hides the world. But most of the time, Arkady stays below. His berth has become a whole cathedral; it is from there that he accesses the Christbody, so he stays there, traveling the hours.

Evgeny forces him to walk the deck a little each day. "You want to live, don't you? You need your strength. Spitsbergen, her arms are strong. She'll wrestle you down and keep you there."

Arkady's above deck when the men sight Bell Mountain through a break in the fog. Their shouts startle him, but Evgeny springs up from below and grasps his shoulders. Somehow, they are dancing.

"We knew your grandfather, little priest. Nikolai Aleksandrovich Afanasyev, the white-trousered hunter! He was a great one. We won't let the long night take you, nor the Sisters, neither."

"Nikolai Afanasyev," someone else shouts. "Part of Starostin's own crew!"

Evgeny pulls Arkady to his chest, and, despite the seriousness of Arkady's intentions in Spitsbergen, the faithlessness and filth of the Pomors, the fear of what lies ahead—despite it all, he sobs into Evgeny's shoulder because this is the first time anyone has embraced Arkady or even touched him for as long as he can remember.

Soon the men rush to their berths and throw sweaters and bottles into their crates. Landfall next morning, they repeat to one another so often it drowns out Arkady's prayers.

After dinner Evgeny lays a paper-wrapped bundle in Arkady's hands. "Here are some thick socks we knit for you. And a seal hat with fox fur inside. You wear it under a sealskin hood. We made you walrus boots during the voyage, see, stuffed with eiderdown."

Arkady recoils. "The Lord is my sole protector," he says. Because people are unpredictable and cannot be trusted. "These trinkets are nothing."

When Arkady is not looking, Evgeny slips the things into Arkady's bag. The Pomors are troubled because Arkady has brought almost nothing and will surely die.

CHAPTER 3

hey leave the lodja moored in foggy Bell Harbor. Before Arkady leaves the cabin for the last time, he stops in front of the ship's stove and studies his warped reflection on the side of Evgeny's great kettle. His black hair is a tangled, dirty halo that he tries to flatten. His hair has always been a problem: too thick, coarse, and curly to lie as soberly as a monk's hair should, but when cut short, the curls spring up, so buoyant and wayward that his cassock and downturned eyes become a joke. Usually, he loads his hair with oil, which stains his clothes but eliminates most of the other problems. Now that he is away from Solovetsky, his hair is a wild bird's nest, with his wide eyes peering out like two strange eggs. His face is one dark question under razor-straight brows. Arkady scoops a bit of seal lard out of a tin by the stove and smears it onto his head in an uncertain bid to tame the curls.

Pasha rows Arkady and six other men in the oarboat over colorless water to a place where a wooden ladder hangs down from the sky. Arkady becomes frightened. The thick fog creates an illusion of light, but beyond it he senses enormous dark things. The air on his cheek seems to be the stroking hand of a drowned child. Before he has a chance to move on his own, the Pomors lift him onto the ladder, and one of them—he does not look down to see who—follows him up so closely that Arkady is practically riding the other man's shoulders. At the top, Evgeny hoists Arkady from the armpits and sets him on a narrow dock. Through the fog, he sees men on shore running toward them. He prays that one of them is the man he's come to find.

While the Pomors unload crates, Arkady tries to walk to shore, but after a few steps, his legs give way, and he crumples sideways with a shriek.

Evgeny scoops him up by the scruff of his coat. "Here, here. The sea will loosen her grip tomorrow. You'll have to be patient until then. Hold tight to me, priest. I'll take you to land."

As soon as their feet touch the seabeaten stones, the Pomors whoop and skip, giddy as children. They hug the men who've come to meet them.

"Today, on the anniversary of the beheading of the Forerunner John the Baptist, I take my first steps into the wilderness," Arkady whispers. He considers this date an excellent sign; for, among other things, wasn't John the Baptist's death the result of the sins of worldly striving? What better day to slough off the chains of society? *Let me come into the pure, open space of your grace*, he prays.

The sea recedes behind him. Stooped and off-balance, he follows Evgeny up a moss-bordered path that fades from boulder to cobble to pebble to soil. He walks slowly while Pomors bound past him like puppies. The fog's outer layers dampen his bare head.

You are just ahead. Your strength will dissolve this fog with one exhale. Your mercy—

Arkady bumps into Evgeny's chest. He hadn't noticed the Pomor turn around, but now Evgeny regards him with a stern expression.

"Listen to me," Evgeny says. "Listen as best you can."

Arkady still prays—*Your mercy is so penetrating that it touches even these heathen beasts*

"Do not go off on your own in this land. Do you understand me? You will be lost in the fog. The ice bears will kill you. You will freeze and die."

Your strength can melt the hearts of pagan overlords and also freeze the world.

Evgeny shakes his head and continues up the path. They ascend the saddle between two ridges and walk down the other side.

Schoonhoven camp was built in layers and at cross purposes over the course of centuries. Evgeny tells Arkady that, long before the Dutch ever came to Spitsbergen, Schoonhoven was known to Karelian hunters under a different name, which is now forgotten.

"Those were the greatest hunters of the north," Evgeny says. "They built their main camp right here, and it served them well. From here they sent hundreds of men up the coast. Barentz claimed it for Holland a century and a half later, but the only reason he ever found it was because his men were lost in a fog just like this one, and they sailed here blind. Hidden behind the boasting words of many captains, fog is the true hero.

"The Dutch broke down the door of the ancient hut, which, by that time, the Pomors—our great-great-grandfathers—used every season. Those Dutch bastards found barrels of brined reindeer meat and dried cloudberries and scurvy grass. Enough to save their rotten lives."

Schoonhoven appears before them, a weatherbeaten monolith at the top of the rise, made of silver driftwood at a chaos of angles. As tall as the monastery's refectory building, it is a ramshackle affair and full of splinters, as if the sea itself tossed up this tangle of wrack held together by cords of kelp. How ugly secular buildings can be. How aimless in the world.

Panting, Arkady pauses on the trail behind Evgeny and spies a small open door on the side of the massive hut and a woman standing there. She is too far away to see clearly, but her skirt blows in the wind. She clutches a baby in one arm while, with the other, she strokes a tethered reindeer. Her head turns suddenly toward the path, and Arkady straightens up. She looks in their direction for a moment then walks back inside, shutting the driftwood door behind her.

"The Dutch ate our food cache, used our fuel, and lived. Instead of thanks, though, the cowards tore down our hut and built a flimsier camp in the same spot and claimed it for Holland," Evgeny mutters. "Many lives were then lost right here, little one, and after all that fighting, Dutch and Pomor skeletons lay together, just over that knoll. Because of their newer guns, the Dutch kept Schoonhoven all through the time of the whales, but after that it was ours again and remains ours still. Your own grandfather spent many seasons here, gleaning the land."

The main door of the hut flings open, and an enormous man sprints toward them, arms outstretched. Arkady dives behind Evgeny.

"Evgeny, it *is* you. You've lost me ten rubles, you devil!"

"Kuzma, the Sister finally got you, I see. You've spent too many winters in Spitsbergen. Now here you are, *proklyatyy darmoyed!* Lazy good-for-nothing, knocking pears out of a tree with your prick!"

The two men clasp each other by the shoulders.

"*Khot' by tebya k chyortu zasosalo!*" the enormous one cries. "May the devil swallow you up, but not before you go sit on a prick. You know that a Sister has had me for two years now!" Kuzma gestures behind him. He is a full head taller even than Evgeny, with a bright-golden beard and pale eyes.

"Brother, we are here," Evgeny says.

"But so late in the season? The storms on the straits! You tempted the Dog with this one."

"We almost didn't come, Kuzma, but there was a night in Arkhangelsk, a long night with many songs and more vodka. We promised Starostin we would come again for the winter hunt. One last time."

"Don't speak to me of endings," growls Kuzma. "You know I'll never leave Spitsbergen, even after the last white fox is sewn into the collar of a fancy whore's cloak."

"The next Starostin, are you? Well, good luck. I'll be back on the mainland in my wife's warm bed."

Kuzma's clear eyes dart to Arkady. "Who is this, a Moscow tax collector?"

"A holy fool."

"Do you know Father Vasily?" Arkady blurts. "Where is he?"

But Kuzma just grasps Evgeny's arm and pulls him toward Schoonhoven. "We've got pickled salmon!" he shouts. "Fried reindeer lips, brown bread, and cloudberry cakes!"

Men swarm Schoonhoven's hall, pulling benches from dark corners, climbing across the rafters to cut down strings of cured fish and lower barrels of honey wine flavored with berries from the mainland. The cavernous hut has many small rooms built slapdash along its walls, and where there aren't makeshift rooms, there are benches and ledges, all cluttered with crates, folded blankets, and a baffling assortment of tools, traps, ropes, clothing, and boots. Arkady looks here and there, up and down, across the main hall and out the small windows to the wall of fog. His eyes won't fix on anything until he spots a huge brass samovar, which bears the languorous, enameled roses of a Moscow drawing room.

For the remainder of that day and into the night, the Pomors busy themselves with debauchery. Led by the now bare-chested Kuzma, a group of men walk to the banya carrying fresh birch branches Evgeny has brought from Arkhangelsk; one or two of their brethren chop driftwood to fuel the sauna. Later, Kuzma, heavily scarred and boiled red, runs naked across the tundra, trailing strings of curses behind him until he plunges into the sea. Man after man follows, steaming and sputtering and renewing himself.

Arkady eats fish and drinks cold, delicious water. Unlike the kvass they drank during the voyage, this water glimmers like polished silver on the tongue. It must be Vespers by the time he drinks his fill of it, but he stays among the Pomors instead of seeing to his prayers. They pile their plates with salmon and reindeer meat. The dozen men of Schoonhoven camp blend with the lodja Pomors into a roar of beards and bad breath, singing and making endless toasts to their precious Starostin and to the great ocean gyre that flings a river of warm water up the coast of Spitsbergen, and within it the walrus that adorn the ends of Pomor spears and turn to gold coins in their purses. The gyre also conjures warmer air along the coast, which serves the reindeer, foxes, and eiders. Without the gyre, there'd be no reason to come here and no stories to tell.

"The very first season Starostin came north, an ice bear knelt down before him," Pasha starts off.

The men have gathered around the great table, swaying in unison. Arkady is with them, annoyed but listening.

"The rest of his crew ran off, but Starostin greeted the beast as a friend. In return, the bear told Starostin the secrets of hunting on the pack ice. At the end of the season, Starostin's sack was full of ringed seal furs! You know what they go for on the mainland. All the rest of his men could only hunt harbor seals, as we still do.

"The Dog wanted Starostin more than any other man. The moment Starostin dropped anchor in Bell Sound, the Dog appeared, sniffing the air. As protector of the island, the Dog's vow is to destroy the ones who kill carelessly or who take and take without giving anything in return. So, he watched Starostin through day and night, waiting for a wasteful move or a careless shot that would maim but not kill. But somehow Starostin knew the place even better than the Dog himself and loved it just as deeply. This made the Dog madder than mad! So, when Starostin finally arrived with a lodja full of lumber and a plan to stay on Spitsbergen for the rest of his life, the Dog howled with rage. For his part, Starostin whistled for the Dog to come to him, and he showed the Dog special gifts of meat and vodka, but the Dog would neither come nor listen. He just waited and watched for Starostin to make a mistake.

"After Starostin built his cabin, he brought his wife Natalya from the mainland because Starostin wanted his children born on the island, and for his children's children to live there, too. When the Dog saw sturdy, rosy-cheeked Natalya picking her way along the beach, he went all quiet and licked his lips.

"The Dog watched the woman all summer as she shot eiders and roasted them up. She fished the streams and walked the slopes, and after the season's calves were weaned, she shot and skinned two reindeer.

"After tracking her for weeks and months, even the Dog was ready to give up. But one day, she came walking over the slopes toward the cabin, carrying an armful of delicate flowers. You see, anywhere else a bouquet of flowers would not even be worth mentioning. But for the Dog, this bundle of sorrel, knotweed, and tiny yellow poppies meant the difference between life and death. In the way he ruled, humans must use everything they took, whether feathers, oil, flesh, or fur. Nothing at all could be wasted or the balance would tip. According to his logic, wastefulness and carelessness would knock the island off its axis and open the door to more and more discord until who knew but the whole world might fall to ruin. That's why he took men and kept their souls for when he might need them.

"The Dog knew what it took for the flowers to bloom this far north, and he knew the small, hearty insects that relied on their nectar and pollen to live through the season. To cut their stems and use the plants for decoration was indeed a mistake.

"He loped toward Natalya, at first growling and then singing his killing song. She looked over her shoulder and dropped the flowers. She raised her musket, but the Dog knocked her down before she could fire. He had planned to run her off the bluffs, but a strike to the throat would do.

"Before he could take Natalya's neck in his jaws, a musket ball whizzed past the Dog's head and tore off the top of one ear. He yelped, and this distraction was enough for Natalya to slip out from under him. For a wild moment, they looked at each other and both realized that Starostin, aiming from the porch of his cabin, had not aimed to kill the Dog but only scare him off.

"Quicker than quick, Starostin was between them with an unsheathed blade, lunging at the Dog and pulling his wife behind him. Although the Dog knew he could still take her right then, he also understood the killing moment had passed. He lived by a code, after all: the rules of the island, where circumstance shifts abruptly, like the wind and weather. A fjord could be piled with old snow and thick ice, with a full season of bear, fox, and hunters' tracks etched across it. And all at once, there'd be a thunderous crack, and just like that, the ice would break up and float away. A seal's head would pop up where the ice had been, and then the curved back of a narwhal, and then eiders. In any event, the Dog slipped out of reach and disappeared.

"All through that autumn, as the dark started rising, the Dog sat on the scree above Starostin's camp listening to the two humans argue: 'Why didn't you kill that beast when you had the chance? What if it had killed me?' And Starostin, reasoning with her as only a Pomor could, 'Certain rules govern this place, my heart. The Dog is part of that. I could no more kill him than kill the sun that sustains us!' Soon enough, winter took hold, and the couple spent more and more time in the cabin. 'If you wouldn't shoot the Dog when I was in danger, I am not safe at all! Why, you'd probably choose a fine ice-bear pelt over me and use me for bait!' And Starostin: 'How can you say such a thing?' And Natalya: 'How can I say such a thing? How could you be so stupid? I saw what I saw. Clipped his ear, and I was about to be torn to pieces!' For weeks the shouting went on and on, and then it stopped.

"For months, the Dog watched Starostin or Natalya emerge from the cabin to carry firewood from their stack or to fill the bucket with snow to melt for water. They no longer spoke to each other. This confused and saddened the Dog, and he whined for hours with his tail between his legs. He did not harm humans for sport.

He meant only to uphold his vow. The humans came to hunt, and the Dog was there to make sure they didn't tip the balance, and when they did, he tipped it back again. He had no experience of the human heart. The arguing had disturbed him, but he found the silence excruciating. He felt sorry for Starostin and for Natalya, too.

"When spring came, Natalya was at the bluff every day, searching the horizon. The only time the Dog ever saw her smile was the day the first lodja appeared. She didn't care that she'd have to wait on the ship another month for the hunters to bring back enough reindeer and seal furs to fill the hull. She packed her things and left Starostin's cabin without looking back.

"Starostin drank with his men and cried in their arms. His Pomors held him up and nursed him through that first summer without her. He would have no children in Spitsbergen after all, and the children of his children would not people the island.

"The Dog retreated inland and stayed away from the Pomor hunting grounds that year. The moon continued to rotate around the earth and the earth around the sun. The ice bears moved across the ice and tundra, and lodjas came and went with the migrating birds, and since that time, the Dog has left the Pomors alone."

In the silence that follows this tale, the Pomors sip vodka from tiny silver cups. Silver-haired Pasha looks into the distance and strokes his beard. The Pomors toast Starostin yet again, and outside the fog keeps a firm hold over the land.

In this lull, Arkady slips in among the men. "Do you know Father Vasily?" he asks, walking from bench to bench, beseeching one sodden Pomor after another like a beggar. "Is he near this place? Where does he live?"

The Pomors smile and gesture for him to sit with them, to drink their devil's brew. They tell him to calm down. "Celebrate," they say. "You've come to a wondrous land!"

Arkady frowns. Each Pomor claims he's never heard of Vasily, but how can that be? Father Vasily is the holy eremite of

Spitsbergen and God's only emissary in this northernmost land. A dazzling soon-to-be saint, Father Vasily is Arkady's own guiding light—his Starostin. Ascending greater spiritual heights, accomplishing more in the name of divine grace than anyone, ordained or not. But the Pomors only shrug at his blessed name.

Father Vasily is the most recent in a long line of northern hermits who embody a holy paradox: Their passion for God draws them away from society into the wilderness, and yet other people, devout or simply seeking forgiveness or relief from the weight of past sins, are drawn to the holy man like insects to a flame. Once the world presses in, the holy man retreats farther away into the wilds.

Vasily began his religious pursuits in the taiga. But perhaps his conversations with squirrels, birds, and the occasional pilgrim were too distracting. After a decade, he deemed his life in the forest too easy, too full of chatter. Vasily moved farther into wilderness than anyone before, including even the Desert Fathers of Scripture, Arkady is convinced. For the past twelve years, Vasily has lived his continuous prayer in Spitsbergen. And these Pomors—what fools!—do nothing but embody the opposite: gluttony, pride, blasphemy, and unfathomable appetite for all that is earthly, from honey wine to their dreadful incantations of Starostin's exploits.

Arkady is sure there is something keen and mocking in the eyes of the men, so he finally leaves. He makes a kind of nest in a far corner of the longhouse among crates and old wool blankets, up against a partition that mostly blocks him from the ruckus.

When Arkady was sixteen years old, the already-famous Vasily stayed at Solovetsky for several weeks while he prepared to go north. Vasily walked along the monastery's paths, deep in contemplation, with the tip of his gray beard floating like carded wool in the breeze. He never attended church services indoors and refused the meager comfort of a dormitory cell. Instead, he built his own shelter out near the island's chain of connected lakes. Arkady, who at that time fished almost every day, watched Father Vasily from between the willows as the older man dragged small fallen branches and bundles of sticks across the meadow to the lee of a small hillock, where he stacked and wove them into a home without ax or nails, chinking the gaps with pieces of turf he cut from the ground with a kitchen knife.

One day Arkady crept up to the hut and peeked inside. On the living grass, Father Vasily had only a bedroll of sheepskin and reindeer hides and an arrangement of books on a birchbark tray: the Gospels, the Psalms, the Philokalia, Saint Athanasius' *On the Incarnation* and Climacus' *Ladder of Divine Ascent*. The same books Arkady has with him now. The hut was snug and secret, like a child's refuge from the grown-up world.

"Why don't you go inside?" A voice came from behind him. Father Vasily was there, blue-eyed and smiling, as slender as one of the lakeside willows. "Go ahead, it's all right."

"I didn't hear you there," Arkady sputtered.

"Of course you didn't. I move in harmony with God's creation, not against it." He made a fanning motion, the same one Arkady used to shoo the hens into their roost.

Obliging, Arkady crawled into the hut and sat cross-legged in one corner.

Father Vasily crawled in after him and settled opposite. "You see? You don't need *all that*," whispered Father Vasily, pointing in the direction of the monastery. His owl-like face tilted to one side, and his bright eyes rolled like marbles in browless, deep sockets before holding Arkady's frightened gaze. "Too much activity and too many voices. Even in the name of the Lord, it's *too much*. Too much weight bearing you down. Too much inertia and opacity in the world, miring you in the muck of men. I know you understand me. I've seen you at the edge of the lake, day after day, casting a flimsy lure into the boundless waters. What do you *really* hope to catch? What are you waiting for? You must cast *yourself*! What you need is to lift off! Lift away! Incorporate the lightness that is God's grace and his gift. Don't mistake me, though. It is not the lightness of flippancy, ignorance, and pettiness. Oh no! It is a lightness that contains the knowledge of good and evil and its infinite permutations. Perhaps this godly lightness is generated by that weight and complexity; it certainly contains all that and reaches far beyond it. I am talking about the endless possibility contained in the simple but profound *choice* to release yourself from the weight bearing you down. Dissolve the solidity of the world! Do this, and you, too, can venture into God's subtle wilderness of grace."

Father Vasily leaned forward and embraced him. With his face pressed against Vasily's beard, Arkady heard the old man's heart pounding with divine purpose. *There is more to life than the lessons, the brethren, the endless recitations, even the bells' clear ringing,* Arkady thought. *Yes. There is more in this life for me.*

Now, in a nest of blankets in a corner of Schoonhoven, Arkady takes up the reins of prayer, the same prayer he has been offering since he decided to follow Vasily to Spitsbergen. *Guide me in lightness. Show me the pathless path into the wilderness of your grace.* And before his heart has beaten three more times, the Lord's beneficent cunning dawns on him: A challenging journey is the only true path. If the Pomors accompany him, or if Vasily were nearby, Arkady would not be risking anything for God! "If I am given easy instructions, I cannot fully lift off and give myself up to this new path," he whispers. "Just like Father Vasily did, I must risk everything."

Eventually, Father Vasily spent his time pacing the shore of the Solovetsky harbor, looking north to a treeless wilderness and into the Creator's unwavering field of vision. Vasily's calling impressed Arkady more deeply than any church elder ever had, and now he wants to become Father Vasily's acolyte. That is his one true aim. Arkady will learn from a master how to survive and flourish as an eremite in the far northern wilderness. And when the time comes, he will atone for his own sins by tending to Father Vasily during the older man's final days on earth.

And after that? He tries to keep this other thought from himself, but it springs forth like it always does: He shall one day be the most northerly outpost of divine grace! He trembles to encounter his ambition and quickly shudders back to the more pressing reality: Without Father Vasily out there somewhere, there is nothing to stave off the vertiginous terror of being in Spitsbergen alone. Again made an orphan, and this time by choice! Quickly he scolds himself. *Have I not come forth from society to pursue the most gracious path? Am I not obeying your will by coming here with nothing, an empty husk, so that I may be filled with grace?*

On the day Father Vasily left for Spitsbergen, Arkady went out to the dock with everyone else. Vasily was at least sixty years old, yet he climbed aboard the monastery's own hunting vessel with such lightness that even years later they called it dancing. He never looked back at the crowd of people waving and shouting blessings to him as the lodja pulled away.

For a few years, the hunters of Solovetsky brought back good tidings of the eremite and, to everyone's surprise, also letters from Father Vasily addressed simply to "the boy Arkady." Then, the hunting declined enough that the annual voyage from Solovetsky was no longer worth the time and risk. The monastery could buy meat from the Arkhangelsk Pomors, and the monks manufactured enough goods at the monastery for trade that they no longer needed white fox furs, walrus tusks, and oil.

When the hunters of Solovetsky returned from Spitsbergen for the last time, they spoke in hushed voices: "He would not come back with us, though we did our best to convince him. He said his true place was much farther north even than our camp."

During the years that followed, Arkady studied the letters and the books he'd seen in Vasily's hut and knew that one day he'd bow his head before the holy wanderer of Spitsbergen.

CHAPTER 4

**rkady** sleeps for hours among bundles of hides, but when he wakes, he feels more exhausted than before, as if he has only blinked. The Pomors are still eating, still drinking, and the infuriating fog still hangs immovable outside. The only difference is that the men's eyes are glassier, they stumble over benches, and their voices are louder and more slurred than the day before. There is spilled food on the floor, and Kuzma lies asleep among the plates.

All through the second day, Arkady paces outside the Schoonhoven hut. He retraces his steps back along the path, back to the dock. He peers down into the oarboat, only to find three sleeping Pomors tucked under reindeer hides like babes in a cradle.

He asks the rest of the Schoonhoven men where Father Vasily lives, but the Pomors just shake their shaggy heads. "There is no Father Vasily," they say. "There is no man of the church on Spitsbergen; there is only Spitsbergen herself, and that is enough for us!" The men raise their cups. Arkady cannot interpret the expressions under their beards and grime and the haze of drink.

After some time, Arkady slumps onto a bench. He watches as Kuzma disappears into a room in one dark corner of the hut. Later, Kuzma returns, flushed and smiling. His brethren clap him on the back. Later in the evening, the Pomor returns to the room. Half an hour later, he is back, again glowing. Could they have icons in there? A small holy room amid their demon hole? On the other side of the door, could there be a row of candles and a small, sacred fleet of emissaries? Could the Pomors be redeeming themselves, even in a tiny way, amid the ruins of their lives?

Arkady approaches the door himself. As he lifts the latch, a cheer erupts, and the Pomors pound their cups on the tables. Only Kuzma frowns and shakes his head. Arkady ignores him and slips through the door. Inside the bare room, a woman faces away from him, squatting over a porcelain bowl. She holds her skirts up around her waist and a thick stream of urine cascades from her most corrupted parts. She glances over her shoulder.

Arkady has never seen a woman's legs. These are thickly furred with copperish hair and are splayed at a most astonishing angle. Under the two halves of her buttocks, he spies fleshy folds so sinful he becomes dizzy. She rises, and her skirt swishes into place.

"Don't wake the baby."

Arkady hadn't thought he'd made a sound, but the woman holds a finger to her lips and points to a cradle. She has a wide, heavily freckled face and an appraising expression. Her thick, red hair falls down her back in two braids. She glances at the cradle every few seconds.

"I have never seen you here," she offers in accented Russian.

"I just arrived."

The woman approaches him. She sniffs him like an animal and looks closely at his face. Arkady recoils. Then, she reaches behind him and sets a small wooden beam into its fitting to lock the door.

Quickly, she pulls off her blouse. Arkady cannot breathe. She lies atop an ice bear's hide. She lifts her legs, letting her skirts fall back.

"Do not tell Kuzma. He will kill you. Get on."

"Brother Jesus Christ, Lord of earth and air and all living things, forgive this twisted soul and my own wretched eyes. She is weak in mind, and she has fallen so very far, but I know she is still within your omnipotent reach. Help her, oh Lord—" Arkady's voice rises higher and higher. "Oh God, have mercy!"

The woman laughs, shakes her head, and points to the cradle and then down to where her legs are spread open.

Arkady backs away and feels for the door. His hand crawls up and down the wall for what feels like eternity until it alights on the beam. He topples it and flings himself outside, and he's immediately rushed by the Pomors. Roaring, they lift him into the air. Kuzma stands back, arms folded across his chest.

"Here is the priest for us!" they cry. "He shouts prayers while he sticks it in her!"

Rocking upon a sea of hands and reeling from the sensations exploding from his painfully engorged penis, Arkady's vision sparks and blurs, and he faints away.

CHAPTER 5

"It was a terrible time. Bears destroyed the cache at Quade Hook. We went as long as we could on the reindeer we'd hunted for our rations, and then we ate our profits. We tried to hunt seal and only caught one. Then we ate eider meat until there was nothing left to kill, just feathers. We ate those, too. There used to be ravens up here, and after we became delirious, we even ate those, so I know my soul is darkened forever."

The Pomor pauses. It is a young man, Vitka, with glossy black hair and a scar across his cheek.

"Soon the long night was upon us, and we were so weak that we slept too much. Of course the Sisters came for us! First it was Ivan because he refused to move from his pallet. Once he lost his will to work, they had him. It was so cold and dark all the time, but I went out for many hours every day. I chipped ice and shoveled snow off the hut. I walked the beach looking for things we could use, and when it became too cold to be outside, I knotted and unknotted ropes. I stayed in the world of men. But poor Ivan succumbed, and within three weeks, he was dead."

Ever since Arkady went into the woman's room, all the Pomors except Kuzma insist on giving him their confessions. After he fainted, they dunked his head in cold water and wrapped him in blankets. They cleared out a small storage closet and put him inside. For two hours now, the men have come in, one after another. Arkady is furious, but he does not let it show. These men could kill him if they wished to, and they probably would with their terrible stories and pagan hearts.

He cannot stop thinking of the woman. The Pomors must be holding her captive. They are having their way with her, all of them! Keeping her in that horrible room with a bastard child and filthy bedding. Arkady himself is as corrupted as a human can be, but these men are worse, far worse.

"I was headed to the same place as poor Ivan," Vitka continues, close to tears. "Even as I wrapped his body in skins and lay it in the empty smokehouse, I could feel the Sisters' cold fingers digging into my arms, trying to drag me into bed, even in the morning. Three nights after Ivan died, the Sisters brought a terrible storm down on my head, and I was so weak from hunger I could barely tunnel my way outside." The man stopped and heaved a great sigh. He looked pleadingly at Arkady. "I knew I would not live unless I made food of my poor friend."

"You *ate* Ivan?"

"It was either that or die," Vitka whispered.

"Then you should have died, you ungodly worm! You should have died!"

Now Vitka put his face in his hands. "I haven't stopped thinking of Ivan's face, his poor frozen face. There is no place in the world for me except here, where men like me face their fates head on." The Pomor rises from the stool. "I see it now, little priest, and I am relieved. There is nothing you can do for me and nothing I can ask. I made my choice on this earth. If I hadn't eaten that raven, none of this would have happened. But I ate it, and I must face my fate with dignity. I will join the Dog's army in the end. That is where I belong." Vitka stands before him, smiling. "Thank you, little priest. Thank you."

Arkady scowls.

Kuzma appears in the doorway and kneels in front of Arkady. He looks intently into Arkady's eyes. "You are looking for Vasily," he says.

"Yes." Arkady leans back, thinking Kuzma might hit him for intruding on the woman.

The Pomor lowers his voice even more. "Evgeny told us to stay silent because you are the grandson of Nikolai Afanasyev. We are supposed to keep you from harm. But by Starostin's beard, every man must make his choices in life and stand by them! And it seems you are determined, so here is the truth: Father Vasily lives at Tusk Bay, in Magdalene Fjord."

"Then I will go there."

"No one has seen him in years. We have no reason to go up there anymore. There are no more walrus up that way, and the whales that used to live up the coast have moved offshore. We get all we need on the lower coast now. No one will take you, but here is a map."

A buzzing joy rises around Arkady's ears, and he has trouble following Kuzma's voice. The Pomor unfolds a thick piece of paper and narrates a route north as he traces his finger up a pencil-drawn coastline. Magdalene Fjord. Arkady remembers the name from studying the monastery's maps of Spitsbergen. Kuzma's finger continues on and on, past coves and fjords with scribbled names, until it comes to rest at the northwest corner of the island.

Lord, thank you for opening this brute's mouth. I am coming. Step by step, the way is coming clear. I will not have an ice bear for a steed, but I will come.

Arkady carefully folds the map. Kuzma turns on his heel and leaves.

Seven more men give confessions, but Arkady's heart beats too wildly for him to listen to their many, many sins. Adultery, greed, theft—one man is undone because he killed a housecat in Arkhangelsk. These men would be punished, severely punished, but not by Arkady. Larger mechanisms at work in the world will cast these men into the inevitable net of fate, and no confession would keep them from being pulled down to their black destination.

That evening, under the same fog and diffused light as midday, the Pomor revels become even wilder. After the supper plates are pushed aside, Kuzma ascends a tabletop with a domra and plays for the men, who soon jump up and join him in the song. While the giant Pomors stomp the floorboards and the unlit oil lamps swing on their hooks, Arkady prays Vespers and packs his things.

From Schoonhoven's abundant storage shelves, he takes a leather rucksack and thick fur mittens. He finds woolen underclothes and rabbitskin socks to supplement those he's brought from the monastery, and the knitted hat, undergloves, and thick scarf given to him by the Pomors. He stuffs his canvas bag with dried fish and meat from Kuzma's larder to supplement the rye flour and dry barley he brought from Solovetsky. He adds a small cook pot, spoon, and tin mug, and thinks himself well-prepared. Solovetsky monks made the leather boots on his feet, and he's kept them well-oiled. He leaves behind the walrus boots. He rolls up a thick wool blanket and a reindeer hide and ties them to the pack along with the collapsible fishing pole he made himself years ago at Solovetsky. Into his coat pockets go his fine knife, whose handle is made from the base of a reindeer antler, the Gospels and other books, and finally one other item, hidden inside a soft leather purse: a theft from the monastery so great that he blushes, even now.

He imagines his starets shaking his head sadly. "All those years, little one, have I taught you nothing?" Back at Solovetsky, as Arkady prepared for this theft, he convinced himself he would die without the contents of this purse, and he is right. He tucks it in the innermost pocket of his vest, and his hand lingers on the worn packet of folded letters that has rested there since he left the monastery.

Come quickly, my child. Come north.

Arkady stops before a closet filled with rifles and smaller guns. He has never touched a gun, and he leans toward the oiled wood and metal filigree as if beholding artifacts from an unknown civilization. Some are huge and battered. Others are sleek and could fit in his pack. *Rifles are carried either in warfare, to create profit, or to protect against the world,* he thinks. *My aims are altogether different. If I take a gun, I will be failing before my pilgrimage has even begun. Even by packing food, I am skeptical of God's plan for me.* Without touching the weapons, he hurries back to the main hall.

Arkady sits on his nest in the corner and watches the men regress into dumb beasts. Some of them are dancing, some lean against one another on benches, murmuring lovingly into their brothers' ears. Kuzma calls them up, and they dance together like a ring of three-day-pilgrim girls in the monastery meadows. The Pomors stumble and laugh, but after a minute or two, something is awry. The circle wavers and splits like a skein of geese. Pasha the many-buckled, silver hair streaming in an unkempt blaze, stands with his arms folded across his chest. A young, red-faced hunter leans into him. It is Vitka the raven-eater. They argue amid a growing cheer. Pasha laughs sharply, and the young one responds by balling his fists and spitting on the floor near Pasha's boot. Kuzma strides over and scolds Vitka, who storms to the other side of the hut. The music continues, and Pasha again joins hands with the men. But only a minute later, Vitka is back. His face is red, and the ropy muscles in his neck bulge. The men laugh.

"You, Pasha!" screams Vitka. "How can you be such a fool? Everyone knows you stole from me."

He shoves Pasha to little effect, but Arkady can see that the gesture offends the older man. The two lock arms and push against each other with their heads down like billy goats.

"Last season, you stole from me. You took two bundles of reindeer and six foxes' worth of profit! *Poshol v pizdu!*"

"Lying bag of meat," Pasha says. "*Poshol ty na khuy.* Go fuck yourself, Vitka. You accuse me of this falsehood in front of my brothers? You should be ashamed." He pushes the younger one off.

All the men howl.

"Shame? You speak *khuetenie* in front of our brothers?" Vitka screeches, lunging again toward Pasha. This time he hits the old sailor wildly, catching him at the neck. "You're the one who should be ashamed. Even the Dog won't take you. Give me what you owe!"

Pasha recoils. "Touch me one more time, and the only thing I will give you are the fruits of my father's teachings."

Pasha lifts a huge goblet to his mouth. Vitka swerves close and knocks it from Pasha's hand. All the men in the hut go quiet.

Pasha slowly turns. "Kuzma, fetch me one of the old axes," he intones and strides out the door.

In unprecedented silence, the Pomors follow Pasha out into the impassive daylight. Vitka remains standing where he'd been.

Evgeny appears with a serious expression. "Vitka, if you need sobering, there is tea and cold water in Kuzma's kitchen. Take your time, boy. Come when you're ready."

What will these animals do next? Arkady stays inside but scurries to the window. In a little time, Vitka strides past him to join his tribe on the tundra flat directly outside the hut. Arkady sees the two Pomors circle each other; each man holds an ax crosswise, neck in one hand and stem in the other. They are drunk, and Arkady sees their mouths moving and spittle flying, but hears nothing. The two figures move slowly and change direction now and then.

Pasha casually raises his weapon, and the ring of Pomors takes a step back. Vitka lunges toward his opponent, clearly intending to move much faster than he actually does. Pasha hits Vitka squarely in the chest with the blunt top of the ax head, and Vitka gracefully falls onto his back.

What a ridiculous display, Arkady thinks. *Neither man can hit the other. They are axes, after all. Centuries have passed since the men of the forest used axes in battle.*

Vitka slowly rights himself and aligns the ax in Pasha's direction. When Vitka circles close enough, Pasha hooks his opponent's weapon with his blade and jerks. Vitka holds tight, letting forth a sharp yodel. Finally, Vitka frees himself and manages a quick slash to Pasha's back. The force doesn't appear to be strong enough even to cut through Pasha's clothing, but Arkady can see that Vitka's first successful blow enrages Pasha. He tries to slap Vitka's shoulder with the heavy side of the ax head, but Vitka feints as best as he can, given his inebriation, and Pasha swings his weapon around his whole body to attack from the left. Vitka is playfully tossing his ax from one hand to the other, which infuriates Pasha even more. With his ax held crosswise, Pasha assaults Vitka's knees, and as Vitka stumbles backward, Pasha hits him again at the waist. Vitka's face contorts as he careens into the Pomors encircling them.

Now the fight runs all to Vitka's favor. He circles Pasha, jabbing constantly about the other man's shoulders. He delivers a blunt blow to the chest and another to the back. He increases the strength of each thrust until Pasha must be thoroughly bruised. Pasha drops to one knee but rises quickly. Vitka whacks Pasha in the head with the ax's stem, and Pasha drops to the ground.

The head? Do rules not govern these pagans? Arkady remembers the weight of Pasha's head on his shoulder. The ropes that bound him and the rainswept sea. "Get up, *Dedushka,*" he whispers.

Pasha does not stir from the moss; he seems very comfortable there. The now-quiet ring of men leans in. Two Pomors come forward, and Vitka shows them his ax. It looks as if they are discussing its virtues. Vitka even accepts a silver mug from one of his brethren and takes a deep drink. With the cup to his mouth, he gazes up at the gray, expressionless fog where the sky should be, and in that moment, Pasha jumps up, surprising everyone, and lands his ax blade deep in Vitka's thigh. Behind the window, Arkady recoils as blood fountains from Vitka's leg, and the young Pomor topples to the ground.

Layers of voices rise as the men surround the fallen one. Pasha drops his ax and turns toward the sea.

The Pomors bring the smell of oxen when they come in. They lay Vitka across the feast table. For once Arkady doesn't run away to hide in his nest. He has never seen wounds of violence, and he can't turn away. Kuzma comes forward with a pair of metal shears, while Evgeny lights lamps and hands them to the men closest to Vitka. Vitka himself lies quietly with flames reflecting off his eyes.

Kuzma cuts away Vitka's trouser leg. Someone brings a bowl of water, and Kuzma splashes it over the wound. Blood bubbles and froths as if from a spring. They bind Vitka's leg tightly above the gash, and Kuzma calls for a needle and catgut thread.

As Kuzma explores the wound, the men feed Vitka liquor until he lies still. Then their voices rise, cursing Pasha's pride and then, later, acknowledging that Vitka did not fight fairly. Pasha is still outside, facing seaward, sitting cross-legged with his ax across his knees.

Arkady leans against one wall of the hut, nauseated. *See how the godless fall apart? So quickly, and for the pettiest reasons—hides, profit, commerce, greed—they slash each other and stumble through their dark lives. God's grace eludes them, though its lantern fills this room.*

By and by, Kuzma's attempt to stop the bleeding grows more frantic. He says a vein is severed and one end has retreated far up Vitka's leg. Although Arkady doesn't see it up close, the wound is probed, even cut further, in search of the vein. Men huddle close around the table. Arkady tries to remove himself through prayer, but his words fly away without touching his heart; his mind is somewhere else.

How quickly a life changes direction, he thinks. From boasts and the company of men to this pale body on the table. From a grandfather's hearth on the Laya tributary to Solovetsky Monastery to Spitsbergen. Swift as the stroke of an ax blade, one life slices away. *But I am here,* Arkady thinks. *I defy those forces. By my own faith I am here, and I am ready to embark on the journey I am meant to take.*

He rises and walks toward the back of the hall and his nest of blankets, where he has stashed all his supplies. There is a door at the back of the hut.

Now is the time to lift off, he thinks.

"Little priest!" Evgeny shouts.

Arkady freezes.

"We need your help."

Arkady turns back to the world of men. He notices all the bowed Pomor heads. Blood and bits of gore cover the feast table, and Vitka lies white as a bone.

"He is dead," Evgeny says. "All his blood flowed away."

Someone goes outside to tell Pasha, and Pasha's cry sends the snow buntings sailing across the tundra.

"We will build a pyre," Evgeny goes on. "We shall send our Vitka off on the long road with a fire that will make Starostin proud. And you, Arkady Afanasyev, you will give a prayer to send him on his way."

CHAPTER 6

he Pomors carry loads of driftwood up from the beach to the crest of a ridge behind the hut, whose top is obscured by fog. They light a fire and tend to it until it is huge and hot. Even from the hut, Arkady hears them discussing what to tell Vitka's wife in Arkhangelsk. They finally decide on the story of an ice bear, which kills quickly. It happened early in the season, when bears still roam south from Ice Sound. Vitka was butchering a walrus on the beach, and the smell of blood drew the bear. Before they carry Vitka's body up, Arkady assures Evgeny and Kuzma that he will follow them. He tells them he must prepare for the ceremony.

Empty, the Schoonhoven hut seems to breathe on its own. Arkady turns from the window, and the silence is a balm. Finally! Alone after so many weeks being pushed, pulled, and cuffed by the Pomors, Arkady closes his eyes. From a faraway corner of his being, he hears the distant bells of Solovetsky. *You are here. You are guiding me. It is finally time.*

He scurries to the bags stuffed with everything he has taken from Schoonhoven's shelves and pantries. He clutches his most brazen theft from the Pomors: a compass. To Arkady, the wobbling needle in this small brass case is not magnetized by earthly forces but drawn only by God's emissary, Vasily. He bundles up his things and leaves the hut through the back.

Outside, the fog leaves pearls of water on his clothes as he hurries down the path to the dock, where he hears the oarboat rocking against its lines. He spares not a thought for Vitka or his own false promise to pray for the dead man's soul. He walks along the dock. He tosses his rucksack and satchel down into the oarboat and carefully climbs down the ladder. With trembling fingers, he struggles with the bow line. *I am coming as fast as I can. Protect me as I come north to your light.*

A bulky shape materializes out of the fog and drops into the stern, rocking the boat so dramatically that Arkady pitches to the side, and his face dips into the sea. Shocked by the clenching cold, he rears back and gasps. The woman sits before him, wrapped in a thick hide coat and fur hood. Her ice-bear pelt is rolled up and strapped to her back, and she carries her swaddled baby in her arms.

"Even now," she whispers, looking over the side of the boat, "Chúdo-Yúda is down there, waiting for the sound of oarlocks creaking. He waits for us." Her eyes dart across the water's surface and along the shoreline. "He can heave himself up on land like a walrus." With one hand, she unties the stern line.

"Wait! Get out!" Arkady hisses as the boat slips free of its mooring and drifts away from the dock. It glides swiftly, as if pulled by something strong and invisible. Every idea and plan he harbors about this journey rattles in his skull.

"I will not go back to Schoonhoven," she says.

"Why not?"

"My time there has been fruitful. I have received what I sought. Now, I can go."

"What about your baby?"

The woman clutches the bundled form. "What about it?"

Arkady has no answer. They have drifted out of sight of the dock. The boat noses through a soft curtain of fog. Arkady hears a splash, which terrifies him. It is true he must keep his eyes open to the mysteries of divine guidance. Wasn't poor Vitka a sacred messenger in his way? Could this woman also be such an envoy? Or is she a mere temptation? He must rely solely upon God's grace. Which is she?

Arkady takes up the oars. He uses the compass and Kuzma's map to follow the rocky curve of Bell Hook as best as he can in the fog, while in the stern the woman coos softly to her baby. It is not entirely unpleasant, and Arkady breathes deeply, taking in the salty underlayer of air near the water and the icy pall of the fog above. Schoonhoven, like Solovetsky before it, and Arkhangelsk long before that, is gone. Reeled over the far edge of the horizon and out of sight for good. The only thing that matters is the path before him. The woman peels back the layers of her coat and dress to reveal a breast. She encircles it with her right hand as milk dribbles onto her lap. She raises the baby to nurse. Arkady looks away.

"I won't let Chúdo-Yúda get us, precious one. No matter how hard he tries, I will beat him so hard that his skull shatters, and he falls back in the sea."

Arkady recoils.

The woman fusses over her child.

"How old is it?"

"Been with me for two seasons now, since I came to Schoon-hoven."

"That long?"

"Maybe more."

"It's so tiny." Arkady has not spent time with infants, but even he knows that a child of two would be bigger than that. "What is your name?"

"Saskia."

Soon they round Bell Hook. The water rises to wavelets, and a cold breeze touches their faces. Bell Sound. The same wind that smoothed the wild grasses on Solovetsky weeks ago now brushes their cheeks. Arkady angles the boat northeast. That way, he prays, they will not miss the coast and head out to sea. Once they come into sight of the northern shore of the Sound, they will turn west until they come to the outer coast. Then it's northward for days and days, rowing unceasingly until he reaches Father Vasily. He keeps the compass on the bench in front of him and thanks God for all his years' experience rowing along the lakes and canals of Solovetsky. Only much later will he thank God for the calm weather during this crossing; he will not realize how lucky they were until he has traveled deeper into Spitsbergen. For now, the wavelets remain wavelets.

"Chúdo-Yúda follows us." Saskia's voice reaches him from farther away than it really is. "I see him swimming below us. I can see his beard trailing out behind. He is shaking his fist at me." She stands, and the boat rocks wildly.

"Sit down!"

Saskia points into the water. "Don't you see him? He is there." She peers down. "In the shadows. Just there!" Her voice rises to a screech, and her child drops to the deck. It makes a surprising clunk.

Arkady leaves the oars and scrambles to where the bundle lies. Saskia is reaching into the black water. He hears a splash coming from the opposite side of the boat. Saskia whirls around, rocking the small vessel even more.

"Did you hear that?" She leans over the other side. "I can't kill him. I didn't get a good hold."

Arkady lifts the damp bundle. It does not move its arms or legs. Under the layers of grimy rags, he finds not a child but a roughly hewn wooden doll stained dark with handling. It has the head of a bear cub, with rounded ears, tiny, wide-set eyes, and a black nose. The mouth has been carved carefully, with an orifice sized for the nipple, and the stains are darker there. The doll has a human body.

"Give it to me!" Saskia lunges toward Arkady in a movement that sends the boat lurching.

Arkady falls backward over the bench.

"You've made it cold. Give!" She snatches the doll away, cooing and swaddling. "Do you know how easy it would have been for Chúdo-Yúda to take it from me?" She again peers into the sea. "He has sunk down into the blackness."

Shaken, Arkady turns back to the oars and curses himself for not forcing Saskia off the boat at Schoonhoven.

CHAPTER 7

wo hours after Arkady begins to doubt that he's rowing in the right direction, and one hour after he swears he hears voices near them in the fog, the boat encounters a raft of eiders. The sturdy sea ducks tilt their black-and-white faces toward him and then return to avian pursuits, which at this moment appears to be dozing. He discerns the faint outline of topography behind the fog. It disappears quickly, but he rows faster, and soon he sees it again. After a few more strokes, he hears waves tumbling over a pebbled beach.

Saskia has been asleep for hours, curled strangely in the bow with her nose tucked under her arm like a cat.

"We've reached the shore," he whispers between strokes. "We've reached the far shore." His doubt, previously tenacious, disintegrates.

Thank you for shepherding us across the waters. We are that much closer to Father Vasily and Mother Mary, who will welcome this harlot unto her bosom and show her the way of virtue. I see now it is surely a divine sign that she accompanies me. ... I can't help but think of Mary Magdalene, and we are going to Magdalene Fjord. Even though Saskia spews pagan foolishness, surely she is your messenger.

Father Vasily will know how to approach the bizarre task of weaning Saskia of her bear-child. As if she hears him, Saskia pulls the doll closer. She was probably brought to Spitsbergen when she was just a little girl and abused ever since. No wonder her world is full of heathen creatures. He hadn't heard anyone talk about Chúdo-Yúda since his grandfather scared him with stories when Arkady was a very little boy standing at the muddy bank of the Laya tributary. Nikolai made the old sea demon as frightening as he could; anything to keep the child back from the river's edge.

The next time Arkady looks over his shoulder, the shore has revealed its layers: sea-licked pebbles growing lighter in color as they extend up from the waterline, and the lowest layer of fog, with the faint greenish tint of tundra behind it.

Saskia startles awake when the bottom of the boat scrapes along the beach. She grabs the bowline and, with her wooden cub in her arms, makes an extraordinary leap to shore. She pulls the boat up easily. Arkady clings to the sides to keep his balance.

"Chúdo-Yúda followed us, and I tried to grab him when I could," she says. "Understand me, I felt no fear, unless he was afraid of me. I wanted him in my grasp, so I could cudgel him to death. He is still dreaming me."

Arkady scrambles to shore and looks around. In the shifting fog, he thinks he sees the jutting roof of Schoonhoven. He looks around wildly. What if the Lord has brought him in a circle? Was he worthy of such divine jest?

"Are we still in Schoonhoven?" Arkady fumbles in his pockets for the compass.

Saskia glances up. "Of course not. Look at these beach pebbles, so different here. They lay there so rounded, and speckled with red. Smell this air." She pushes her face into the breeze. "This wind comes straight off the inland glaciers. It is colder than what we get across the sound at Schoonhoven this time of year and stronger out on the water—there, see the ripples farther out? We are south of Deadman Spit. It protects us for now. But the wind is rising. We'll need a shelter."

Arkady tries to sound confident. "We must rest now, and then we'll continue in the boat along this shore, until it comes to the open sea. Then, we'll row north for many days and follow the coast to Father Vasily." Perhaps it is a blessing to have someone who knows this land to guide him north.

"I must feed my child," Saskia mutters.

"Can't you see that your child has the carved face of a bear?"

"Do not speak. You don't know anything about it."

"May God have mercy on your poor, twisted soul."

"*You* are the twisted one." Saskia steps close to him and points at his nose. "You come here with nothing. To *this* place? With nothing! No tools. No warm things. Who but a fool would come without a rifle? You steal from the Pomors," she points to the boat and then to the compass in his hand. "They did nothing but nourish you, and you stole from them. You are wrong to be here."

"God has instructed me to come here. He asked me to come forward, away from my brethren, and to continue walking north, without worldly fortifications, to approach his uncreated light. The invitation is to trust in him completely. Now I am here, with you. The Lord wants you to peel back the layers of illusion under which you have been living. Do you want to emerge into his grace?"

"We must gather wood. We must build a fire. We must eat. We must stay warm. That is what I know. You've made many mistakes. The Dog may have noticed you already."

Arkady steps closer, and Saskia moves back. "This child you have. Why does it have a wood grain along its face and body?"

"Don't you speak of it."

"How can it breathe when you wrap the blanket around its face like that?"

"Shut up, beast! I have found a way to survive. You must do the same."

Together they move the boat farther up the beach and explore the piles of driftwood, until they find a protected space behind several huge logs, where Saskia builds a fire. Arkady hauls his bags up and lays out the hides and blankets. They eat salted reindeer meat and bread and a little water from Saskia's walrus bladder. She stares at him from across the fire. Facing the warmth of the flames, Arkady struggles to keep his eyes open, even when Saskia unbuttons her dress and nurses her doll. He falls asleep to her cooing, which, as he slips beneath the waves, is a comfort.

CHAPTER 8

weat streams down his back. Arkady throws off the blankets and lurches awake. Sick with the feeling that adversaries surround him, he jumps to his feet and the bright, blurred landscape spins. A huge, black shape bounds out of his peripheral vision. He closes his eyes until the world stops tilting. He waits until he feels the pebbles under his feet and normal pangs of hunger in his belly. He opens his eyes, and for the first time since he left Solovetsky, he sees a canopy of radiant sky. All across it, clouds in the shapes of dragons, ships, carriages, and riders form a westward procession. The fog has lifted.

Today is September first, the beginning of the Church year. He breathes in the scoured air of Spitsbergen. A blue the color of Mary's robes forms what could be called a protective shell across the world. Anywhere else it would simply be beautiful. But as Arkady casts his eyes across the land, that crisp blue illuminates a vast and jagged range of gray peaks rising straight up from the sea to the east of him.

Streaked with snow and cascading rivers of shale, the crags' steep angles shock him, as do the sheer number of mountains, like line after line of infantry in an army of giants, reaching as far as he can see into the unknown interior of the island. For the first time, he wishes he'd left Solovetsky with the blessing of his elders instead of their curses. Their benedictions surely would sustain him more than any of his own weak prayers.

Northward, the beach disappears at the base of a bluff. He looks up the bank behind him and thankfully sees a ledge of moss and tundra and, behind that, a thin band of rolling foothills that quickly gives way to the scree slopes of the giants. He climbs up the bank and sinks to his knees. For once, the sea sparkles with sunlight. Just above the waves, five dark birds ride the lowest drafts. *You have lifted the fog from my eyes!* He looks around with rising excitement and notices the oarboat is no longer where they'd left it.

He searches the beach and then across the sound. He looks farther offshore. There may be a speck, way out there, but he can't be sure. It could be an eider, or a seal. Or Chúdo-Yúda. He searches the beach again. Saskia is gone.

Arkady bows his head. How will he reach Father Vasily without the boat? How quickly he'd regarded the strange woman as his protector. Now, she's gone, and he is left only with the terrible discovery of his own foolishness. What to do now? He fumbles in his clothing, unbuttoning first his coat and then his vest to get to the thin packet of letters.

Within a year of Father Vasily leaving for Spitsbergen, Arkady wrote to him. He gave the letter to the monk-hunters on the eve of their annual voyage to Spitsbergen. In the letter, Arkady asked Father Vasily what qualities were necessary for an eremite's life. All through that summer, he speculated what Vasily's answer might be. Steadfastness? Courage? Clarity of thought or purity of prayer? Arkady recalls his excitement, and then his dismay, when the reply finally came.

Now, on the north shore of Bell Sound, he unfolds the worn letter: *My child: You ask which qualities of heart make this life possible. Here is my reply: Hunger for solitude and thirst for the raw elements of life. You must be able to look into yourself unwaveringly for an unimaginably long time—so long that you no longer see a self in your reflection; instead, you see a single airborne seed! A droplet of rain! A primordial ember! You see your grandparents' grandparents and the children of the child you may never have. You see your sins fanned out like chaff above the threshing board. You see past, present, and future as it really is.*

Arkady looks north along the thin strip of navigable terrain: his future. Without a bit of fertile soil in which to germinate, Father Vasily's words soon float away. Saskia will not come back. Arkady perceives her and the boat for what they really are: symptoms of his lack of faith, nothing more. He will leave behind the mirror-world of men and women, guns, warm coats, and provisions.

Behind him, high up on a stone ledge, the Dog watches these events unfold and waits to see what Arkady will do next. And behind the Dog, the cliffs rise like screams frozen to stone.

CHAPTER 9

"Have you ever wondered why we keep dozens of hens at the monastery, but we don't eat many eggs?"

On his seventh day walking north from Bell Sound, the voice of Father Ilya, Arkady's spiritual father at Solovetsky—his starets—arrives as if the old man walks beside him.

"Have you wondered why we give worms from the garden to our flock of hens instead of keeping them in the ground? It's true that when we cut ourselves in the kitchen, we use egg membrane to wrap our wounds, and, yes, we decorate eggshells for Easter. But neither of those is the egg's holy purpose. Think, Arkady. Think. We keep so many hens. Why would that be?"

Even though Arkady is utterly alone, and perhaps because he is, memories crowd in so vividly that he repeatedly forgets where he is and fancies himself back at Solovetsky with Father Ilya looking down at him, his teacher's question manifested by a shaggy, raised eyebrow.

Like Arkady, Father Ilya grew up in the monastery, just as Ilya's own starets had, and probably his starets before that. How old had Arkady been when they'd discussed the monastery's hens? Arkady stops to think. He stares down at the gray beach stones. He remembers the monastery still felt new to him then, so he couldn't have been more than eight or nine years old.

Of course, Father Ilya hadn't given Arkady the answer. But he leaned down close, his sour kvass-breath whooshing across Arkady's face as it would for the next fifteen years. "The hens are little holy mothers. Why would I say that?"

At the time, even though he had no inkling of the answer, Arkady knew that what Father Ilya was telling him to do was run to the chicken coops right then and open his mind, or else he'd remain a fool in this world.

As he walks up the coast of Spitsbergen, Arkady worries the lapel of Father Ilya's wool coat. He wears it thrown over his shoulders like a cape, attached by one button at his neck. He keeps his eyes centered on the ground ahead of him. This is partly because the stones require careful navigation and partly because, even after many days walking, Arkady can't bear to look into the far distance ahead of him. The terrible crags rise to the east. To the west, the sea emits its continuous hiss. Arkady prefers to walk on the ledge of tundra above the beach, but for two days now, his boots sank too deep in mud up there, so he edged back to the shore.

Today is the anniversary of the nativity of the God-bearer— the Holy Theotokos: Mary. She who foreshadowed He. That is what brought to mind Ilya's homily of the hens in the first place. Arkady ran to the hen yard as fast as he could. It was summer, he remembers. A particular, ethereal Solovetsky light gilded the surface of everything. He ran out of the boys' dormitory courtyard, where Father Ilya watched him go, and continued along the south wall of the cathedral. Past the cloisters, the monks' refectory, the herb garden, and one of the smaller forges. To the west were hostels for the three-day pilgrims of summer: two for men and one for women. Ahead were the stables and barn.

Several bearded monks walked around different parts of the hen yard, singing and tossing handfuls of cracked rye in short, swishing arcs. Arkady stared at the hens and tried to think. One of the monks came out from a coop with a wooden bowl of speckled eggs. Arkady opened the gate for him.

"Where are you taking them?" he asked.

"Come, and see for yourself," the young man said softly.

Arkady trailed behind as they walked past the stables.

Solovetsky manufactured many different goods. Through the forges came everything from nails and horseshoes to cast-iron pots. The cobblers made boots to sell in Arkhangelsk, Novgorod, and even Moscow. Monastery carvers lived and worked on the island. There were a dozen manufacturing buildings on Solovetsky, and many of them housed two or even three cottage industries. The young monk and Arkady walked among these buildings, past a group of potters loading a kiln with the earthenware vessels that would later be filled with the monastery's famous pickled cabbage, which was sold to three-day pilgrims on their way home, along with dark bread and bottles of raisin-sweetened kvass.

The monk walked inside a whitewashed stone building with huge windows that Arkady had never visited before. Arkady crept up to the workshop's open door. Easels were scattered in spots of sunlight across the room, each with a monk seated or standing before it. Beyond the easels were wooden worktables. The monk set down the bowl of eggs on one of the tables. He waved Arkady in, and Arkady stepped as softly as he could among the monastery's most treasured artisans.

He was still too young to recognize an icon for the cataclysmic event that it is, but just seeing human hands giving icons shape and expression excited and troubled him. He had only ever seen icons in church, usually by the candlelight that made saints' painted eyes dart every which way, taking note of the sin surrounding every man and boy. He had not yet learned that it was not the artist's brush strokes or even his skill that created an icon, but the conjoined power of divine will and earnest prayer.

The monk from the hen yard showed him how an egg yolk was removed from its white by several back-and-forth pourings between shell halves. The monk collected the yolks in a deep ceramic bowl and mixed them using a wooden whisk, which, Arkady later learned, was itself a blessed and holy object.

"The egg mixes with the powdered pigment and then can be painted," whispered the monk. He bowed and handed the bowl of yolks to a very old man. "Brother Nicolef has been the monastery's pigment mixer for almost seven decades. There is no other like him."

The monk bowed again and gestured that it was time to go. As they walked back, the monk explained that, besides the icons in all the monastery churches, chapels, and, of course, the main cathedral, the Solovetsky studio made thousands of small Saint Savvatii icons every year for the three-day pilgrims to buy as a reminder of their pilgrimage. Savvatii was the consecrated, four-hundred-year-old founder of the monastery.

"I gather eggs after Matins every day except Sunday. Join me if you like," the monk told him.

Father Ilya was still in the courtyard where Arkady had left him. Perhaps he was waiting, or just following the hours. Arkady never knew if Ilya had planned for the whole thing to go as it did: for Arkady to start gathering the eggs and working in the icon workshop.

"Icons!" Arkady shouted as he approached. "The eggs serve God!"

"Good boy. But also, understand: Icons do not merely sit atop their wooden panels. They occur inside the old stones of these islands. Saints reside within the glass panes of our windows, at the bottom of our water buckets, and beneath the surface of our lakes. Out there," Ilya gestured toward the monastery gates and the harbor, "trodden by every single three-day pilgrim and hidden inside each plank of our blessed dock, is an icon capable of guiding our destinies."

Arkady continues north on the beach as a cold breeze plays with the empty sleeves of Ilya's heavy coat. A boy's starets is assigned to him on the day he arrives at Solovetsky. For eighteen years, Ilya tended to Arkady as if the boy were a tiny garden.

Arkady was lucky. There are stories of pairings that did not fare so well. And when the boy is grown, he takes care of his mentor during the elder man's waning years. Arkady had known this fact of monastery life from the beginning. But before he can be ensnared by a different, darker memory, he speeds up across the rocks and sand.

"My sins are more numerous than the stones of this beach," he mutters. "I am as lowly and humble before you as lichen."

Gliding atop his pillar a few feet away, Simeon the Stylite tries to warn Arkady that by now he should have stopped for the night. Arkady's obliviousness to his unforgiving surroundings has disturbed Simeon ever since the saint arrived seven days earlier on September first, his feast day.

Simeon is especially worried because of the huge black Dog tracking Arkady, and the saint urges caution in any way he can, but Simeon's resources in that regard are limited since Arkady is hardly laying himself bare before God. Simeon finds he cannot contact even the most remote layer of Arkady's consciousness because this human is living almost entirely in the past. This replaying of dramas is common for those first setting out in the wilderness, but Simeon is surprised that someone raised in a monastery would fall prey to the phenomenon so soon and so deeply.

In any case, the seasons change quickly on Spitsbergen. Each day holds less light than the last, and even after such a short time here, Arkady should perceive the danger, but he doesn't.

Open your eyes, Simeon urges silently. *You are giving the upper hand to the cold and the dark. Remember my story—atop my pillar, braving the weather and winds. What qualities of mind do you suppose I needed to withstand the elements?*

But Arkady walks on with his head down and no ears to hear.

CHAPTER 10

inally, Arkady stops to rest. The land is in shadow, as if an enormous bird of prey is flying overhead, but it does not darken further. A breeze rises, so Arkady carries stones up from the beach onto the mossy shelf where he will sleep. He judges the wind as best as he can and stacks the stones into a windbreak, plugging the holes with turf that he cuts out of the ground with his antler-handled knife. He gathers small pieces of driftwood to last through the night. Using the hatchet, he peels shavings for kindling. He collects moss to replace the dried stuff he will use as tinder. Then, he fetches the soft leather purse from the inside pocket of his vest. Inside the purse are the flint, striker, and tinderbox from the monastery's main kitchen. Here is what he stole from Solovetsky.

The flint he doesn't fret over because this piece had been chipped like all the others off the monastery's big block. And the brass tinderbox could easily be replaced. But the striker is different. Once, when Arkady had a fever, Father Ilya brought him to the kitchen for some willow-bark tea. They sat on the hearth, and his starets picked up the small piece of iron and told him its story. Three hundred years earlier, a monk, out wandering the island, found the striker near one of the lakes, entangled with the skeleton of a man. A Norseman, it was said. The striker bears a simple design, the steel hammer-struck and curved into an oval shape, with the two ends bent into delicate curls.

"I need this to live," Arkady says aloud from where he kneels on the mossy ledge, surrounded by wilderness. "That's why I took it. Did not the holy martyr Sozon break and steal part of a gold statue? These are pagan tools now in the service of God."

Sozon comes to mind because the saint's feast day was just a few days earlier. But from where the saint sits a few paces behind Arkady, with the great golden arm of that statue lain across his lap, Sozon himself shakes his head. *Mine was an entirely different circumstance. Be careful where you tread.* Sozon hefts up the golden arm. *I sent a message, yes. But I gave this gold to the poor, and I died a horrific death for it.*

Arkady makes a spark in the tinder and blows it into the nest of dry moss. He drops the tinderbox and feeds shavings to the ember.

For years, Arkady sat by the monastery's hearth fire each morning. Then he'd run to church for Matins, and after the service, to breakfast. Then, in a crowd of dispersing boys, he walked to the hen yard to gather eggs for the icon workshop. Every boy at the monastery had such tasks, monitored from afar by his starets. Some boys moved quickly into more skilled jobs, but Arkady's stayed the same. Another boy, Maksim, began helping Brother Nicolef grind pigments after only a few months of collecting eggs. Arkady hid his jealously the best that he could. But he complained to Father Ilya.

"Maybe you are not meant for those duties. Did you consider that before you came to me with your whining?" his teacher responded.

"I have been collecting eggs for so long. Why am I not mixing pigment like Maksim? It's not fair."

"What do you mean, *fair*? I don't understand you. Isn't God's will the force behind each and every movement we make on this earth?"

"But—"

"Before you go on, open your ears. I know you lean into your prayer with honesty and humility. You would be surprised at how many boys don't. Do not discount the value of these qualities in yourself, Arkady. Do not place too much in them, but don't discount them. Do you understand me?"

Arkady did. But he also watched Maksim closely, hunched over the sacred minerals and pigments like an alchemist, grinding and mixing. Barely a year later, Maksim was mixing his pigment with yolk tempera. Three years after that, Maksim stood behind one of the icon painters, observing. After that, he became an apprentice painter. After that, Arkady tried to stop watching the other boy but couldn't.

Arkady has made a decent fire. He unpacks his portable larder and counts what he has left. Nine fat dried salmon, more than a pound of smoked meat, several pounds of cracked barley, and a little salt. He warms half a fish on a stick, and as he eats, he considers his success thus far. He hasn't needed his fishing pole yet, and, considering the fish he has seen rising in the shallow mouths of streams along the beach, he'll reel in plenty. Tomorrow, he'll see what he can catch, just to be sure. The many streams flowing down from the mountains have kept his water jug full. He has not yet felt hunger, the map remains tucked safely in his pocket, and he rests in the comfort of two pairs of Pomor-knitted socks and woolen long underwear; his starets' coat, fox-fur hat, and mittens; a wool blanket; and a reindeer hide, fur-side in, wrapped over it all.

Arkady drowses behind the windbreak, curled around one side of the fire. Some distance away, Simeon stands on his pillar at the waterline. He watches the sea, which is as glassy and polished as obsidian. Now that it is quiet, Vasilissa creeps into view. Since her feast day on September third, the girl-saint has mostly stayed out of sight, but now she sits near the fire, warming her hands. The light flickers over her misshapen face and her few patches of hair. As is his usual practice, Moses (September fourth) keeps his distance, kneeling at the outer edge of firelight with Sozon, keeping watch for the Dog. They all turn as Mary, Mother of God, approaches the camp. She has just arrived; the hem of her blue robe is already black with mud. The others nod in greeting and make room around the fire.

CHAPTER 11

he next afternoon, as the sun dapples the water, Arkady catches a gleaming salmon at the sandy mouth of a little stream. The fish is small but fat, and Arkady leans his fishing pole against the high bank, guts the salmon, and eats it raw right there. The flesh is firm and delicious, especially sprinkled with the last of his salt.

"Praise be!" Shouting to God, Arkady leaps to his feet. Fish will be bountiful! He rejoices to himself, and almost immediately, he spies a huge Cross standing on a rise some distance north. *See?* he thinks. *I utter thanks to your impeccable mercy, and here you are, made tangible.* "Could it be Father Vasily?" he speaks aloud, his mind suddenly reeling with the idea that his journey might be much shorter than he'd thought.

All the saints shake their heads.

"It is a sign. Surely it is a sign that I am on the right path!" He will pray Vespers tonight at the foot of that Cross.

Arkady rinses his hands in the surf. He hefts his pack onto his back, picks up the satchel, and sets off at a swift pace without looking back. Suddenly, and for the first time, he truly believes his northward journey will be successful. He will eat fish, be sustained, and, by the time he reaches Father Vasily, he will have entered the holy light of the true pilgrim. He will have found his true spiritual home.

All the saints call out and gesture for Arkady to turn around, to go back to the salmon stream, to pause and reflect before charging ahead.

Soon, he is close enough to see that the huge Cross has two boards angled up from the crossbar to form a triangle. An old Promise Cross. Just beyond it is a tiny wooden hut, weathered gray. Is it possible someone is there? He sees no smoke, and yet his hope rises. He hurries on.

Some distance ahead, Moses crouches behind a granite boulder. Like a scout on a battlefield, he gestures for Arkady to take cover.

Gliding on his pillar, Simeon the Stylite whispers, *This doesn't look good.*

But Arkady can't see what frightens his saints: A new, massive figure looms up from behind the Cross. He is a huge, grimy Pomor dressed in reindeer skins that are falling to ribbons, as is his own skin. His tangled hair falls in a knotted mat all down his back, and his tundra-tinged beard reaches his waist. High on his exposed cheekbone blooms a rosette of orange lichen. He screams at the saints and throws stones that crash to the beach and splinter the driftwood.

Arkady walks right up to the Cross and kneels at its foot. He prays for a long time while the Pomor continues his tirade: *All of you stay away from here! I survived the storm and built this Cross in good faith. I remembered my promise. But you took me the very next night, during the very next squall? Was I a joke to you? Stay away from my grave, or I'll pummel you with stones. I will grind you to dust.*

Sozon vies for the Pomor's attention by waving the golden arm. He wants to explain that that isn't how things work with them, that he has misunderstood a saint's function. But the Pomor catches the golden arm with a good-sized stone, and it spins out of Sozon's hands and lands on the beach with a clang. All the saintly ones take cover except Vasilissa, who is already hidden.

Oblivious to the otherworldly commotion, Arkady crawls through the partially collapsed doorway of the old hut, but no one is there. There are words carved into one of the time-beaten planks —a message?—but he doesn't recognize the language. He can't bear to stay there for long, so he makes his own camp farther up the beach.

CHAPTER 12

agging memories chew at the edges of Arkady's mind as he trudges onward with his saints in tow. He grows more and more sullen as the visions break up the present moment and pull his attention ever backward. The sun blesses him with its light. Storms are not yet on the horizon. And yet, the hopeless dramas of the past pull Arkady into darkness.

Over several years, Arkady watched Maksim become the monastery's rising icon painter while Arkady eddied in rotating, unskilled positions. When Maksim was just eighteen, one of his Savvatii icons was presented to the Tsaritsa in Moscow. The message she sent back to Solovetsky was that Maksim should paint some of the other saints. She suggested the Archangel Michael, which caused the brethrens' tongues to wag: "One so young! Michael? It will go to his head!"

But Maksim seemed to save all his energy for painting and prayer. He had no close companions, and his starets did not fuss over him or build him up. Steadily, his fame as an icon painter grew, thanks to the three-day pilgrims.

They arrived at the monastery every year between May and August, as they had done for the past century. There were more of them during Arkady's years at Solovetsky than at any other time in the history of the monastery. This was partly because of the roads that now crosshatched most of Russia and partly because the monastery had decided to make it easier for the pilgrims to come by building two big hostels in Arkhangelsk and adding another steamer to its fleet of ferries. And lastly, it was because women were now allowed to make the popular pilgrimage to pay homage to Saint Savvatii, pray, and endure what they considered the ascetic life of the north.

By the time Arkady was twenty, the three-day pilgrims enraged him, and, in his heart, he knew that the monastery patriarch, Father Leonin, had been wrong to increase their numbers. He disagreed with this Archimandrite on more than just this issue. Since Father Leonin had arrived at Solovetsky, Arkady had endured homilies in the refectory on the harmony that can exist between the layman's and the holy man's lives.

"We can be of most service if we exist together with, not separate from, the laymen," Father Leonin said. "Only then do we have the greatest chance of helping the most people to salvation."

This was a silly thing to offer monks living on a remote archipelago—anyone could see that.

Arkady also knew the real reason the monastery had bought the second steamer and built the hostels in Arkhangelsk. Now that roads connected the vast, different regions of the country, and artisan products flowed steadily into Novgorod, Saint Petersburg, and Moscow, there was less demand for Solovetsky pottery, bread, and forged goods. But those same roads brought visitors to the monastery; a new economy of pilgrimage was rising. During these years, thanks to the three-day pilgrims, icons had become synonymous with the monastery on the White Sea. Specifically, Maksim's icons. Maksim himself lived in a simple cell in a loft above the icon studio. In fact, he rarely left that building and, by all accounts, was as humble a monk as the one feeding the hens.

But one night, after the midnight office, Arkady took a short walk out in front of the monastery's great walls to enjoy the midnight sun's rosy light. After contemplating this beauty, he made his way back toward his cell to gaze from his small window once more, breathing in the peaceful scene of the island at rest. Suddenly, he saw a pilgrim, a woman, trotting past the stables, in a direction that was certainly not toward the women's dormitory. From his window, he followed her progress across the cherry orchard and kitchen gardens until she disappeared between two manufacturing buildings.

Of course, he didn't know which direction she'd gone, so once he reached the place where he'd last seen her, he peeked in the windows of the brickworks and the leather-working studios. Then the cobbler shed and forges. He crept up to the last building in the row, the icon workshop—Maksim and his assistants were known to work through the white nights when the Spirit moved them.

At first, nothing seemed awry. He looked in on the studio, empty save for Maksim himself, standing at his work easel. Arkady had to admit it was a beatific scene. He almost turned away, except he noticed something strange about the canvas in front of the painter. Instead of a thick, golden mandorla in the upper half of the icon, there was a head of feminine curls. Leaning in and squinting, Arkady realized that Maksim was painting a layperson. A woman! And then he discovered the woman herself, sitting so still that Arkady hadn't even noticed her, and he gasped. Here was the monastery's most famous acolyte, using the sacred pigment for a cheap layman's picture? What a blaspheming, greedy, worshipper of false idols! He'd always known there was something unholy about Maksim. Righteous anger flooded his mind.

Even now, trudging northward, so far away from the incident in space and time, Arkady's outrage radiates in a palpable heat, and the fist of the past lands a quick punch to his gut.

To break free, he forces himself to feel the mildness of this day. With his hat and mittens firmly on, the breeze across his cheek is refreshing not bracing. The mosses give a satisfying spring below his step; he reiterates to himself how much more he likes walking up here, along the green bench, as opposed to the beach.

He works to stay in the present moment, but despite his efforts, and despite Simeon the Stylite's continued shouts and hand waving, which had begun the day before when Arkady spotted the old Promise Cross, Arkady has no ears to hear. He still does not realize that he left his fishing pole far behind at the salmon stream. He's already replaying the next part in the story.

Arkady burst into the icon studio, and with the clattering of the door, the laywoman leapt up in surprise.

"How dare you use the sacred pigments this way?" Arkady said. "Doesn't this negate everything you've ever painted and everything you will ever do? How can this be, Maksim?"

"My lady, that will be all for tonight," Maksim said, ignoring Arkady.

The laywoman gathered her shawl around her shoulders and hid her face as she left the workshop.

"What is your name?" Maksim asked. Rather kindly, which angered Arkady. They had delivered eggs to the studio together, years ago. Did Maksim not recognize him?

"Arkady."

"Arkady, the truth is that Fathers Leonin and Kristof are well aware of this practice. It is one of the ways of the world that brings a significant amount of benefit to our monastery. It is a hidden economy, yes, but not a blasphemous one, according to our Fathers, who represent God's will on our island." Maksim smiled as he continued, "Similar to the escapades of our boys during the summers. Acceptable in the larger context of the Church as part of the world of men."

It was true that an unspoken agreement among startsi and church elders was that boys in the monastery school should taste of the world so that each boy could make his own decision about whether to stay on as a man to join the brethren. During the summer months between the boys' fifteenth and sixteenth years, the youth could be seen in rowboats out on the lakes, wearing handsewn approximations of laymen's clothes, with three-day-pilgrim girls and boys in tow.

"I make these paintings for nobility. This one," he gestured to the wood panel, "was commissioned for two thousand rubles. All of which the monastery receives."

Arkady had never heard of anything in the world that cost two thousand rubles. It was more than he could imagine. "And you make many of these?"

"One every three days during pilgrim season."

Sixty thousand rubles each summer. This mind-boggling sum would be enough to run the monastery for a year.

Maksim held his hands palms up. "Whether we prefer it or not, we all are of this world, Arkady. And the monastery needs these benefits to run. Do you understand what I am saying?"

Arkady backed out the door. Maksim turned to his easel and calmly put his pigments away.

On the Spitsbergen horizon, peaceful clouds rise. Moss springs underfoot, but not far below that, soil gives way to solid ice. Surfacing into the present moment, Arkady breathes deeply to center himself. *Lord, I am unworthy of your love, yet I beg you to wrap your arms around me and sustain me during this trial. Cool my passions. Help me to keep you at the forefront of my thoughts and thereby banish the vicissitudes of worldly care.*

Five minutes later, Arkady was back at Solovetsky. After what he witnessed in the icon studio, he ran straight to his starets. When Father Ilya heard of the night's drama, he looked out the window of his cell for a long time, watching the pattern of gulls as they circled above the monastery gates. Then, he turned and patted Arkady on the arm.

"Well, we'd better go find Father Leonin."

"Right now?" Arkady had never had a private audience with the Archimandrite.

Ilya splayed his hands. "You're a grown man now, Arkady. Do you want to tell him what you saw, or don't you? The choice is yours."

"I want to tell them."

"It is the Archimandrite's breakfast hour. He'll be in the refectory. Come."

They found the Holy Father with a cloth napkin tucked into the collar of his vestments, and hands clasped around his soup bowl. When Ilya and Arkady appeared beside him, Father Leonin looked up but continued to eat. The other Fathers at the long table turned to watch as Ilya nudged Arkady, and Arkady stepped forward.

"Holy Father, forgive my boldness in approaching you at table. Forgive me for approaching you at all. But last night I discovered something that I'm sure you will want to know about."

Father Leonin raised his eyebrow at Ilya and tore a chunk of dark bread off the loaf on the breadboard. Arkady described the laywoman scurrying across the orchard and sneaking into the icon workshop and what he saw when he followed her.

"Maksim was using the sacred icon pigment for this crude picture!" Arkady whispered.

The eyes of the other priests and monks swerved to the Archimandrite as if magnetized. Arkady had expected a collective gasp or at least the signature rustle that signaled a disturbance among the brethren. He realized all these men already knew about the lay paintings. Which meant that Ilya must also have known. Ilya's lips were pursed, and his eyes, too, rested on the Archimandrite.

Father Leonin pulled the napkin from his collar and rose from the bench with a lurch. He looked at the row of questioning faces down one side of the table and back up the other.

"If we do not provide these portraits, *as the Tsaritsa herself has requested,*" Leonin turned his head sharply toward Ilya, "we will lose a quantity of annual revenue that will make it necessary to increase the number of our three-day pilgrims by five hundred per month during the summer. This will mean that we'll need to build annexes to all our existing dormitories, add a refectory, and endure the effects that more pilgrims will have on our monastery grounds. How many of you would like to see that happen?"

No one moved.

"How many of you would enjoy seeing this happen?" Leonin paused. "Arkady?"

Frozen, Arkady could not speak.

"Then I consider the matter settled." Leonin walked away from the table and out of the refectory.

After his studies that afternoon, Arkady searched the monastery's library and archives. It wasn't long before he found the name of the Bishop of the Archdiocese of Moscow. Arkady supposed that this Holy Father was the next logical step. He wrote a simple letter telling him everything.

Fifteen versts north of the Promise Cross, Arkady's feet hurt badly. He's limping when he comes across the ruins of two ancient, huge hearth rings. Their crumbling, red brick walls stand knee-high and enclose black circles of bare ground. When he pokes the stony material with his foot, it flakes like charcoal.

His patron saints gather a short distance away. He has found the disintegrating remnants of a copper pot nearly twelve feet around, which had once rested atop these brick hearth walls. Two hundred years earlier, Dutch whalers used the pot to render the famous Spitsbergen whale oil. Kegs of it filled their hulls as they made their triumphant way south across the Greenland and Norwegian seas, and down across the North Sea to the port of Amsterdam. From there, the oil dispersed by cart and ship to light the lamps of the world. All the saints push together, but even they are not strong enough to right the old rendering cauldron.

A little way upslope, huddled together in an indiscriminate mass, sits a group of six Dutchmen who, over the centuries, have turned the color of driftwood. They wear wide-brimmed felt hats and sit with their knees to their chests, staring at Arkady like vacant-eyed chessmen carved from walrus tusk.

Arkady carries enough food for at least another week, but he'd planned to be moving faster, and by boat, skimming along the coast during these last days of full light. He'd hoped to reach Father Vasily before his stores ran out. By now, and especially with the loss of his fishing pole, which he is not willing to go back for, he knows that will never happen.

As he walks on, and not for the first time, he wishes Saskia were still with him, even with her carved doll and frightening superstitions. Despite his good boots, a layer of skin above his right heel has rubbed off. He guesses he's walked more than ninety versts since he started out, but without bells to mark the time, and across such rough terrain, he can't be sure. And the weather is turning.

The next day, seeing Arkady's worsening limp, Simeon the Stylite, Mary, and Sozon gather close around him, with Sozon scuttling ahead to move the more awkwardly sized rocks out of Arkady's path. Moses stays ahead of the group, carrying a stone in each hand to hurl at the Dog. But the newest ones—three sisters martyred in Bithynia during the first years of the fourth century— lag behind.

Simeon whizzes back and forth so the girls won't feel abandoned, but by midday they are far behind the rest. The others had hoped that little Vasilissa might turn to these new ones for comfort, but the girl is nowhere to be found. The lovely martyr sisters, Menodora, Metrodora, and Nymphodora, commemorated on September tenth each year, huddle so closely together that they are a lavender- and rose-colored jumble with dark hair and darting eyes. They whisper among themselves and softly exclaim each time one of them stumbles and is pulled back up by the others.

CHAPTER 13

few days before Lent, in the cold and dark of the Solovetsky midwinter, Arkady happened to overhear two novices in the refectory wondering aloud who the next promising icon painter might be.

"Has something happened to Maksim?" Arkady inquired.

"He is banished," said the novice.

Arkady's letter, sent six months earlier, had reached Moscow, and the correct action had been taken.

Usually, when acolytes or priests left Solovetsky, the brethren prepared a special service with hymns and tokens of appreciation. But here was nothing of the sort. He wondered if it were possible that the Tsaritsa's hand itself might have been slapped over the ordeal. He had done the right thing! He had finally done something important and Godly. Even within the regulated cogs and structured wheels of Church bureaucracy, *he* had made this happen.

Thereafter, Arkady found himself friendless. Those who formerly shared meals with him no longer made room. Those who had offered amiable nods now averted their eyes. An invisible border separated him from others during studies in the library, and even in church, surrounded by dozens of brethren all connected by the word of God, he was alone.

This was also the time that Father Ilya became ill. Arkady understood that, without his starets as an advocate among the society of monastery elders, his unpopularity would rise unchecked. This is when Arkady became serious about his plans to go north.

He studied the writings of the Desert Fathers and Theophan, Bishop of Tambov. He memorized all thirty rungs on the ladder to Heaven and read as much about the Northern Thebaid as the monastery library allowed. Since his petition to live in one of the island's small huts far from the monastery was declined, his studies remained decidedly bookish.

He gave thanks for all he'd received at the monastery, but it was the annoyed acknowledgment of an adolescent. Soon the Jesus Prayer became his only home. He felt that he'd been called to shed the world and give himself fully and only to the journey of his prayers. Commerce and worldly business blanketed Solovetsky, and this problem, condoned by the elders, grew worse all the time. His hatred of this worldly intrusion pervaded his days, perhaps even more insidiously than the prayers taking root.

In May, a few days after Ilya took to his bed for what would turn out to be his final months, he summoned Arkady to his side. "You are not going to like what I have to say to you." Ilya's soft face had caved like the flank of a malnourished animal. Arkady found it difficult to look at its unpleasant new topography. "But please temper your reaction with awareness of God's plan for you, or at least pray for the virtue of patience to see you through."

"What is it?"

"You've been called to help during mealtimes in the pilgrim refectory. Just for the summer, little one. When autumn comes, you will be back to your usual schedule."

"The pilgrim refectory? Why me? It is only much younger boys who work there. Much, much younger! I am twenty-four years old. There is no one over sixteen serving in the refectory!"

"It has been decided that that is where you will serve God for the time being. In the women's refectory."

"That is the worst place in all of Solovetsky."

"You allow your emotions too much power. This hinders your journey into God's light."

Arkady turned away. He noticed that Ilya's chamber pot was brimming and foul. Flies sat in a row along the brass rim, greedily rubbing their forelegs together.

"What choice do I have?" Arkady asked.

"What choice do any one of us have but to serve God as we are guided to do?"

Arkady bowed his head but could not bring himself to say more. Trembling with rage, he left the room without tending to Ilya's pot.

Arkady clenched his teeth for the duration of his last summer at Solovetsky. Now, recalling it all as he trudged along in Spitsbergen, he wished he'd kept his eyes open to the particular beauty of the place so that his stores of memory would have been richer, more comforting, and perhaps could have sustained him longer as he faced Spitsbergen's darkest reaches. He could recall the network of monk-built, moss-lined canals that connected the island's many lakes, where he'd spent his favorite hours floating near a shore full of windswept, spindly birches. But what of the afternoon light glinting off wavelets in the harbor? The ethereal aroma of northern wildflowers in bloom in the meadows? Over time such things as the thick beeswax candles that filled each chapel and church, the main kitchen's fragrant herb garden, and even the unique resonance of a room full of prayers faded away in the face of new trials.

As it was, during that last summer, he perceived nothing but sin sucking the life out of a once-holy place. He served pickled herring and sour cream to women of all shapes and sizes, and all he saw was their common bondage to the evils of the world. He worked alongside the boys from the monastery school who, for this one summer out of their lives, were given permission to flirt with the women. These lust-filled fellows, Arkady was horrified to observe, were bold and forward not with girls their own age but with the mothers.

Perhaps because they had been raised by innumerable fathers, the boys conflated mother and lover and went out of their way to display their readiness for trysts at the expense of daughters who vied desperately for the boys' attention. Judging by the number of clucking women who lingered by the refectory door after meal-time, the boys were not being turned down.

Arkady didn't know whether Father Ilya suffered from something other than age itself; the monastery healers often did not speak in medical terms. All he knew was that Ilya could not eat, move, or relieve himself without help. Arkady was expected to forgo his studies and even church services to tend to his dying teacher. So, every day, before and after he endured the frippery of female pilgrims, Arkady sponged Ilya's face and body, changed his sheets, and aired his cell. Ilya had grown quiet and watchful in his decline. For almost two decades, Arkady's starets had greeted him with a smile and a wink. Now, Ilya just stared from his bed, his face owlish and unreadable. At times Arkady thought Ilya was deep in the world of his prayers, but as the summer reached its prime, Arkady wasn't so sure.

"Teacher, what's your name?"

Arkady had just read to Ilya from the Philokalia. He asked the nonchalant question as he tidied the sheets around the old man and prepared him for sleep.

"Who do you think that I am?"

Ilya stared straight ahead and spoke in a rasping monotone that Arkady had never heard before. Arkady saw the candle flame reflected in Ilya's dark pupils, which were so large that they blotted out all but a sliver of white.

"Tell me your given name."

"I am the light of the world." Ilya's voice didn't seem his own.

Arkady stepped back from the bedside. "Who?"

"I know where I have come from and where I am going, but you do not know where I come from or where I am going. You know neither my father nor me. If you knew me, you would know my father also."

Arkady gaped.

"I am going away, and you will search for me, but you will die in your sin. Why do I speak to you at all? Very truly, I tell you: before Abraham was, I am."

"What is *my* name, Teacher?" Arkady whispered.

"You are the son of man."

Arkady shook his head. "You don't recognize me?"

Ilya turned his head suddenly to look straight at Arkady. "I recognize all of my children."

Ilya reached out his claw of a hand. Arkady recoiled.

"All right. It's time to sleep now," Arkady whispered. "I'll blow out the candle."

"No matter," Ilya rasped. "I can see in the dark."

The next morning, Arkady stood outside Ilya's room for a long time, unable to enter. He could not bear the thought of Ilya's cold, grasping arms reaching around his neck as he lifted the old man out of bed to hold him over the chamber pot. After some time, a group of boys passed through the courtyard. Judging from the tools and buckets they carried, they were on their way to the stables. Arkady recognized one of them as a particularly ardent boy from the pilgrim refectory. The disgust he usually felt toward the boys and their fleshy obsessions faded. He experienced a shiver of relief he could almost call ecstasy when he perceived that he would not have to care for dying Ilya any longer. *His* Ilya was gone, that was certain. What was left but a physical husk as insubstantial as this boy's fleeting passions? Anyway, shouldn't Arkady spend his time preparing for his true, northern calling?

Arkady called the boy over, and soon it was agreed. After weeks in the refectory with these youths, he knew that their biggest problem was finding a place for trysts. Due to time constraints and the monastery's regimented schedule, venturing far afield wasn't an option, though there were many secluded groves and meadows on the island. But locating a private place among the monastery's droves was difficult because cells were shared among three or even five souls. The prospect of one's own, dedicated room for a few minutes each evening would have been very difficult for this particular boy to refuse.

Before Matins the next day, instead of going to Ilya's room, Arkady hurried to the stables and fulfilled the boy's early morning chores among the goats. It was the work of a neophyte, but Arkady suddenly did not see it as the insult that it was. After morning service, he fulfilled his refectory duties. He went about his day, picking up the boy's afternoon chores, as well. And after the pilgrims' evening meal, he went straight to the library to continue his studies of the northern ascetics.

While the rest of the monastery brethren prayed in the Transfiguration cathedral, the boy, fifteen years old, led a buxom, grayhaired pilgrim from Novgorod through the hidden tunnel that led from outside the monastery's west wall to the cellar of the main dormitory for tonsured monks. The boy listened until he was sure that no one else was present and then led the pilgrim—whose two daughters and husband prayed fervently in one of the pilgrim chapels—to Arkady's own cell, where the boy then pushed her roughly to the stone floor and tried desperately to discover how a corset was made to release its bounty. She, even more eager than the boy (for when would she have this opportunity again?) pried him off for just long enough to make the necessary adjustments.

And so it went through July, until one day, a Church Father whom Arkady recognized but didn't know, called him into one of the monastery's smaller chapels. Inside, Archimandrite Leonin himself stood facing the small iconostasis, his palms together and head bowed. Arkady stopped some distance behind him, glancing every which way until, after ten, then twenty minutes of silence and stillness, he let the world of the Jesus Prayer overtake him.

During the course of the summer, Arkady had noticed the emphasis of his internal voice shift to the second phrase of the prayer. He knew from his starets and other teachings that these shifts in tone and focus were one of the first perceptions of a mind gradually releasing its grip on the vast heart of a man. He was taught to pay attention to these divine vicissitudes; they marked the way on a holy treasure map, which led to one's own place in the pocket of the Lord.

Jesus Christ, Son of God, have mercy on me, a sinner. Son of God. Son of Man. God-man.

Arkady felt a tingle of recognition, for wasn't this the crux of a question so profound that it engendered centuries of monkish study across the world? How can Jesus be the Son of God? How is it that he is both human and divine? Arkady thanked God, and even Father Ilya, for planting these questions in his mind. Isn't this what a true hesychast, alone in the wilderness, should ponder?

Lord Jesus Christ—

"Arkady."

Father Leonin turned to face him. Illuminated by the sunlight streaming in the door of the chapel, Leonin appeared almost beneficent, but Arkady would not forget the older man's devotion to worldly commerce and cunning.

"Your starets has been called to the Lord."

Arkady gulped. He hadn't thought it would happen so quickly. It had only been three weeks since the boy took over Ilya's care. Why hadn't the boy told him?

"Yes," Arkady said.

"Apparently his body was in quite … a state."

"Oh?"

Leonin stared at Arkady, who stared right back at the most highly ranked Solovetsky elder. "Tell me, Arkady: what were Father Ilya's last words?"

"He said, 'Have mercy on me, a sinner.' He had been reciting the Jesus Prayer, and he passed after the last line."

Leonin continued to look at Arkady with a blank expression. "Is there not anything else you wish to tell me?"

"Father Ilya was the best starets any boy could have. I am very grateful that he treated me with the care and—"

"Arkady Afanasyev, you will now surrender all your monastic duties. Take a moment now to hear me and to understand that for a period of two months, beginning right now, you are not eligible to receive the Eucharist. Our goal is to restore you to full communion by Nativity, but let me be clear: you are receiving a punishment that was decided by the council of elders of Solovetsky as an appropriate penitence after your abandonment of your starets on his deathbed." Leonin anticipated that Arkady was about to speak and raised his hand. "Silence."

The Archimandrite walked past Arkady, who hadn't yet quite absorbed this newest change in fortune. From the doorway, Leonin turned back to him.

"For all the hours of the day that you are not attending services, you will work on the main dock, chiseling debris from between the planks. On occasion, if our cooks deem it necessary, you will help carry kitchen slops to the sty, but you are forbidden to prepare any food that will enter the mouths of the brethren."

The Archimandrite drifted out of sight among the dappled stones of the path back toward the Transfiguration cathedral. Confounded by his new station and shaken that his plot with the boy had been discovered (how? He would flog that fornicating husk!), Arkady ran back to his cell, where, to his horror, he found a set of wooden-handled, Solovetsky-made chisels neatly laid on his bed.

CHAPTER 14

rkady limps relatively alone through the late afternoon, while above him the low-slung sun sends golden bands of light shifting across the faces of the mountains. Sozon, Mary, and even Moses drop far behind him in an effort to help the three sister-martyrs, whose struggles have become a major distraction to the others.

The sisters have torn their robes and skinned their knees. They've been in tears numerous times each day; they are not at all equipped to keep up. Their ineptitude annoys Simeon the Stylite in particular: Surely in their many centuries of roaming the world in service of humans, these women would have built up their stamina. Or at least grown some calluses. To escape their whimpers, Simeon glides out over the frigid shallows. His pillar leaves a very faint wake, which Arkady has no eyes to see.

Up until now, the saints had hoped that together they might function as Arkady's second sight. Indeed, with the addition of the three sisters, they may well have reached a sort of divine threshold beyond which they could have awakened Arkady from his backward-facing reveries into the wonders of the present moment, and thus onto a true path of the Spirit.

Theoretically, they could have succeeded, and given more time, perhaps they would have. But the sisters prove to be a fatal distraction because just at the moment that Moses, the group's self-appointed sentinel and scout, kneels to help untangle Metrodora's trailing shawl from a driftwood snag, a twelve-year-old female ice bear rises like an apparition some distance behind them. Her head is a level, predatory triangle. She moves swiftly toward the saints. She is hungry and calculating and has not seen another of her kind since a roaming male of her species devoured her two yearling cubs three months earlier. She had been about to turn inland and travel north up the icy spine of the island to the pack ice when she smelled something unusual on the beach.

Simeon the Stylite sees her first. He yells a warning before gliding toward the others. If he can bring them up onto the pillar they might be saved. Mary runs up the beach toward Arkady, believing that somehow her deep, though impersonal, love for the wayward human might protect him, if only she could reach him in time. The bear shifts to an easy lope. Moses and Sozon stay behind, helping the sisters, but Sozon soon wastes the group's only real defense by hurling the golden arm directly at the approaching bear, who swerves casually out of the way. Moments before the bear sends the sister-martyrs back to the long, spiraling road from whence they came, Menodora, Metrodora, and Nymphodora turn toward Arkady's receding back and bow, willingly giving themselves so that he might be saved.

Arkady looks over his shoulder just as the bear raises her bloodied face. Prey has been scarce here, in the vicinity of Lixets Rocks. She has not eaten since she felled a reindeer almost two weeks earlier. Arkady's eyes go wide. The bear's yellowish coat glimmers against the dark beach.

My God, will it be like this? Will he be torn apart, devoured by a beast?

He trundles up the beach, willing each effort of muscle and bone to make him into something he's not: agile, fast, smart enough to get away. He drops the satchel that holds his lifeline: the food and his books—the Gospels, a prayerbook, the Psalms, the Philokalia, Saint Athanasius' *On the Incarnation*, and Climacus'

Ladder of Divine Ascent—his only solace. Then, he forgets his limp and runs for his life.

Behind him, the bear makes quick work of Sozon and Mary and then chases Simeon through the shallows until she's close enough to bump his pillar and throw him neatly off. Moses is the last to succumb, and then the bear mauls Arkady's dropped satchel, scattering flour and devouring the dried fish and meat inside.

Arkady runs and prays and runs. *It can't be time. Not nearly time, not yet.*

The ice bear sniffs the air. Soon, very soon, the earth will turn its face from the light. She'll hunt seals from the pack ice under a sky illuminated by a depthless amphitheater of stars. She gauges the distance between Arkady and herself. Then, she smells something else. To the east, a black shape picks its way down from the scree. It trots toward her, but its eyes are fixed ahead. She goes silent and bares her teeth. When the Dog approaches, she lunges and scares him off. Then she removes a bit of shale that has lodged uncomfortably between two pads in the underside of her hind left paw. She turns back to her kills and scavenges what she can.

CHAPTER 15

s it turned out, chiseling caked dirt and other accretions from between the planks of the monastery's main dock suited Arkady better than serving meals to pilgrims. From his reading, he knew that the work of the hands is a crucial component for those serious about a life of the Spirit. He knelt in an attitude of supplication with towels tied around his knees for padding, carrying out his duty with as much humility as he could muster, given his great anger toward Father Leonin for allowing Solovetsky to edge ever closer to becoming a marketplace, souvenir stands and all. Arkady's desire to leave the monastery grew as he watched three-day pilgrims disembark from the steamers with their pocketbooks and gaiety and hungry eyes. He prayed for God to show him a new path, and when, after only three weeks on the docks (he had chiseled his way through eighty-one planks), his fate approached in the form of a speck on the horizon that grew into the shape of an old lodja, he was not surprised.

Evgeny stepped casually off his ship. "Greetings, little priest. We are Spitsbergen-bound and have come for supplies of flour, grains, pickled cabbage, and a barrel of scurvy grass. Nails, too, and pulleys and sheaves from your foundry."

Instead of ignoring the heathen's request, as he would normally have done, Arkady stood up. Dirt cascaded from his canvas apron and fell into the sea. The Pomor eyed him curiously.

"Of course. Give me a list of what you need, and I will fetch it."

"A list?" Evgeny laughed. "Wouldn't that require paper and pencil, not to mention the patience to write it?"

Soon, Arkady had procured not only what the Pomors requested but also Evgeny's reluctant permission to join their voyage north. Arkady assured him that he'd been training for the ascetic life ever since he was a boy, and that the Church Fathers had given their blessing.

"We are departing tonight at the stand of the tide. Surely you'd not be ready to leave so soon."

"I am ready now."

It was Arkady's resolve, and the obvious fact that he was being punished by the Church, that Evgeny let him aboard. Certainly no one else approved.

"We are taking him to his death," said the Pomors.

"That may be so," replied Evgeny, "but a man must be given an opportunity to test his conviction. And did you hear his name? Arkady Borisovich Afanasyev! This is the son of Boris Nikolayevich Afanasyev and the grandson of our own Nikolai Afanasyev, may his soul rest before Starostin's great hearth."

The Pomors nodded. Even if Arkady didn't recognize the forces that moved him north to the land of his ancestors, who were they to refuse passage to such a one?

The monastery fathers wholeheartedly disapproved of Arkady's plan to go north. They had been watching him; they knew which books he'd been reading in the library, and it didn't take much speculation to see what he had in mind. After dinner in the elegant parlor reserved for the elders, over steaming cups of Chinese black tea sweetened with fresh milk and raspberry jam, they bickered about whether to intervene. Some felt that Arkady would surely die in the northern wilds, so his plans must be stopped. Others shook their heads and said the monastery would do well to rid itself of a troublemaker like Arkady. He would never be an asset to the Church, and he had caused enough problems already. In the end, they let him go.

Just past midnight, when the summer light was at its most beautiful, Arkady passed through the holy gates of Solovetsky for the last time. As he walked onto the dock, all the icons that dwelt within the planks pressed their hands upward in an effort to touch the monk's heels in blessing.

CHAPTER 16

ithout the extra burden of the satchel in his hands, Arkady should have walked more easily, but new blisters on the balls of his feet cripple his progress, and he replaces the lost satchel with a walking stick. He worries more than he should over the loss of the oarboat. If it weren't for that madwoman, he'd be much farther up the coast by now, he thinks, maybe even to Magdalene Fjord.

He limps across the tundra plain that stretches ahead of him as far as he can see. It is patchy like the shedding hide of a reindeer. His burning feet sink into the uneven tussocks and moss, causing more work for each step to count as movement forward. Under a sunset dotted with the variable shapes of clouds, he picks his way along, stepping on islands of bright lichen and pillows of moss, and leaving behind deep footprints in the vegetation. Large, downy feathers blow across the plain. Once, a pod of a hundred small, bone-colored whales passes offshore, making its way north. Leaning on his stick, Arkady watches them roll and dive.

If this should be my end, so be it, he breathes. But deeper within, a rage bubbles up. *In good faith, I came here. You would not still my heart so soon… you wouldn't. I must reach my teacher, Father Vasily.*

There is an even dusting of snow on the shoulders of the mountains to the east, and nights are growing colder. Soon, these hours-long sunsets will fade to dusk and then quickly to darkness. Arkady's mind still hovers above Solovetsky but now from a greater distance; instead of replaying his dramas, he revisits favorite routes through the stone canals that connect the Solovetsky lakes. Between his prayers, he remembers specific patches of dark, lush moss and the brackish fragrance of the waterways and the way the oars creaked in their locks as he rowed to his best fishing spots. He can't imagine a more wonderful pastime than fishing at Solovetsky for delicious trout. This leads him back to the fact that he has very little food, so very little. Readily, he asserts that, of course, prayer, not fishing, is the most wonderful pastime in the world.

It has been two days since the ice bear tore through his food supply, and while Arkady maintains a vague sense that he's lucky to be alive, he can't shake the feeling that he's being followed. He looks over his shoulder at the wilds behind him. He spies his first reindeer this way. This shaggy creature wears an elaborate crown of antlers and grazes on similarly branched lichen. But something else he cannot yet see also is there.

Let it be you. No one ever said you do not creep up behind. I am a sinner, and the fear of ghosts is close to the fear of God. Let your terrifying power raise my hackles.

On the morning of what he believes is a Sunday, Arkady awakens and sits up, wrapped in hide and wool. Overhead the clouds withhold light so that nothing can soften the dark stone of the mountains.

Near him on the tundra, the ground is cracked into hexagons. He made camp here because of this appealing symmetry and because of a small lagoon that reminds him of the monastery's lakes. He pulls off two layers of socks and examines his feet. The blisters are ripe, and the surrounding flesh red and sore. His heel has bled through his sock. He packs moss onto the wounds and leaves his boots off.

He is familiar with the glazed-over feeling that dominates his senses. Everyone at Solovetsky knows what it's like to be hungry. He understands that he must put his mind to work on this problem of food, but for now the best he can do is stare at ripples on the water.

Jesus, you sat in the wilderness. I sit in the wilderness. You encountered temptation and evil and withstood it. But I am weak. This place frightens me.

He hears a rustle. Behind him a brown-white haunch and flick of a tail disappear behind a boulder. The shape doesn't emerge on the other side, and when Arkady finally turns away from it, there is a loon floating in front of him.

Loons breed on the lakes of Solovetsky; he has seen them all his life. But not in such close range. It glides across the water toward him until he can see its blood-red eyes.

"Good morning, sir," his disused voice croaks. "Or ma'am."

If loons really were among the makers of the world and do play a part in the ushering of spirits—which, of course, Arkady believes they were not and do not—then he should speak to this one with courtesy. He does it because he is spooked and also because, during the time he has been walking, he has felt his grandfather's presence close by.

The loon cocks its head.

"This pond seems awfully small for you."

He can't look away from the bird's stippled markings. He pulls the reindeer hide closer around his body.

"Not one, not two, but three times you dive down to the very bottom of the waters," Arkady whispers to himself, hearing his grandfather's voice. "And after you surface from the third dive, why, your mouth is full of mud! And with this mud, you create the world."

When he was very small, Arkady slept in a wooden cradle in the shape of a boat that his grandfather carved for him. The boat hung by two ship's lines from the low ceiling near the hearth, in his grandfather's cabin on the banks of the low-slung Laya tributary.

Inside this craft were fox furs and sheepskin, and as Arkady lay there, the old man would sit on a stool by the stove, rocking the cradle with one knee, carving chessmen and talking until Arkady fell asleep. Who knows but Nikolai kept talking even after that, sending stories and pronouncements up with the wood smoke to hover above the estuary and drift out to sea.

"Loons live all year round near the mouths of rivers," his grandfather's voice continues. "They do not travel south on the great bird way like the geese do. They remain here, diving for the souls of the dead. The dead travel along north-flowing rivers, you see. Here, where our Dvina meets the sea, the loon collects souls and gives their eyes to the Mother Below. Why do you think loons have such sharp bills? They use them to skewer those eyes! Without possessing the eyes, the Mother Below cannot bring those souls back round again. These are the processes that keep our world intact."

Nikolai was tall and lean, not huge and unkempt like Evgeny and the other Pomors. He wore colorful wool shirts from Novgorod and store-bought trousers. His white beard was long and tidy. He smoked out of an ivory pipe whose bowl was carved into the shape of a fist.

Only once as a child did Arkady see the great, white fur trousers and parka for which his grandfather was known among the other Pomors. As he watches the loon watching him, Arkady feels Nikolai so close that goosebumps rise on his arms, and he looks over his shoulder.

The story travels this way: When Nikolai was a young hunter on Spitsbergen, he once lay injured inside a small, dark hut. During that season, none of the usual hunting grounds had been fruitful. Reindeer retreated up the mountains. Seals hid among the northern floes, away from most Pomor field camps. And when Arkady's grandfather hiked to his favorite eider colony, where he was usually met by a hundred-thousand fussy sea ducks and half as many down-lined nests—enough to fill the enormous canvas bags he'd brought with him and planned to carry back to Advent Bay harnessed to a willow-framed backpack—he saw nothing but a vast, empty ledge sprayed with bright green lichen. For the first time in memory, the birds hadn't come.

Nikolai had only brought enough food for the journey out; every year since he was fourteen years old, he'd feasted on eggs and ducks while working at this camp. That first day, walking among the rock ledges, he searched for eggs. Perplexed and tired, he set his foot where he shouldn't have, and the stone tipped. Nikolai fell from the rock ledge, and on the way down, he twisted his knee. Crawling back to the hut took most of his remaining strength. At the threshold, he turned his eyes to the sky. In this place, a mistake could mean your life.

His knee swelled so that he could not walk. He lay on the hut's thin bed, while outside the bright sunlight illuminated the empty rock. He carved chessmen from a supine position to keep his mind busy, and all the while, he sang. He had opened the hut's only window, a small one right above the bed, for light to carve by, and with hope he would hear eider calls. He was just drawing a deep breath to start in on another song when the immense head of an ice bear poked through the window.

The bear was so close that Nikolai saw its black nostrils flare and contract, and the air around his head rushed to the animal with each of its inward breaths, and a puff brushed his eyelashes with every outward one. He smelled the creature's strength: the discrete layers of its many seasons of killing and the sweat of its unmapped travels.

So, this is the way, Nikolai thought, bathed in the bear's musk. *This is the way I will reach the long road.*

The bear's eyes darted in an unusual way, and Nikolai realized it could not yet see him in the darkness. He shot out his arm and slashed the bear's face with the tiny woodcarving blade. The half-made chessmen tumbled to the floor. Without emitting a sound, the animal withdrew its head. Nikolai leapt out of bed and hopped to where his musket lay on the table. By the time he'd gotten his hands around the gun, the bear had thrown its weight against the hut's door. For two centuries, these bears had lived parallel lives with the Pomors and, before that, the whalers. They knew men and muskets and doors.

Nikolai fumbled with the powder horn while the bear slammed against the hut. He filled the barrel and stuffed in a tuft of wool for wadding, but his hands trembled so much that he dropped the first ball on the floor, and it rolled away. He pushed the second one into place just as the bear broke through. Nikolai stumbled backward on his weak knee and crashed to the floor as the bear bolted toward him. He fired. The bear fell on top of him with force. Nikolai lay there while the bear groaned, shot through the skull. It took time for the creature to die, and Nikolai cried for it as he struggled to breathe under the bear's weight.

Nikolai never told this story to Arkady himself, but the old man's friends took every opportunity. Afterward, Nikolai walked forty versts back to Advent Bay on his injured knee, dragging the ice bear's bloody pelt behind him. The Pomors acted as if he'd only been away for an afternoon hunting trip; they didn't comment on the hide. But a few weeks later, his brethren took up the whalebone needles their grandfathers had carved for them and together stitched the fur garments that Nikolai would wear until the end of his seafaring days.

The loon preens and beats its wings against the water. It pedals its feet, seeking the air. Unlike most of their avian brethren, loons are made of solid bone, not hollow, because these birds are made to sink to the underworld. Arkady is sure the pond is not wide enough for the bird to fly. But it gains surprising momentum as it pumps its way across the surface. When it reaches the far shore, it continues running and beating its wings right up onto the mossy bank and across the plain. It runs and runs and finally, tucking up its webbed feet, takes to the air. The bird banks west and glides over the sea.

Its flight: impossible, then suddenly proved. Like my faith. Do not fault me my stumbling through the past. How could I do anything else? My heavy failings will pour out of me on this journey. I will shed what I can on my way to you.

Still wrapped in hides and sitting under an orange-streaked sky, unable to stand and continue walking north toward Father Vasily, Arkady reaches into the pocket of his starets' coat and lightly touches the two dried fish that have rested there since the ice-bear attack. Swiftly, he pulls his fingers away.

Arkady stays at the lagoon. He prays. Not unceasingly, and not from the deepest closet of his heart, but at times with great effort. He can't bear to walk on his aching feet, and the day passes before him. He understands that the cold is wedging itself into him, but he does not yet perceive how quickly one season gives way to the next in this place; each night is longer than the last, and each day the sun is weaker, more diffuse, surrendering to the inevitable.

Loneliness grips him and scatters his thoughts. He scans the horizon, searches the sea's riffles and swell, and looks nervously north.

Behind him, sitting in the lee of a granite boulder dropped by a melting glacier eighty-five hundred years earlier, whose whale-like surface is adorned with massive rings of centuries-old orange lichens, the girl-saint Vasilissa strokes the summer coat of an arctic fox who sits in her lap, alert but calm. Alone since the ice bear killed the others, Vasilissa is tiny, silent, and even more hidden than before, though she still trails Arkady and creeps close to his fire after he falls asleep. Hungrily, she pets the fox. The creature raises its nose and sniffs. When she feels the fox's desire to move, Vasilissa's grip tightens around the animal's body. She uses more and more strength to keep the animal still, but soon it snarls, and she cannot bear for it to hate her, so she lets it go. The fox shivers to rearrange its fur and flicks its tail twice. Then, it steps lightly out from behind the boulder and trots toward Arkady.

The day is Friday, September fourteenth. Arkady's misplaced Sunday prayers dissolve in the air.

Theoretically, each patron saint helps the next one find his or her bearings and acquaints them with the terrestrial situation into which they've materialized. Before, Simeon had carefully flagged down Sozon, Moses, and the others, explained that there was the Dog to watch out for, among other perils, and briefed the new-comers on which particular types of protection Arkady required. But the ice bear threw things off, and so does Vasilissa's solitary and uncharitable nature. Those who now arrive blow away like eider-down across the tundra.

Vasilissa is not in the habit of watching the landscape behind her, so she didn't even see one-eyed Paphnutius appear, leaning heavily on an acacia crutch. As a result, he wanders south and away from the human he was meant to protect. On the twelfth of September, in a riot of confused shouts, the martyr Julian appeared. He probably would have found Arkady despite Vasilissa's negli-gence, but his entourage of forty beheaded companions required most of his attention. Vasilissa observes them for a minute, but she has no interest in the messy, bloody men, and she walks on. Next came Cornelius the Centurion, the first pagan recorded by the Gospels to convert to Christianity. Without a notion of which way to go, but with admirable confidence, Cornelius strode inland along a narrow river valley that ultimately leads to a glacier. Dressed mostly in metal, in a helmet adorned with dyed horsehair plumes, Cornelius is a fighter, and well-trained. The Dog took him right away for his army.

So, Vasilissa remains relatively alone with Arkady, barely keep-ing the Dog at bay with her presence. She hides behind the boul-der, and later, once Arkady has scared off the fox for the second time, the creature returns to curl up in her lap, and the girl smiles for the first time in centuries.

CHAPTER 17

n the morning, Arkady tucks his flint, steel, and tinderbox into the pocket of Father Ilya's coat, which now he wears continuously, fully buttoned, day and night. He packs up the rest of his camp and ponders the mossy indentation that represents his earthly form. A cold breeze lifts strands of his dark hair. His beard suddenly itches, and he rubs his face with mittened hands.

Truly, it is better to fast than to starve. What else can we humans do but exert our puny will and, by the contours of our effort, see the framework upon which the universe is draped? What else can we do? My earthly husk is hungry, though my spirit still feeds.

The clouds have retreated to the sky's upper reaches, and an elongated sunrise stretches a pale-yellow arm across the horizon. This triggers a strange glow over the tundra plain: a variegated chorus of green and stone.

Arkady moves on. His body has benefited from a day of rest, but each step still hurts. He crosses a subtle point of land that ebbs into a narrow beach. Here, the stones reveal the outflow of a stream, whose course has eroded a rift in the mountain. Far above, Arkady hears but cannot see a waterfall. He drinks from the stream like an animal.

Foxes follow ice bears. That is their way. Foxes can hunt on their own, of course. In Spitsbergen, they specialize in ptarmigan and nesting sea ducks. But mostly they follow bears out onto the ice. Arkady cannot say that foxes have faith, though his grandfather might have said so. But foxes operate on the promise of left-behind blood and entrails. Foxes follow ice bears. But this one follows Arkady.

He drinks from the stream and watches the fox pick a delicate way across the wet tundra.

"The animals live by rules unknown to us. Mysterious rules, little one. Rules we could learn from. If you are going to be wise about things, which I know you shall, you will keep your mind open to the very different rules of the four- and two-legged creatures of the earth. Do you hear?"

Hindsight will change any interpretation, but even as young as he was when his grandfather said these things, Arkady heard nervousness in Nikolai's voice. By then, his grandfather had become thin, and he'd developed a rough and painful cough, which the old man cursed colorfully and continuously. Arkady must have been six years old by that time.

"Now that you're seaworthy, you must read the landscape of birds. It can tell you much about where your vessel is, and what types of wind lie ahead and behind."

His grandfather was bent over a cedar chest. He was packing. Always loquacious, Nikolai now poured forth a torrent. Even a child could sense something was amiss, but Arkady was so excited to finally go to sea and become a real Pomor that he didn't heed the balance tipping in his grandfather's voice: as if the old man recited straight from a pagan almanac, emphasizing lessons, which his grandfather usually avoided.

Nikolai lifted something from the chest. Trying to hide it and simultaneously appear casual, the old man turned away from Arkady and headed for the door. But a fold of white fur slipped from his arm, and what little boy wouldn't exclaim and beg upon glimpsing such a thing? And so, finally, the old man put on the furs and instantly transformed into something wilder and more frightening than the boy could have imagined. When Nikolai pulled up the hood, Arkady screamed, terrified that his grandfather, who by this time also was his mother and father, and whose usual place was near the hearth, could shape-shift so completely. Even now, it hurts Arkady to think of it, but again hindsight flavors all memories, and he has conflated this small betrayal with the larger one to come.

After he has been walking for some time, Arkady turns on his heel and kneels down with one arm outstretched. He extends one quarter of one dried fish (a full eighth of his last remaining food) southward and waits. After just a few moments, the fox edges up, sniffs the savory tidbit, bares his fangs, and plucks the torn fish from where Arkady has set it on the stones in front of him. The animal growls and retreats out of sight with the morsel.

From behind a driftwood log, Vasilissa frowns, confused by the human's kindness. Each night when the fox comes to her to sleep with its tail curled luxuriously at her neck, she feels its ribs poking a little closer to the surface of its body. All night she hugs the animal tightly and watches flat, gray clouds drift overhead. With the animal close to her, she is part of this immense place; she creeps, hides, and persists just like the delicate purple saxifrage blossoms she saw when she first arrived on the island. With the animal near her, she is stronger. By loving it, she is somehow more able to consider helping the human, although for now, she does not.

Nikolai carried his sea chest on his shoulder, and little Arkady trotted beside him, dragging his own small sack of clothes. They followed the dirt road along the tributary, whose silted brown water seemed to hold up logs and birds with a consistency more like pudding than liquid. The fragrance of mineral-rich soil emerging from snow-thaw moved through the air, and Arkady's newly knitted sweater itched wonderfully. He leapt over puddles and skipped along the muddy track. They stopped in the village for the old man to buy six fat skeins of tobacco and a package of sewing needles.

Then, they turned toward the small harbor, still several miles upstream from the sea, where they encountered some of the men who would join them on the voyage. Blending with the mist, the men smoked pipes and murmured as they walked.

Arkady had never known such joy as when he finally reached the end of the dock and climbed up the thick wooden plank to be lifted aboard the lodja. This was his birthright. His people. Nikolai smiled then looked away.

Then, they were underway, tacking across the river for almost two hours and then running before a fair southeasterly breeze straight into Dvina estuary. There, the ship found strong winds funneling into the White Sea, and poor Arkady, not three hours into his first voyage, fell into a terrible seasickness that unmoored him completely from any life he had known.

Now, the tundra plain extends its wide palm along the coast, and Arkady trudges in a daze of hunger through the afternoon and his most painful memories. His prayers only skim the surface of things, and he can't shake the feeling that his grandfather is walking just behind his right shoulder. Instead of a comfort, though, the presence unhinges Arkady's composure so that, for two hours, he can't keep from looking over his shoulder every few minutes. Once, when he turns, the fox is following closely behind him, and, using some of his small store of willpower, Arkady tears off a second chunk of dried fish. This time the fox takes it directly from his hand. Walking on, Arkady sucks his fingers for the salty residue. Then, he unwraps his prayer rope from around his wrist and slips it into his pocket.

The rest of Arkady's first voyage is a void in his memory. When the lodja reached Solovetsky Monastery for supplies, he must have been delirious or unconscious. He can't remember arriving there or the Pomor crew stowing barrels and crates of food and forged hardware from the monastery's workshops. Thankfully, he does not remember his grandfather lifting him from below deck, where he lay curled around a stanchion, and carrying him ashore and through the monastery gates.

When Arkady finally woke up, he was in a warm bed tucked in the corner of a room smelling pleasantly of beeswax. He stretched, sat up, and through a window, watched a bald man in long robes sweep sand from a stone path. Then, he bolted outside.

"Where is the lodja? Where am I?"

The monk, Father Ilya, knelt so he could look straight into Arkady's eyes. He didn't smile. "Your grandfather means for you to live with us. He felt he must go to Spitsbergen. He's left, my child. He is not coming back."

Arkady spun around, expecting to see Nikolai pop out from behind a tree, chuckling at the joke, bending down with his arms outstretched to scoop him up. But he was not there.

The third time he offers the fox a piece of fish, Arkady trembles with hunger. Vasilissa watches from the slope just above them. The fox will not go completely hungry today, and she is glad. She decides she will flag down the next patron saint. The human deserves a kindness in return for this one.

Below her, by the curve of a stream, the fox plucks the last of the fish from Arkady's outstretched left hand, and, quick as he can, Arkady grabs the animal by the throat with his other, gloved hand and holds on. He's decided he can bear the animal's claws but probably not its teeth.

Arkady will never forget the way the fox fought for its life. It drew both its hind legs close to its body and thrust them at Arkady again and again, faster than he thought possible, with its claws outstretched. It used these powerful tools to shred the wool in one section of Arkady's coat and to gash the skin of his right hand and wrist, and once even his face, as he fought to secure those legs. The fox writhed and used its front claws as shield and sword both, but a man's arms are longer than a fox's reach, and when a creature is gripped by the throat, it is difficult to persevere. After he secures the hind legs, Arkady shuffles on his knees to the bank of the stream and plunges the fox into the icy water. Unfortunately for the fox, the water is just deep enough, and Arkady's hunger just strong enough, for the man to succeed.

Vasilissa watches Arkady struggling with the fox and gradually understands she is watching a battle to the death. Her sight periscopes back and upward until she is a cloud observing a tiny diorama far below. But when the human finally raises the fox's limp and dripping form, the whole scene collapses in on itself, and the next thing she knows, she is crouched on desert sand, eyes squeezed shut, with her hands covering her ears. There is a crowd of sweating, screaming men, and the strength of the sun on her bare and bleeding back terrifies her as much as the men do. She feels the hot oil hitting her shoulders and hair, and she even hears the crackle of the torch just before the shouts fade in the face of the searing pain that fills and then bursts her open. Then, inevitably, the pain unto death blooms into something else: She is no longer a little girl. She is a figment, a force, and a bright, small terror adrift in time. This knowledge fills her mind and heart, and the old, familiar pain of burning to death fades as suddenly as it arose, and she is back in a stark northern land, kneeling on a cushion of intricate moss filaments, clenching her fists.

Vasilissa rises and turns from the human world, because she can. She glides over the ground. She continues up the scree slope, away from Arkady and his pathetic travails. Before long, she meets the Dog on his way down. He wants Arkady.

No, she says. *He is mine.*

The Dog smells death and furious power on the girl.

Vasilissa will be folded into the mysteries of Spitsbergen, comforted by the crags, and nourished by endless plains of ice and stone. In some future form, she will emerge from this sanctuary, but for now, she disappears.

CHAPTER 18

rkady eats the fox over two days, and soon he is hungry again. He has bandaged his right forearm with a dirty strip of fabric cut from the hemline of his shirt, but the ragged cuts from the fox's claws are hot and already swelling with infection.

I am in danger. I feel my own death on the path behind me. Guide your miserable brother. You are a perfect crystal, and I am nothing but a clump of sod.

Worldly care has prevailed. His prayers are only of the mouth, not of the heart. He puts his prayer rope around his left wrist, but it barely helps him. He is still taking the first steps toward God.

After a life in a monastery? After so much practice among the brethren? After all that, I am a worm, a tube, living to eat and only eat. It is better to fast than to starve. Better. Always better.

He teeters in the storm of his thoughts. He cannot keep hold of any one of them for long enough to see it through to a meaningful point.

I am simply struggling in the wilderness as countless others have done before me. This is a natural part of the holy path. But no! I am nothing. Less than nothing. A cursed fool. Not even my family wanted me. I was born to be alone and wandering.

After Arkady realized his grandfather was not hiding behind one of the monastery's stone columns, or waiting for him on the beach, he let Father Ilya comfort him, and soon he blocked himself from the inner realms of his broken heart and moved into the semblance of a regular life. He was seven years old and living among a group of boys for the first time.

Since summers at Solovetsky are short, the brethren allowed the littlest boys to run free for much of the time between services. They each had assigned chores—in the kitchen, for Arkady—but fishing, gathering firewood, minding geese, and running errands for the blacksmiths constituted part of the fun, especially when those tasks were part of large-scale games that spanned much of the monastery's main island. In good weather, they played Game the Bear, the Pike and the Crucian, and Wizards. Arkady, who had never had friends of his own, was breathless with love for the carousing boys. He pushed his grandfather out of his mind, ate his fill in the refectory every night, and fell asleep exhausted and happy in his little room.

When the first northerly winds reached Solovetsky at the end of summer, Arkady's grandfather's lodja returned. He heard the monks discussing it. They wondered why the Pomors were visiting again since the only thing that ever brought them to the monastery were supplies for the hunting season, and this ship was returning to Arkhangelsk. Arkady wondered if his grandfather would take him back to the mainland. But he didn't want to leave his friends.

After breakfast, Arkady lingered in the refectory as long as he could, helping more than usual to clear tables and sweep the floor. But as soon as he stepped outside, Ilya gestured him over to where he sat with a Pomor on a stone bench. Arkady didn't recognize the man, whose huge legs and mane of matted brown hair suddenly seemed to Arkady to be a disgrace here in the monastery. Or anywhere in the sight of God, he realized.

When Arkady came over, the Pomor knelt in front of him and said that Nikolai was dead. The Pomor said many things, but after those initial words, Arkady's ears filled with a roar, and all he could do was stare at the silver clasp on the Pomor's vest, forged into the shape of a great tree with a dog sitting at its base, front paws crossed.

"Nikolai brought you here so that you will grow strong in your mind," the Pomor said, gesturing to his own temple. "Strong in your mind, in your body, and in your heart." The Pomor leaned in closer. "That's the only way a Pomor can survive in the northern hunting grounds," he whispered.

The Pomor laid a leather-wrapped bundle and a small wooden case in Arkady's arms.

"He will resemble his grandfather," the Pomor said, standing up. Then, more softly, "The old man wanted to die in Spitsbergen."

The wooden case held a set of ornate chessmen carved from walrus bone. A few years later, Arkady traded it away to another boy in exchange for something in which he soon lost interest. The other gift was the antler-handled knife.

"Arkady, what do you have in exchange for the knife?" Father Ilya said.

Arkady emptied his pockets and found two shells from the beach and three blue-glass marbles. He held out these things to the Pomor, who solemnly took them and then touched the boy lightly on the shoulder and walked away.

Now, Arkady sits cross-legged on the tundra and uses the same knife to shave fox cartilage from bone. The knife's grip fits perfectly in his hands. He sucks on the last filaments of meat and stares at the gray, shifting sea. When the food is gone, he plunges the knife into the ground next to him, covers his face with both hands, and cries for his grandfather and for himself.

If he were a lucky or merely a different man, this rift in his heart—this pure grief for lost family—would have cleansed his soul and healed his old wounds. He would have wedged himself into it and broadened it into a life as a true hermit of God. Perhaps he would have been inspired to choose this lonely beach—the site of his awakening—as his permanent home. He could find firewood nearby all year round, and even wood for a new fishing pole. He could fish the stream just ahead of him; he still has time to catch enough for the winter if he begins right now and fishes every day, all day. He could dry lichen for tinder and build a sturdy hut out of notched driftwood tree trunks.

But before he has presence of mind enough to follow that path, a wooden door slams in the distance, and Arkady jumps up and runs toward the sound.

CHAPTER 19

head, the tundra plain recedes from the shoreline leaving a wide, flat expanse of beach. As he moves forward, Arkady searches wildly for whatever made the sound. At first, he can't see the hut since it's made from driftwood that has weathered to the same dappled gray as the beach.

But there it is, equidistant from the shore on one side and the foot of the mountain on the other: a cabin with a metal chimney that sends a healthy ribbon of smoke into the sky. Magdalene Fjord is still at least 160 versts away, but Arkady's hope surges toward the shelter that Vasily would provide. It is something he has never been without, and for the first time—right there, in his sudden longing—he sees what his choice to leave the monastery really means. *Did I not come here to learn, to be tonsured myself? God forgive me: I can't survive on my own.* He strides toward the hut. Roasted vegetables, he hopes. Potato stew? Bread.

Originally, it had been his intention to skin and cure the fox's hide so that no part of the animal went to waste. But after a botched attempt, he'd been too hungry to follow through with the undertaking, and he'd left the mangled carcass behind. Father Ilya and the brethren taught all the boys thrift, but without the men looking over his shoulder, Arkady couldn't be bothered. What's done is done.

An upside-down oarboat lies on the roof of the hut. Nearby are two sawhorses and a heavyset bench facing the sea. Leaning against the side of the hut is a shovel, and sunk into a chopping block is a respectable ax. A massive pile of cut wood sits just to the east of the hut atop a thick layer of sawdust. The woodpile rises as tall as the shelter itself, and barely visible beyond all that is another oarboat. Surely one of these can carry him to Magdalene Fjord, although the sea has been rough and will only get rougher. As he nears, Arkady hears music. He pauses. Instead of going straight to the door, he sits on the bench, transported by the simple melody of a stringed instrument. Usually, secular music is just a distraction from holy light, but after so many days of hearing nothing but his own crunching footsteps, this unexpected reel is heavenly.

After a few minutes, the music stops. Before Arkady has time to stand, a wiry man wearing a matted sheepskin vest and oil-stained leather trousers emerges from the hut and squints in the relative brightness of the world. He is beardless, with a pocked face and dark, thinning hair, and he clenches a wooden pipe between his teeth. He strides to the pile of firewood and doesn't see Arkady until on the way back. Arkady stands, and the man looks him up and down without stopping. The man disappears back into the hut and slams the door behind him.

The music starts up again. Because he can't think of what else to do, Arkady sits back down. He looks at his hands, one of them crisscrossed by his homemade bandage. He examines his dirt- and blood-stained palms and then the grimy backs of his hands. *Have I already blended to Spitsbergen's permeating gray? Am I an invisible specter so soon? Is it a sign that I should pass this cabin and keep walking toward Father Vasily?* He wonders. *What do I need with this unseeing man? But what of the boat? Surely there is a chance he'd give it to a man of God, if I may call myself such a one. I am a hollow husk. Show me how to exert my will in Your honor. In Your grace. Please, God, I want to sit by a stove. Jesus Christ, have mercy on me, a sinner.*

Taking courage from the prayer, and tucking his fears behind it, Arkady approaches the weather-beaten door. He gives two quick knocks then rubs his knuckles. Right away, the man answers.

"Ah, men jag trodde att du var en ande. Du är verklig, är du riktigt. Då antar jag att du ska ha lite te. Kom in, vandrare."

As the man makes these incomprehensible sounds, he glances at Arkady then searches the distance behind him. Arkady is taller, but the older man is coiled with a latent energy. He makes a rapid motion with one hand, and Arkady follows him inside.

"I am just a pilgrim," Arkady murmurs, overwhelmed by the sudden smell of life indoors.

"En rysk! Vilken fruktansvärd tur," the man mutters. A Swede, it seems.

The hut is very dark and hot. Like Nikolai's ice bear, Arkady sees nothing at first. Soon, a crude table and two chairs appear in the foreground, and many shelves line the walls. In the murky light, a smoke-darkened metal stove emerges at the back wall next to a narrow bed. The Swede picks up his strange fiddle, which has buttons and reeds as well as strings, and sits on a stool by the door. At the back of the hut, Arkady notices another person standing at the stove. The heat sucks Arkady's breath out of him; he blinks, trying to regain his bearings. The red-haired figure turns toward him and, in the murky heat, resolves into Saskia, who holds out a steaming cup.

Arkady cannot speak. He accepts the tea and looks at the damp, coppery strands of hair sprung free from her braids. The constellations of freckles covering her face and her arms below the rolled-up sleeves. The Swede swipes his bow across the fiddle's strings and moves his other hand up and down the row of strange wooden buttons. He ekes a jarring tune out of the instrument. Saskia nods encouragingly at Arkady, wiping her hands on a white apron that she couldn't have had with her when they left Schoonhoven, could she have? Arkady nervously looks around for a cradle or other sign of Saskia's bear-child but doesn't see one. It dawns on him that he could be dreaming.

"Thank you?" he ventures. His hands are shaking.

"You are alive," Saskia asserts, clapping her hands together once. "I was sure the Dog would take you right away. You made so many mistakes! After we parted, you must have done well. But you're hurt." She points to his arm.

"You didn't return to Schoonhoven," Arkady says.

Saskia seems larger than before. Her familiarity startles him; he didn't think he had much of an impression of her to begin with, besides the first indelible image of her squatting on her haunches. She helps take off his coat and settles him into a chair.

"The mountains called me." Saskia laughs as she unwinds Arkady's filthy bandage. "The fjords whispered for me to continue north! My mother called for me from her grave at Wijde Fjord. A voice called out, and I heeded the voice. Don't get excited, though: it wasn't your god, little priest."

Saskia crinkles her nose when she uncovers the parallel cuts along Arkady's arm. Pus fills each red crevice.

"A fox," she scolds. "No other creature here that size. Let's clean these up."

"Is that our oarboat outside?"

"Not ours anymore. Just mine. I will stay here awhile. The company of men is my weakness." She laughs and swats at the Swede with the hem of her apron.

The Swede plays the strange harp fiendishly. Every time Arkady peeks at him, the grimy man glares back.

Saskia turns back to the stove and pours water from a tin pitcher into a kettle. After so long outdoors, Arkady feels like the hut's walls are closing in on him. A panic clogs his throat.

"He works for Stockholm traders," Saskia says. "I don't know which. He has been here since spring, and he will stay until next Easter. His name is Kol. I do not yet know if he is a good man or a bad man."

"How long will you stay here?"

"I will go north. But the winds are bringing winter. I may stay here for some time. I prefer company during the long night."

"Where is your child?" The words fly from Arkady's mouth before he can stop them.

Saskia smiles and pats her stomach.

Has she eaten it? Arkady thinks, forgetting for a moment that the bear-child was made of wood.

Kol jumps to his feet. "*Pratar alltid bland er! Kan inte du hålla tyst?*" He sets down the harp and goes outside.

"Can you understand him?" Arkady asks.

"Yes, all but his words. You should introduce yourself. You are being rude, little priest."

Here, in this place so far from Arkady's society of brethren, and indeed so far from any society at all, he can't seem to alight on what to do. Should he leave immediately? Saskia's presence is confusing. Certainly, she is mad. Yet, conversing with another human is deeply comforting. The stove, even though it is made of rough metal, is the only hearth he's seen for many weeks. He would be a fool to leave before Saskia produces a hot meal, and if Kol invites him to sleep under a roof, he will not refuse it.

What is happening is Your Will. Have mercy. I barely have ears to hear.

After rinsing Arkady's arm with warm water, Saskia fetches an onion out of a wooden crate, halves it, and rubs the cut side into the wounds. Laughing at Arkady's shrieks, she then spreads a thick layer of honey over the gashes. Arkady reels as she wraps his arm in a new cloth cut from her apron, but no longer from pain. He's dizzy at the sight of this food.

"See, you are lucky!" Saskia says. "If you hadn't found us, those cuts would have killed you. Now, go introduce yourself to your host."

Outside in the gray light of dusk, Kol sits on the bench with a red tobacco tin on his lap. He glances up when Arkady comes out but continues working on the tobacco, pinching flakes from a strip of the plug he's cut and packing his pipe. He closes the tin and tucks it back into his vest pocket and brings out a small box of matches. The lit tobacco is fragrantly earthy. Kol sighs, his eyes cataloging the sea.

"My name is Arkady Afanasyev. I am a novice from Solovetsky." Arkady points to the prayer rope coiled around his wrist and reaches inside his coat pocket for his prayer book, which bears a gold filigree cross on its cover.

Kol narrows his eyes.

"I am going to Magdalene Fjord to find Father Vasily. That is my path here on Spitsbergen."

"Vasily," repeats Kol.

"Do you know him?" Arkady drops to his knees before Kol, who responds by frowning and gesturing for him to rise.

"*Det gamla dåre. Samla ägg och frysa ihjäl, och säger att det är Guds vilja. Endast ryssarna.*"

Arkady smiles. "You know him! I can tell. Thank you. Thank you, Kol."

Kol again shakes his head with a disgusted look. He shoos Arkady with his hands and points back to the hut. "*Lämna mig att röka i fred.*"

Arkady interprets this as an invitation to stay for supper.

CHAPTER 20

During the weeks that he'd been walking, Arkady maintained only a vague sense of light sliding into darkness. Because he is an animal himself, moving in and through the terrain and involved with its myriad changes, from subtle to catastrophic, he did not consider the whole, even though by the time he reached Kol's hut, Arkady had been wearing every piece of clothing he had, plus the wool blanket draped over his shoulders. It is only when he sits near the Swede's sad little metal stove, belly full of potatoes fried in seal fat, and gazes through a window and sees Spitsbergen thus framed by the tiny hand of man, that he realizes the planet has reached that point in its orbit, and that devastating angle, that signifies the beginning of winter. He contemplates the simple fact that his journey could end very badly.

But I cannot waste time fretting over the long night, he reassures himself. *I am here. I must face it with humility, even if it means death.*

Saskia sits across from Arkady, smiling at him over her tea. Before supper, she indicated that Kol's employer owned most of the provisions in the hut, and only the minimum could be spared for unexpected guests. She tells Arkady that Kol has been decent enough to take her in for the winter but that Arkady shouldn't expect to stay himself.

"I would not consider it," Arkady says. "I am on my way to Magdalene Fjord and Father Vasily."

"You won't make Magdalene Fjord before the long night. There's an old Pomor camp at Advent Bay," Saskia says thoughtfully. "But maybe it was abandoned after the whales left. I remember a large hut there, like Schoonhoven, probably with a cache. Since the northerly winds have already picked up, it's too late to go by boat. But you might make it there on foot before the long night if you go quickly and if the Dog lets you pass."

"If it is God's will," Arkady says. He remembers stories about Advent Bay from his grandfather. He pulls the map from his coat pocket. "Can you show me where it is?" He smooths the worn paper over the table.

"No one is there, but unlike these company men," she raises an eyebrow toward Kol, "the Pomors do not lock their huts." Saskia points to a place much farther north than Arkady expects.

Kol had been leaning against the wall, looking out the window and polishing his pipe on his shirttail. In addition to potato fritters, Kol had eaten meat and carrots out of a tin. Now, he motions for Arkady to put on his overcoat and come outside. Kol picks up an unlit lantern and strides north on a subtle path Arkady hadn't noticed before. Arkady hurries to keep up. Outside, the world seems brighter, but also silent in a way he hadn't perceived before he'd arrived at Kol's hut in the first place. The presence of human voices quiets the land.

"*Jag kommer att skrämma skiten ur dig,*" Kol barks. "*Kom igen. Du kan inte komma undan det!*"

They reach a shed almost the size of the hut. Built on top of a natural shale foundation, the shed's walls include a low, stone-and-mortar construction, and above that, half-logs notched together. The roof is one large piece of metal set at an angle. Arkady thinks Kol has asked him to help with some kind of work.

Kol makes a show of retrieving his matches, theatrically shaking one from the box, and preparing his glass lantern. He fiddles with the wick and adjusts the vent. Arkady shivers. He wonders whether rain or snow would fall if the heavens opened up. No birds disturb the surface of the sea, and none slice through the air.

When he glances back at the hut, Arkady thinks he sees someone standing outside, but when he looks more closely, no one is there.

Finally, Kol's flame licks and sputters. From his vest pocket, the Swede produces a key. Arkady has rarely seen these instruments; they are unknown to most Solovetsky monks. He remembers his grandfather's sea chest, with its rusted keyhole and the ancient tool that opened it. The workings of locks and keys are a mystery. Now Kol raises the lantern and motions Arkady close.

"Min vän. Min goda, goda lilla vän."

Kol opens the door, smiles, and gestures for Arkady to enter first, which Arkady does without thinking. Perhaps naïveté is the downfall of those raised in the Church. Perhaps it is simply Arkady's own particular weakness. But Kol's is the prank of a schoolboy, and Arkady walks straight into the trap.

Inside the shed, the huge, bodiless heads of ice bears gape toward Arkady. With their hides folded beneath them and their paws jarringly crossed, it seems as if the rows of animals are simultaneously roaring and praying. None of the bears has eyes, and the sockets provide a godless portal into the void. Arkady screams and instinctively turns to bury his head into Kol's shoulder. Kol is heaving with laughter, and, immediately after sensing it, Arkady jerks back, aghast and having wet himself, although not enough for anyone to notice. He backs out of the shed.

After Kol recovers, he retrieves a saw from the depths of the bear shed and again motions for Arkady to come. At first Arkady does not follow him farther up the little path, which winds between mossy tussocks, but Kol chides him. Kol's movements are reassuring; he has had his fun. Arkady follows.

Kol takes him to where he has hung a slaughtered reindeer from a pulley attached to a driftwood pole. The Swede strides to the pole. He motions for Arkady to grasp the ropes, and together they lower what can only be bear bait. The pole and the carcass wear a dusting of skua droppings. Once the reindeer is on the ground, Kol shoves the saw into Arkady's hands and motions for him to use it on the reindeer.

"Oh, I am not skilled in such things," Arkady says. Again, he considers simply dropping the saw, continuing north right now, and never returning to Kol's stove nor civilization in general ever again. But his pack is in the hut. His service book and psalter, too.

Now, Kol launches into such a dance of pantomime—eating motions, gestures aimed at the hut, and expressions of Arkady's larger journey—that Arkady finally relents.

A corpse is just a corpse, he reiterates. *Without the presence of the Divine spark, there is no difference between sawing through an animal's remains and sawing through a log.*

The reindeer is half-frozen, and it takes some work to deepen the gashes that Kol had already put across its belly and chest.

The blood will draw the bears, Arkady reminds himself, and bears mean money to this merchant of bodies. *This man gave me sustenance and shelter. Sustenance and shelter,* he repeats the words to himself. *But it is only You who can provide true sustenance and true shelter. That is the only truth I must carry with me. Nothing else matters, not even this chipping bone and frozen meat.*

Out of the corner of his eye, Arkady sees the swirl of a fox's tail a short distance away on the beach. The fox pauses for a moment, sniffing the air. Arkady looks away. He hears his grandfather's voice: *Animals carry the spirits of their brothers.*

Spattered with blood, Arkady finally returns the saw to the Swede, who claps him on the back and again lifts his hand to his mouth as if he is eating. After they raise the bloody and virtually dismembered animal once more onto its ghastly pole, Arkady walks back to the hut with his head down. Kol returns to the shed.

Inside the cabin, Saskia still labors over the stove, muttering and scrubbing the cylindrical chimney with a clump of lichen. She does not turn when Arkady enters, but she starts the kettle to boil.

"I do what I can, I do what I can, little mother." Saskia is somewhere in the middle of a soliloquy. "But this grandfather will not be appeased. I scrub and I scrub, but this design is no good, and you give little heat. It annoys him. He tells me to build a proper one, but how could I do that? Am I on Russian soil? Am I a stone mason? And he fights. Oh, he fights with you, I know. And the other one, she seethes in that stream, trembling with rage. This place is no good, but I will stay. I do what I can."

Arkady ignores her as long as he can but soon gives in. "Kol forces you to clean it? I must agree: it is a pathetic stove."

"Not Kol. The grandfather." She glances up at the hut's one rafter. "*That one*," she whispers.

Arkady realizes she's referring to some kind of domovoy, a peasant superstition, a house spirit. He purses his lips and shakes his head. Heathen rubbish follows every Russian. "*Makes* every Russian," Arkady hears his grandfather's voice add. One must be vigilant to shake it off.

"And there is one in the stream behind the hut. But *that* one," again she looks at the rafter, "pisses in the stream, and so she torments him. They fight, and now he takes it out on me because I can hear them and I can see them." Saskia hands Arkady a tin cup of tea.

"But this is a Swede's hut, not a Russian's."

Saskia laughs. "Are you so ignorant? This was first built by Russians. Outside, you can see shards of brick where the stupid Swedes threw away the real stove. That one is still angry about it. I do what I can, but it never will be enough. They fight. Oh, that's what they love the most."

"You were born in Russia, then?" Arkady asks.

Saskia laughs again. "Of course not. But the Russians have been up here a long time. Not as long as me, but long enough for the gyre to carry *them* here, too." She gestures upward.

"What do you mean?"

"The house spirits and all the others. So many layers of them. Been coming here since the beginning of our time. You've seen them, haven't you? Brought over the sea and across the air, to this place. The Norsemen called the gyre a serpent that turns and turns way down in the ocean with its tail in its mouth. Its turning brings all our stories northward, past, present, and future. They are here."

Arkady looks frantically around the cabin because he cannot meet Saskia's eye. Nikolai spoke of such a thing, but Arkady was so young, he only remembers fragments. Arkady wants to run away and almost does. But his eyes finally settle on a paper wall calendar, and he rushes over to it. Even though it's in Swedish, he can decipher the days; Kol has penciled an X over each day that has passed. Assuming Kol has not yet struck one today, Arkady deduces the present by subtracting thirteen from what the heathen calendar shows, to get September seventeenth. He tethers himself back to the Church calendar.

Kol returns after a little while, carrying a bulging canvas bag with a shoulder strap. He clears his throat and waits for Saskia to turn. She does not, and Kol bangs the bag down on the table and exclaims sharply. She finally sighs and turns around.

"Som en symbol för mitt tack för hjälpen, här är lite mat för resan." Kol gestures grandly to the bag, facing Arkady but looking at Saskia.

Arkady looks back and forth between them.

Saskia shakes her head and shrugs.

Kol points at the bag, and then at Arkady. *"För honom. Att ta med honom. Mat."*

"I think that's for you," Saskia says. "He is an old goat."

Arkady goes to the bag, but Kol stops his hand.

"För senare. När du går."

Kol gestures northward and makes eating gestures again, and soon Arkady understands this is a gift for later. He nods in thanks. Kol also opens a tin of meat for Arkady to eat with his tea.

"You are walking along a country road," Saskia speaks softly from across the table. "You meet three men. Each has his own horse and cart. You are on a long, long journey. Not unlike the one you've embarked on here. Each of the three men offers you passage on his cart. The first man has a beaming face and introduces himself as the Sun. The second man has blue skin. He is Frost. The third man, who has tousled hair and puffy cheeks, is the Wind. Which one do you go with, little priest?"

"Well, I surely—"

"Think carefully now."

Arkady looks from Saskia to Kol, who is picking dirt out from beneath his fingernails with a huge, stained knife blade. "The sun, of course," Arkady says. "I go with the sun so that I may be warm for my whole journey and travel through one long summer day."

"Fool!" Saskia yelps, thumping her fist on the table. "You will not last long in this world. If you sit in the cart of the Sun, he will burn you with his heat. Father Frost will freeze you. But the Wind can cool the heat and send a warm breeze from the south during cold weather. Wind is the master of both elements." She shakes her head. "No matter, no matter."

CHAPTER 21

Arkady lies between two gamey reindeer hides on the floor of Kol's hut, but he cannot fall asleep. Strangely, in the dim light filtering through the hut's tiny window, Saskia still stands, cleaning the metal stove, occasionally scowling and looking at the rafter. In the two hours since Arkady and Kol returned from refreshing the bear bait, she has not paused in this activity. Earlier, she brushed off Arkady's feeble attempt to converse. Kol shook his head and his fist at her, but that was all, and soon the Swede disappeared under the hides on his pallet. It seems to Arkady that Saskia's cleaning has become more frenetic as the hours stretch on, and although he is perplexed, he doesn't interfere.

After a long time, Kol erupts from his bed. "*Woman! Du kan inte fly. Kom till mig snabbt nu!*" he shouts.

The Swede stands, hopping from one foot to the other wearing a dirty red woolen shirt and grayish leggings over his sticklike legs. Arkady squeezes his eyes shut against this vision.

"I have already given you what you want, demon!" Saskia replies. "No more."

Arkady hears a resounding clang and what surely must be cursing from Kol. When he opens his eyes, Saskia is poised with two long metal spoons in her hands, pointing them at the Swede, who has been hit in the shoulder with some other utensil.

Kol lunges for Saskia and takes a swipe, managing to hook her apron string into his hand. This he pulls on, but Saskia won't budge, and soon the strap rips free.

"Ack!" yells Saskia. "You pig!" And she hurls a tin of meat at Kol, who ducks.

Their sparring continues for some time. Now, Kol cackles and inches toward the woman. He lowers the waistband of his leggings to reveal a capable instrument of carnal sin.

Arkady is about to leap up to intervene on Saskia's behalf, when he sees that the woman is smiling. She begins to fiddle with her clothing. Again, Arkady squeezes his eyes shut. *Oh Lord, may it not be so. May it not not not not not be so!*

His path is clear: Leave now. He knows that neither she nor he will try to stop him. Why would they? Arkady is nothing but a mouse here, stealing crumbs and glancing sidelong at two tricky cats. His way is northward on that long, roadless road to Father Vasily.

But he does not go. After Saskia's and the trader's shrieks collapse into groaning, and after he hears the slapping of skin against skin, he opens his eyes. From between the table legs that separate him from Kol's sleeping pallet, Arkady can see them fornicating intently. Saskia's bodice is open, and she's splayed atop the wiry Swede with her head thrown back and her prodigious form sinking him into the hides in a rhythm as regular as storm waves crashing against the shore. Arkady spins into a tingling ether, and his breaths come shallow and harsh. His hand creeps toward his waist and then fumbles below.

After Kol and Saskia's grappling peaks, Arkady waits for a long time. Then, as gently as he is able, he collects his things. He picks up Kol's gift bag and, on his way out, catches a look at his reflection in Kol's cracked wall mirror. His beard has grown thick, his hair matted. His first thought is that he belongs outside, where he blends with the gray and black stones. He closes the door quietly behind him and enters a blue realm of shadow ruled by an icy breeze that heralds the true onset of the cold in Spitsbergen. The sea is a chaos of whitecaps moving southward. Even if Arkady could drag the oarboat to the water's edge by himself, he couldn't make headway against that wind. But Saskia said he might make Advent Bay on foot. He must continue on.

Two miles north of Kol's hut, Arkady stops to take stock of his new provisions. Pulling his hat lower against the cold and exhaling bright-white clouds, Arkady wonders what warming food might be inside the bag. But when he opens the flap, sawdust sails out. He digs through the dust, but amid the shavings and a few stones, he finds only one sack of yellowed, clumped flour.

"Brother Jesus, what is this?" Arkady's voice drops through the air like a gray stone joining the infinity of gray stones that encrust these shores. "The sawdust is my heart and soul. It seems that this husk does not have the strength to find You after all. Or Father Vasily."

Arkady removes the stones from the bag and dumps out the sawdust. Some of it floats horizontally with the wind, and he watches until it merges with the night.

From where he stands, just behind Arkady's right shoulder, Saint Eumenius shakes his head. Could Arkady not use the fine sawdust as tinder or even to fill his socks for warmth? Eumenius, a Desert Father, strictly adheres to fasting and is known as a shepherd of men venturing into the wildlands. He has grown annoyed by his long wait for Arkady just outside the door of Kol's hut. The patron saint is pleased to finally get going.

CHAPTER 22

rkady continues north with a feeling of dread. His hollow prayers bounce around his mind to no effect, and he flounders while looking for the smooth thread of faith. His frosty breaths are shallow, panicked. *I will die here*, he thinks. *That is the only outcome that was ever possible. How could I have been foolish enough to think otherwise?*

He stumbles, and Saint Eumenius thinks the human will turn back. They usually do. That is their downfall, from Orpheus to Lot's wife. The saint sighs and glances out to sea. A pity, he thinks, but not a surprise.

Arkady stops. He unbuttons his coat and pulls out the letters from Father Vasily. He knows each page by heart, but he opens one just the same.

Dear Arkady,

None of the others write to me anymore. But you continue. Why? Do not be addicted to your own suffering. Do not fill up your psyche with desire. Move humbly into Uncreated Light. Do not be frightened of that wide-open space, which I see mirrored in the vast land where I dwell. Let this pure Light fill your heart. Do not try to force meaning from texts and teachers, or even the liturgy itself. Let the Light enter you! Let yourself be Lighted!

Arkady keeps walking. Twice a day, and then once, he mixes stream water with Kol's rancid flour and boils a thin porridge over a fire. After eight days, the flour is gone. Again (so soon!), he loses track of the calendar. His knees and heels ache continuously, but the gashes on his arms are healing. On the morning of the ninth day, Arkady pauses at the stormy shore. For the first time, he understands that he is a vessel not for worldly care, or even for hope, but for prayer and nothing else. He surrenders his life into God's hands and prays only that the weight of his sins, specifically his arrogance and disregard for Father Ilya, may be forgiven and fall away.

The bands of amber and rose in the sky have dimmed to gloomy overcast, and the nights, each one longer than the last, bring full darkness and freezing cold. He walks north, always north, first over beaches and then across another great tundra plain. The mountains have retreated inland on this part of the island, and he finds the whole place more bearable with them at a distance.

Now, Arkady resides in a holy fast. He drinks deeply from tiny streams, always managing to pick his way across them on stones or by walking inland to a narrow passage that he can jump over. At night, he lays his fires using driftwood sticks and dry seaweed and lights them using the Viking striker, and though he is awakened often by his roaring stomach and the rustlings of the wild, the fire nourishes his spirit, as fire has nourished the spirits of men since the beginning of their time on earth.

During the day, his head aches, and he feels an increasing vertigo, so he picks up a stick and uses it for support. He has trouble focusing his mind, even on his prayers, but he uses all the power he can conjure to stay true to his original purpose.

Father Vasily, are you here with me? he asks the deepest corner of his heart. *You must be with me. You rise up from this mossy ground, and you lean out from the roiling clouds. You are here in the wind.*

He reads and rereads Father Vasily's letters: *Brother Arkady. The Divine Light is so bright it reveals the world beyond the world. I must share this with humankind. There is no one here to behold the Light and the secrets it holds. I thought my way was solitary, but now I see. Like a father to his son, I will pass on the Light to you. Come to me. Come quickly! The Light permeates me. We are becoming one.*

Mercy from his increasing agony finally arrives in the form of a true vision: All at once, Arkady smells and then sees the tart, bubbling yeast sponge that lived on the shelf above his grandfather's brick stove.

Cradled in a shallow, lidded porcelain dish painted with the figure of a bogatyr, the yeast's omnipresent aroma was never particularly notable when Arkady was a child, but now it is a divine gift. He hears the hollow knock of the wooden ladle against the mixing bowl as Nikolai stirs in the flour, and a fire crackling under the flat iron pan. The ladle tips, the batter sizzles, and bubbles form as the thin pancake cooks; a minute later, golden filigree laces its edges. Now, he is sitting at the small pine table with a plate of steaming blini before him. He tears off a piece. God, how the crisp edge gives way to the velvety middle! Arkady smiles: all those years with his grandfather, he had been ingesting the most perfect food in the world.

He folds the pancake into his mouth. He tastes the particular, heavenly union of melting butter and Ustyansky honey, and it sends Arkady into such a reverie that, when anything threatens it—the sound of a wave crashing into shore, the moan of the wind, or the ping of a stone skipping away after he trips over it—he fights reality with more blini. Blini with sour cream from Nikolai's heifer … maybe a few spring onions on top. Blini folded to hold chunks of lamb. Blini and raspberry jam!

From where he sits at his grandfather's table, Arkady looks behind him over his right shoulder, through the many-paned window, at the small kitchen garden. It must be midsummer; set on the black loam like gems are two rows of plump and tightly furled cabbages. Ah, shchi. Savory cabbage soup. A staple at Nikolai's and also at Solovetsky in every season, in many forms: using the outer leaves of the cabbage only, or using sorrel leaves in addition, adding fish, which was common at the monastery. But Arkady's favorite was sour pickled cabbage soup with chopped apple, onions, potatoes, carrots, horseradish, and dill. And the sour cream! Beyond the garden, Arkady can just see the heifer's black-and-white haunch. If he could, Arkady would eat just the cream. Great mouthfuls of smooth, thick cream. He moans out loud.

Beyond the kitchen garden is the track into town, and beyond that, the silty primordia they call the Laya tributary. The Dvina is the heart of the region, raking her countless fingers across the land and the people, dragging them northward to the sea. Since the beginning of time, the pull of this place has been northward. Every fish Nikolai ever caught in the Dvina was swimming north, he claimed. And what fish he pulled from those waters!

He considers the countless serious crimes he's committed by abandoning unfinished meals in the refectory over the years as he hurried out to play, and later to study. Great chunks of dark bread baked with molasses and full of caraway seeds and raisins. Half-full bowls of soup, tidbits of beef and haddock, stoneware cups of kvass and tea. He recalls that, on the day he left Solovetsky, he was so afraid the Pomors would leave him behind that he skipped a last monastery meal. It would have been warm kasha boiled in milk, with nuts, stewed fruit, and butter melting on top. It would have been tea sweetened with honey and perhaps bread and salt-cheese. He shakes his head. For many hours, Arkady's spirit is lifted and sustained by the memories of the food of his life, from the many varieties of delicate, otherworldly forest mushroom (fresh, roasted, fried, or pickled) to the simple life-giving potato.

After making camp for the evening and drinking a single, large cup of spring water for supper, Arkady lies down under his reindeer skin and blankets and stares at the flames. Instead of his prayers, he thinks of the fox. Salivating, he considers each charred bit of the animal's savory meat. He recalls sinking his teeth into bite after bite. Suddenly, he is overcome with tears by the sheer abundance of food the small animal provided and the depth of his physical and spiritual inadequacy in Spitsbergen. Lying on his side, he buries his face into his meager bed. There were still scraps of meat on the bones when he discarded them! *What a useless larva am I*, he thinks. And miles behind him, those bones still lay where he tossed them. If only they could sustain him now. If only he hadn't been so idiotic as to toss away the food inside the food: the marrow. It is at this point, after the tears subside, that he knows his holy fast has ended, and he has begun to starve.

CHAPTER 23

aint Eumenius walks just behind Arkady, and as the days accumulate, so do other patron saints. They scan the horizon and, at first, discuss the perils of Arkady's situation. This group is mostly generals and ascetics, with a combined experience of the wild much greater than Sozon and his company had possessed. They take bearings on distant mountains and peer out over the water for approaching ice bears. They speculate about the weather: When will winter descend for good? When will the winds rise? When will sleet plummet down from above? They wonder where Arkady is going.

Saint Eumenius leads discussions of Arkady's position, especially in regard to this approaching cold. Several patron saints agree that, if his feet get wet, he is lost. The cold is the greatest danger, not starving. Others say that, without food and specifically fat, Arkady will die very quickly. Each day, he uses more and more energy, which is not replenished. Eumenius appoints two men to keep a lookout for any seals that may have washed up on the beach, but they find none, and even if they had, they cannot directly alert Arkady, who is lost in reverie most of the time and not praying with his mind in his heart, which would increase his chances of heeding his mostly invisible allies.

Some patrons think Arkady will run out of fire-making tools and freeze to death. *He actually threw away sawdust, which he could have used to start the fire!* one complains.

But without beeswax to bind it, the sawdust would have done little good, another argues.

The poor man hasn't even noticed that driftwood has mostly disappeared from the beaches, says somebody else.

And he didn't collect any before, when it was plentiful, the first patron adds.

He's too weak to carry such a load! comes a voice from the back.

Eumenius hushes the others. *Can't you see he needs us? Stop this chatter,* he scolds them with a stern look. *The most important thing right now is that he keeps moving and stays ahead of the storm that is coming. Can't you see the direction of the wind? He must move. We must work.*

And so, for a long time, the saints bow their heads or else stare at Arkady as he bobs along ahead of them. Each in his own way concentrates his various powers—fortitude, patience, mercy, love—on Arkady's small, hunched back.

Eventually, Arkady comes to a shallow inlet. He must wait for the tide to recede before he can determine whether he can walk across its exposed mudflat or whether he must dip inland to walk all the way around its shore. He stands at the edge of the water, looking down but not seeing. For the past few hours, Arkady has been comparing the relative merits of raspberries and blackberries. He welcomes the respite as a chance to think more deeply on the question. He is about to turn away and lie down against a log farther up on the beach, but something (the combined concentration of the patron saints, like the concentrated force of a sunbeam through a glass?) keeps him at the shore long enough to understand that some of the stones dancing beneath the shallow water are adorned with tiny snails. He kneels. He sees his salvation: a meal.

The berries tumble from his thoughts, and tiny whorled shells take their place. The work of collecting feels as if it passes quickly, even though he is at it for two hours. The act of foraging opens Arkady to other culinary possibilities: he finds fronds of leathery kelp and immediately cuts a piece to chew on as he works. By the time he builds his fire and submerges the snails in seawater, he has kelp slices and some other soft, thready sea lettuce to add to the broth. Beside him, Eumenius nods approval, although he doesn't believe Arkady has the fortitude needed to extract the minute amount of flesh from each mollusk. Even if he eats all three hundred snails he's collected, the protein will not sustain him until his next meal. He will need to gather and eat these tiny prizes continuously, and, of course, that would be at the expense of precious time. Eumenius is certain that Arkady must hurry to reach his ambiguous goal before winter overpowers him. The other patrons believe that it is vital that Arkady eat as many of the snails as he can before he proceeds, but they do not speak against Eumenius. Two patrons have already been ostracized for contradicting the Desert Father. These saints wander away together across the plain, where the Dog, who has been keeping his distance, soon apprehends them.

Arkady stays at the snail inlet, watching the tide recede and then return, using the butt of his knife to crush the tiny shells, but not with so much force that the gobbet is smashed. Arkady eats all the snails and then gathers another potful. He chews kelp and drinks the broth. He eats another potful of snails, this time leaving half of them in their shells, and eating those, too. Many hours have passed by now, and it is dark. Still ravenous and chilled, somehow he sleeps. And when he wakes, he is very cold, but again he dips his hands into the icy water to forage. He twines kelp around his neck to carry forward and cradles his full pot in his arms. At low tide, he walks across the inlet, trailing his patrons behind him. They speculate whether his feet will stay dry. This time, they do.

The next day, weaker by far than at any preceding time, Arkady gathers lichen to boil. Discovering the snails has opened his eyes to the few other edible elements of the terrain. He mixes in a little seawater and cuts a length of kelp for the broth. He drinks it. He walks another mile then frets because he is hungrier than ever, uncontrollable shivers and pains rack his body, and skin cracks on his lips and hands. Again, his mind plunges into the meals he left half-eaten at table: mashed salt cod drizzled with oil and Solovetsky sea salt, ground lamb baked in dough, pickled cherries in a jar, kasha with butter, kasha with honey, kasha boiled in fish broth with sorrel and mushrooms. He can't stop, and he doesn't want to.

Look at his fixed gaze, barks Saint Eumenius. *Again, his mind strays. He is so weak. He must be stronger! Brethren, come to his aid using all your force.*

The other patrons glance at one another. Some of them scowl. Eumenius is a know-it-all, and they're tired of it. The poor human is doing the best that could be expected of him. What he needs are loving guides to lead him forward not an overbearing schoolteacher. They keep quiet and shuffle along the beach.

Arkady is certain there is someone walking just behind and to the right of him. It's a familiar, unnerving occurrence. He looks over his shoulder again and again. He feels that the figure, whoever it is, may be speaking to him, but he cannot quite hear it. In fact, Eumenius speaks constantly to Arkady, pointing out the level of the tide, updating the monk on the direction of the wind, the consistency of the beach over which they travel, and the ominous bank of clouds that approaches. All this navigational input is meant to help Arkady, but each of the elements that Eumenius points out is beyond the realm of Arkady's perception.

On the twentieth day after Arkady had left Kol's cabin, one of the patrons walking by the edge of the sea finds the waterlogged body of a black guillemot. The seabird was a yearling who had been injured on one of the last days of nesting season on the rocks. Her lameness prevented her from flying south with her brethren. She fished successfully for a full month—quite a feat—until the fish moved out to sea, and then she starved. Her last thought before perishing was a kind of memory of the glinting sides of a dense herring school as it flashed in a mob in the undersea gloom. She died on the water, which is the way of her kind, but the wind came up before her body could sink, and four days later, she was pushed all the way to shore.

The saint that spotted the bird, red-bearded Stefan of Serbia, drops to his knees and prays for Arkady to see it, too. But Arkady passes right by, unresponsive to Stefan's plea, which, Stefan is certain, would cut through the psyche of a less-troubled soul. From a few feet away, Eumenius shrugs and motions for the entourage to keep going, but Stefan takes matters into his own hands by throwing a rock into the shallows near the bird. Still, Arkady does not heed. Surely, he must have heard the splash? The saint throws another, heavier stone toward Arkady, and then another. Eumenius furiously waves his hands for Stefan to stop, his face a contortion of disapproval.

Listen! Stefan says, with the intention for Arkady to hear.

Eumenius waggles his finger and points upward, shaking his head. Arkady turns.

What have you done? Eumenius scolds a few minutes later while Arkady sits at the shore, pulling feathers from the thin body of the guillemot. *Have you sunk so low that you resort to earthly means? Do you, one of the Appointed Ones, lack faith? If that is so, you are destined to dwell in these wastes for all time!* Eumenius froths at the mouth. *Do you not recall our training? All the days and nights and centuries of your apprenticeship? Spiritual means belong to us. Spiritual. Not physical. Have you lost all sense? Do you forget that there is a particular way for these things to unfold? Would you disrupt His machinations?*

Stefan defies his elder. *Let my action speak for itself. I will not waste breath on your tirade. The man eats. He lives. We can help him; therefore, we should.*

You interfere where you should not. Without trust in God, he will die anyway, if not in flesh, then in spirit. Why do you prolong his torture?

Stefan shrugs and turns away. He knows what will come next.

You are banished! Eumenius says.

Stefan lifts his arms in mock surrender. He takes a long look at Arkady's rapturous face then wanders away. Within a few minutes, after each gives Arkady an apologetic look, all the other patrons turn from Eumenius and hurry to join Stefan. Furious at the mutiny, Eumenius stamps his feet.

CHAPTER 24

ortified by the guillemot's meager flesh, Arkady hobbles on with slightly more vigor, though his body is weak, and the cold has nipped him hard. A wind rises. He retracts his arms from the sleeves of his many layers and walks with his hands tucked into his armpits. He believes he will die before next nightfall.

Saint Eumenius, too, has grown broody. This is not the first time other saints have chosen to leave his side. He has remembered that, during his earthly life, no young novice appeared as heir to his spiritual wealth. Essentially, like the human, Eumenius has always been alone.

At dusk, there is no driftwood in sight. Although it hasn't rained, the stones on the beach are slick. In a daze, Arkady limps to the base of a tundra hillock. He will spend the night in its lee. He positions himself under every layer he has and then mimes laying a fire. He builds the framework of invisible kindling and sets within it a nest of dry tinder. He brings out the flint and the sacred striker and lights a spark that immediately blinks out. He puts the fire-lighting tools back in their pouch and into his pocket and closes his eyes.

Some hours later, Arkady cannot sleep anymore. In the piercing cold, he walks with his head down; he faces inward, mind and heart. One moment he is a boy in the empty monastery kitchen, drowsily slurping shchi and listening to the hearth fire pop, and the next moment, he's walking next to Nikolai on the dirt track into town, leaping over puddles and raising a stick in some long-forgotten victory. He leans against Father Ilya while his starets teaches him how to read. He contemplates the wood-grained hull of the lodja that carried him to Schoonhoven, half-listening to the Pomor stories, which are really his grandfather's, and likely his own.

Then, dredged from a deeper place, he is very small, standing on a stool at the back window of Nikolai's house, looking at a starry sky. Out from the forest beyond the field comes a figure carrying a lantern. The woman is barefoot and wears only a white nightdress, but it's not her. Another figure emerges, skipping. Not her. Then a group of them come out, and there she is among them, holding her own lantern. Her dark, unbound hair mingles with the stars. He reaches out to her, but she doesn't see him. The way that he wants her has no precedent. She and the other women circle Nikolai's hut. One of them digs a furrow all the way around the house, while the others sing and drop bundles of herbs in the turned soil. There she is again, running barefoot toward the homestead across the meadow. He shrieks as the lantern light bobs out of sight, and then he is coughing, coughing, and his grandfather is there beside him, scolding him back to his bed.

When Arkady returns from this reverie, the wind pricks his eyes, and he stumbles. A jumble of bones crunches under his feet. The bones are porous, weathered by the tides and no good to boil for soup. Ahead of him, as far as he can see, great piles of them cover the beach. Stupefied, he trudges on as if pulled by an invisible thread. He opens his mouth, unsure if he will scream or laugh.

"The hand of the Lord came upon me and brought me out by the spirit and set me down in a valley full of dry bones," Arkady says, immediately startled by his own hoarse voice. "He said, 'Mortal, can these bones live?' And I answered, 'O God, you know!' Dry bones, I will cause breath to enter you, and you shall live. I will lay sinews on you and will cause flesh to come and cover you with skin and put breath in you."

Arkady drops to his knees. He caresses the bones, which seem to be those of giants, and lets his forehead touch them. Rich salt tears flow out of him as his mind drops into his heart. He slips from his struggles into a vast, open space.

"Suddenly, there was a rattling, and the bones came together, each bone to its bone," he whispers. "I looked, and there were sinews and flesh and skin upon them, but no breath. Then He said to me, 'Mortal, say to the breath: Come from the four winds, O breath, come from the gyre. And breathe upon these slain, that they may live.' And the breath came into them, and they lived and stood on their feet, a great multitude.

"'Die to yourself!' I hear on the wind. I am listening. You will open my grave and bring me up out of there. You will put a new spirit within me, but can I live?"

Arkady glides across the bones without stumbling, lifted by the same spirit as that ancient multitude. And who's to say that, beneath his feet, those great walrus bones did not feel a quickening, that they leaned toward the bodies from which they'd been cleaved? For a century they'd lain there, unmoving except by the forces of tide, ice, and wind since their slayers coasted out of the bay in their lodjas and oarboats, laden with ivory tusks and numinous oil.

"Can these bones live? Can they?" Deliriously ardent and moving faster than he had in days, Arkady brandishes a walrus rib ahead of him. He walks across the slaughtering beach known far and wide as Sentinel Bay among the Dutch, English, and Russian huntsmen of centuries past. Arkady whacks himself on the shoulder with the walrus rib. "You know. You know. You know you know you know you know you know." He clobbers himself on the other shoulder. "Can they live?"

"Oh stop," Eumenius says, stumbling as he hurries along behind. He is no stranger to the ravings of dying humans. "Is that really necessary? See this stream? You need to drink water. Stop here, you fool."

Arkady whirls around. "Ah! There you are." He points the rib at his patron saint. "Get back!"

"Calm yourself," Eumenius whispers. He hadn't realized Arkady was close enough to death to see and hear him. "You must concentrate. You. Need. To. Drink. Water."

"Stay back, Dark One. I am not thirsty!"

"Stop that nonsense," Eumenius says uncertainly.

But now Arkady is staring fiercely past Eumenius. The saint whirls around, and the true sentinel is there behind him, close enough for Eumenius to see the great coat of blue-black fur gleaming and the twitch of a tattered, wolflike ear.

"It is Koshchei the Deathless at last! The only one who never dies," Arkady whispers. "But these bones live!"

Arkady rushes past Eumenius to lunge at the Dog, who steps lightly to one side. Arkady falls forward onto the bones. He feels an icy wind against his face. He grasps his antler-handled knife. When Arkady rises, the Dog's lips are pulled back in a smile.

"The Dog," Arkady says. "You want men, but you live by a code. Nikolai told me about you."

Without taking his eyes from the Dog's face, Arkady grabs Eumenius by the arm. Astonished, the saint opens and closes his mouth and then looks around, desperate for a witness to this unprecedented event.

"I will not join you," Arkady says.

He pulls Eumenius close to him, wrapping an arm around his chest. Quickly, before the saint realizes what is about to happen, Arkady sinks the blade of his knife into his patron saint's throat, and in that motion forsakes once and for all what the Church taught him.

"Here's my offering," Arkady says to the Dog as Eumenius falls. "Take this one instead of me."

Arkady walks on, wiping his knife blade on his coat. The Dog watches him as it sniffs the wilting saint.

While Arkady walks, he cuts his hair away. As it drifts off, it takes with it the drama and comedy of his life up to this point. Because Solovetsky was theater, he realizes, and nothing more. Yes, he found refuge in hymns and candlelight, but he knew nothing and sought to know nothing. Arkady's vision of Father Vasily, that great northern hermit, falls aside in a whoosh of dusty robes and falling sticks. So quickly? Yes, and at long last.

At the northern edge of Sentinel Bay, the walrus bones give way to a smooth beach, and after his passions settle, Arkady is overcome by the cold.

He walks as far as he can and then finds an enclave tucked away from the wind, which has been rising every evening and now whips past with great force. As he settles down to die, dark clouds blow across the sea. After some time, the clouds pass, and blinking stars emerge. To these celestial bodies, he releases all that he still holds: words, mostly. Some memories, a shred of hope … and all ties to his kin and the rest of humankind. He does not dwell on it because he believes that earthly concerns are no longer worth his time. Indeed, he can no longer feel his arms and legs.

Fading in and out of the wind and the moments of his life, Arkady stands again at the window of his grandfather's house. This time he is not a boy but a man. The rich, blue color of the night and the dark-green woods stun his senses. He feels the colors like a warm cloth on his brow, and then he sees the lantern light bobbing among the trees. Again, the women emerge, laughing and barefoot. Some carry scythes. Some carry the skulls of animals. Nine maidens emerge and then three widows. With his forehead pressed against the window, he looks for her. And, as if she'd been standing with her back pressed to the cabin just out of sight, she appears at the glass, terrifying Arkady with her sudden presence then destroying him with longing.

Around the glow of her lantern, moths circle her head, and the shadows of bats flit in and out of sight, brushing against her dress. Twigs and leaves rest in her tangled black hair, which hangs loose to her waist. While the others howl and plough a single furrow around Nikolai's house that is meant to release the healing power of the earth and annihilate the coughing sickness that afflicts the village, she looks at Arkady curiously. Through her gaze, he receives strength from the small handful of people who have ever loved him: Father Ilya. Nikolai. Boris, his father. And even she, the moth-wreathed woman, his mother.

It is not much, but with the scrappy determination of an orphan, he uses that strength to stand once again in the encroaching darkness. As he turns his face northward, winter's first snowflake catches in his eyelashes.

CHAPTER 25

For the next ten hours, Arkady walks in the hush of a gentle snowfall and, every so often, kneels to dig a handful of soil out of the ground with his hands. He feeds himself the soil, and, as his body ushers small amounts through his esophagus and into his stomach, he renews his oath with the earth to stay alive. He is not sure that the spirit of his mother wishes him well, but, for the moment, she functions as a protective force working in harmony with his need.

Arkady ascends a mossy slope laced with snow. Pinnacles of granite frame white-dusted tundra meadows, and he moves through them glassy-eyed and quiet. He walks at a diagonal away from the sea, past strange stone rings and geometrical shapes made by the forces of ice and time. After some time, he hears the gurgling sound of a stream; he finds it running merrily between two mossy banks. It is too wide for him to cross, so after he takes a long drink, he follows it seaward until he reaches a headland where the stream narrows, then falls in a cascade to the beach far below. Near the edge of the bluff, he jumps across.

All around him, boulders and spires frame a view of the dark, wind-tossed sea. He has reached the southern lip of a wide fjord. Looking to the east, he can't see where the great arm of water ends, and he senses correctly that it extends for miles. The distance straight across to the north coast is not vast, but certainly insurmountable.

Hunched like a much older man, Arkady hobbles ahead with tattered sleeves and mud-caked trousers. He is ready to walk the entire length around the fjord. He passes more boulders and enters a small open place. He continues walking, almost missing his salvation, but as he passes, the shape of one of the boulders doesn't seem right. He turns back. Even though no one is with him now, he clears his throat and announces the unlikely sight.

"An izba."

And it is true. The cabin, made from whole, silver logs and thick shingle, is just like any other in the town of Arkhangelsk. Arkady walks back to it as if in a dream. The cabin's steeply pitched roof protects a small window on each wall, and steps lead up to a shallow covered porch. The fretwork around the shuttered windows is carved into the filigreed shapes of birds, bears, and vines. Its head beam is carved in flowers and waves. Crosswise, the roof beam, where it extends above the porch, is a dog's head. Arkady moves toward this place, unsure if it resides in the earthly realm or whether it is the manifestation of his soul's inner closet, or more likely, a door to the afterlife.

Some way away, there is a creature sitting on the beam of a weatherbeaten Promise Cross. Arkady can't discern its exact shape, and its casual, gravity-defying perch makes him uneasy. Its head is bowed over its work; is it braiding rope?

Arkady turns away. "Never mind, never mind," he mutters. Not even ghosts will keep him from the izba. Slowly, Arkady climbs the cabin's seven front steps and lifts the iron door latch.

The cabin is dark and cold and smells faintly sweet. The first thing he sees is a great, plaster-covered brick stove built along the north side of the cabin. He closes his eyes and thanks God, Mother Damp Earth, and Spitsbergen. A Russian stove.

With shaking hands, he opens a wooden cupboard. He lifts a half-empty jar and unscrews the lid. He dips in his fingers and pulls out a clump of crystallized paste. Tears pour from his eyes. He almost breaks the glass in excruciating pleasure. Honey.

In the middle of the room, a wooden table stands with two rough chairs pulled close. On the table, nestled between two half-melted candles, is a cloth-wrapped bundle. He lifts the folded edge. Inside is a round loaf of dark bread. He taps it: ancient. Someone has carved a bowl out of the top of the loaf, and this is filled with coarse salt. How many times has he pulled bread off a loaf like this one? In Nikolai's house, in houses scattered all along the Laya tributary and beyond, and of course at the monastery. Someone, sometime, set out this bread and salt for a traveler. In this forsaken place, where guests are so few. He reaches for the antler-handled knife among the pockets of his coat. With some difficulty, he hacks off a piece.

I am as a hatchling in the nest, reaching for food. Bless this loaf and the person who set it here, wherever he may be and wherever I was when he did it. As I consume this bread, please let me peck my way out of the egg of my folly.

He dips the bread into the salt and gnaws off a morsel, which softens into a sour, nourishing mush.

Neatly stacked ceiling-high along the western wall is split wood, some bearing the hulls of barnacles, and some of it oak and birch from the mainland. Still half in disbelief, he packs the stove's metal firebox. Then he fumbles with his tinderbox, flint, and steel. The flame catches, and he is saved.

Arkady warms his fingertips. After the fire takes, he adds two more good chunks of wood and closes the firebox door. Trembling, he listens to the sound of a fire crackling in the belly of a great stove. He considers again the likelihood that he has died and that this izba is his first waypoint on the long road with no end.

He runs his hand along the metal grate and the iron kettle on the stovetop, thanking them in advance for their warmth. Then he looks above the cooking place to the stove's upper reaches, the flat surface over the heat, designed centuries ago by the most beloved, unknown Russian: the stove bench, accessible by a ladder. Straightaway he climbs up to it and finds many layers of old hides. Before he can even cover himself, his own exhaustion pins him down. Just before he slips into unconsciousness, he realizes that, even though there has not been enough time for heat to penetrate the masonry of the stove bench, the old, straw-stuffed pillow under his head is already warm, as if some creature had been sleeping there and just now risen.

CHAPTER 26

Arkady wakes with a gasp. Covered in hides on top of the stove, feverish, weak, and with his eyes still closed, he hears a soft tinkling sound. At first, it seems quite natural that his mother sits nearby on her low stool, always with her hair unbound to draw in the many energies adrift in the air. Her cylindrical lacemaking pillow lays in front of her on its wooden frame. She always sketched her own lace patterns on paper. Arkady used to stare at those patterns pinned to the work pillow: webs of diamonds and hexagons holding together a cosmos of stars, or worlds of flowers, leaves, animals, and water. She worked so quickly, lifting many pairs of wooden bobbins and passing them between her hands, twisting and looping, then pulling tight. Pinning down the lace and picking up more bobbins, hour after hour after hour.

As he awakens more fully, the tapping and clinking sounds persist, and he's too frightened to open his eyes. Finally, after a long time, hunger forces him to move. And when he slowly raises his eyelids and swings his legs over the side of the stove to look blurrily around the cabin, he sees that the sound comes from a simple wooden ornament: a bird with outstretched wings tapping against the windowpane, and not from a ghost at all.

The stove warms him from below. He raises his hands in front of his face and examines them. They are black in every crease, hardened and scarred from the fox's claws and his crazed digging in the hard ground, and from prying off snails. He marvels that, though his bones ache and his mind is scoured, he is yet alive.

I am naked here and unburdened of piety. But nothing replaces what was starved away. I am a husk waiting to be filled.

Arkady lowers himself to the floor and walks gingerly to the window by the door. The mountains lie quietly under rounded domes of snow. With their jagged edges softened, they are more like ancient peasants nodding off in a row on a bench by the river than the threatening chorus already receding from Arkady's thoughts. Looking out, he can't see two new, huddled patron saints sitting on the porch bench with their arms around each other for warmth. He turns back to tend to the fire.

The izba possesses an eerie, swept-clean quality. It is difficult for Arkady to know how long the place has lain vacant. No dust coats the seats of the two rough-hewn chairs. No mice or birds have damaged the pillow or the hides. The iron cook pot bears no rust. He moves slowly around the cabin's one room, creaking over the smooth floorboards, noticing one detail after another, and finally he realizes that, this far north, none of the small erosions *would* be expected: no mice live here, neither do the usual nesting birds—dust itself isn't even a significant product of the massive seasonal grindings and storms of this mostly snowed-in land.

The front door is on the east side of the cabin, and the west-facing wall bears the massive stack of firewood and a window on the sea. On the north side, the stove takes up almost the whole width of the cabin, with only enough room for a cupboard and a chopping block to one side. The south side is bare except for a shallow loft near the rafters. In the middle of the room there is an outline of a square in the floor.

The place certainly isn't the Pomor camp Saskia told him about. Not in the right place as far as he can tell, and she described a camp even larger than Schoonhoven. Why hadn't she mentioned this one, knowing he would likely walk right by it? Arkady pads across the cabin, smiling at his good fortune.

A few lacquered bowls and cups sit stacked on the stove shelf, and two pots, one birchbark bucket, and a neatly carved wooden ladle.

A broom. Even tattered curtains that have mostly fallen from their rods. This is not a company hunting hut; it had been someone's home.

As he stands in front of the stove, Arkady runs through a rush of thoughts: *What if the cabin's owner returns? It could happen at any moment! What if I starve, even though I've found this place? What if I am delusional, or dead, and this place is not what it seems to be? What if an ice bear tracked me here?* From a newly opened spaciousness, he observes these questions without much emotion. He shrugs and walks to the table. The simple act of pulling the chair out, seating himself, and resting his arms on the smooth wood pleases him so much that he lays his head down for a while to enjoy it.

Later, Arkady notices a tumble of wood and cloth in the corner of the room opposite the stove. Something about one of the small pieces catches his attention, and by the time he reaches for the rectangular panel, his hands are trembling. Who will be gazing out from the other side of this small window? What portal awaits?

Through a thin haze of cracks, Saint Nikolai Chudotvorets gazes at Arkady from an uneven background of gold. He is the beloved Wonderworker, or the Eighth Apostle as he is known in the countryside, because of the old story that he accompanied Christ during the Savior's supposed pilgrimage across Russia. The most merciful of all the saints, Nikolai's expression is amused, encouraging, severe. His left arm cradles the Holy Book; his right hand is raised in a gesture Arkady has seen thousands of times. What he had previously interpreted as *Don't you dare!* was now, suddenly and quietly, *Here, listen!*

The folds of Saint Nikolai's dark-blue robes cascade over his arms and eddy as they flow from him. Fitting for the patron of seafarers to be clothed in water. That, and his ability to help those in immediate danger, is why he is here, of course. The izba must have belonged to a Pomor. Arkady brushes dust from the icon, rehangs it, and straightens the panel's corners. He even smiles back at the Wonderworker. After all, Saint Nikolai also serves as the patron saint of orphans.

CHAPTER 27

fter moving the table aside, Arkady uses all his strength to pry the trapdoor up from the floor, but only one finger fits in the brass ring of the handle, and it's an awkward ordeal. The trapdoor lies in the exact center of the cabin, and the wood has expanded and contracted so many times that the door and the flooring have practically fused, and Arkady is weak to begin with. He works and works, sometimes falling over from the effort. Finally, he threads the brass ring with the iron oven poker and, though deeply gouging the trapdoor where the lever touches it, wrests it open. A sweet, familiar smell emanates from the cellar, as if from a saint's tomb. He uses the ladder to descend into the darkness below.

Because the izba was built atop a stone foundation, Arkady can stand almost at his full height at the bottom. He holds a candle aloft as he peers out from the center of his small flickering radius.

"Oh God, what treasure is this?" The sound of his own raspy voice startles him.

All around are birchbark containers: bushels, covered baskets, buckets draped with burlap, and even a few large hardwood chests. These are the vessels of Russia. Every cabin, house, and hut has them, except in the most dire circumstances. He cuts the twine that binds the lid to the basket nearest him. Inside, for the first time in his life, Arkady sees the face of God's mercy: tea. The smoky fragrance makes his eyes turn upward in their sockets. He carefully relids it and moves on. Rye flour. Barley. A barrel of dried meat. He rips off a big piece with his teeth and chews it up. Another of kasha.

Crocks of lard and even oil of some kind. There is so much here that Arkady reels, almost certain now that he really has died. He finds a basket of dried berries. He shoves them into his mouth.

I will live, and I will taste pleasure. What heaven is this? Cranberries.

In one of the chests, wrapped in fine wool blankets, he finds an old, gleaming musket and bags of clumped but fragrant gunpowder. Also lying there is a fine ax with a filigreed head and an elaborately carved wooden handle.

Who lived here? Whoever it was possessed great weapons, greater than Arkady had ever seen, and brought enough provisions from the mainland to live here for a very long time. Who would live here? A strange feeling rises like an evening mist above the Laya tributary.

Arkady climbs back up the ladder, out the front door, and down the seven steps. Three patron saints stare after him.

The cold knifes his face, and snowflakes drift horizontally in a stiff wind blowing off the sea. The pinnacle rocks in their snow-hoods angle toward him as he searches right and then left. Then, he walks slowly past the house.

The Cross is taller than he is and leans slightly toward the sea. Its crossbeam is empty. Behind it, a great pile of lichen-covered stones marks a grave. He looks all around the stones and examines the Cross but finds no inscription. He crawls on hands and knees, pushing aside feathery snow to search the low faces of the boulders nearby. There is no engraved stone, no human indication. But he realizes he needs no outward sign after all. As soon as he'd seen the musket and the ax, he knew. There is only one person who built an izba like this on Spitsbergen. He heard about it from his grandfather many times, not to mention Evgeny and his brethren, but Arkady never believed the stories. Somehow, he had ended up in the home of the chief-turned-pagan-god of the Pomors. The true patron of seafarers on the White Sea: Starostin.

CHAPTER 28

or a few days, Arkady rests in the izba, then he gets to work. He eats a breakfast of kasha and cranberries, muttering gratitude to Starostin and the Wonderworker. He doesn't even notice he's lost the thread of the Church calendar once again. Instead of tending to his prayers, he finds a ball of waxed thread and a needle in one of Starostin's cupboards. He uses a bit of reindeer hide to patch his wool overcoat and reinforce the cuffs, which are unraveling where the fox tore through them. He makes a new lining for his hat and uses strips of hide to wrap over his stocking-clad feet. He folds dried meat and biscuits into his pocket, buttons into his warmest clothes, and shoulders the magnificent ax.

In the space that has opened up in his heart, he now desires only to work with his hands and see what is before him. This is a good thing because winter is almost here.

Along with the ax, he carries four long strips of reindeer hide. He steps carefully across the tundra and rocks, with his head down in the wind. Far below, the sea roils darkly. The cold nips his lungs. The air is a descending ocean of gray. The sky is all layers of diffuse light where the sun leaves only a faint impression. Arkady's mind is the same: an unfamiliar territory of flitting memory and large open spaces. The hulking figure of a man sits upon the crossbeam of the Cross. The sight barely registers in Arkady's peripheral vision; the moment tells him it's more important to gather firewood than to reckon with ghosts.

He moves slowly east along the fjord, scanning the bluff for a way down to the beach. His mind rests in certainty: even though he now has food and sturdy shelter, he'll die without fire, without heat. Even with the wall of stacked wood inside the izba, the winter will require much, much more. Twice he sees driftwood lying in tiny coves below, piled where high tides and storms left them, but the bluff is too steep; he can't reach it.

Finally, after half an hour of walking, Arkady follows a narrow streambed down to the beach. He walks some distance back to a lagoon he'd seen from the bluff, which is sheltered from the open ocean by great piles of driftwood. Most of the wood is silver and dry except for a light dusting of snow. After resting for a few minutes, he draws out the ax to cut a round from one of the logs to serve as a chopping block. Driftwood isn't the best fuel, but it's the only option. He emits his breath in puffs of white cloud and relaxes into the work, letting his swing become an extension of his arms, honing his movements to eliminate anything extraneous. Soon, he sheds his coat and, later, his fraying wool sweater.

He makes one trip back to the izba dragging a load of wood bundled in reindeer hide, which he attaches to himself by long straps. His hands are half-frozen. As he draws near, one of the patron saints on the porch rises from the huddle. He is an old man with sleepy eyes, leaning heavily on a staff. Arkady recognizes him right away.

"Father Savvatii," he says, dropping the leather straps and walking forward.

Saint Savvatii, eremite of the White Sea and founder of Solovetsky Monastery, holds out his hands. "Arkady Afanasyev, you have emerged into the inner chamber of your heart. You have ears to hear and eyes to see. You've no use for us now."

The old man reaches out as if to embrace Arkady, who rushes toward him, tears flowing freely. Before Arkady can get there, though, the saints dissolve. He passes through the place where they'd been. He stands there quietly, scanning the sea and the coastline, waiting for something else to happen. Then he hitches himself back to the wood and goes on.

By the time he returns to the izba with the second load, Arkady is nothing but a vessel for working muscle and bone. He drags a bigger load behind him and carries pieces of wood strapped to his back. His eyes glaze, and his mind stills to a gentle hum: *If you want to live, you must do this again tomorrow. And the next day. And the next day. And the next.*

The following day goes much the same, except Arkady packs more food and eats more before he leaves the cabin. Despite his aching legs and arms, he reaches his stream-path in almost half the time it took him the day before. On the beach, with the hissing sea at his back and the sky above him dark as a shadow, he chops wood and the whole time regards it as the lifesaving heat Starostin's great stove will soon produce. Running through his mind are not prayers, not memories, not hopes for the future or any idea of a future at all.

On the third day, Arkady trudges back to the lagoon in a fine mist of sleet and resumes his work, but he's only been at it for a few minutes when his numb hand slips on the long neck of the ax. A knot, hidden under the surface on one side of the driftwood he's cutting pops the ax head away and down in an unexpected diagonal, straight into the front half of Arkady's leading left foot; the blade slices through his boot, cleaves the flesh and bone, and lodges itself in the cobble beach. Arkady takes in a great breath and then drops silently to the ground.

CHAPTER 29

For some time, the world wobbles on an axis of pain. Then Arkady's eyes flutter open, and he utters a yawning cry. He pushes himself up onto his elbows and, from an almost sitting position, wrenches his left leg free of the ax blade. Screaming, he struggles to stay conscious. If he does not, he could be finished. When he can muster it, he lifts his leg off the ground and crabs himself sideways along the beach, facing back the way he came. Each time his wounded foot taps the ground, which happens with almost every exertion, Arkady squeezes his eyes shut and prays to die.

Is this where it ends? Sliding along the ground like a shelled insect?

A swoosh of freezing wind sweeps low across the bluff. He is wet and muddy already, and he has not yet made the climb from the beach onto the streambed path; his wound is filthy, and he sees the exposed edge of a splintered bone. He drifts in and out of lucidity, guided forward only by the gentle wooden tapping sound of his mother's lacemaking bobbins. Then, that disappears, and all Arkady can do is convulse—gulping air and willing his hands and one good leg to move together as he pulls himself forward. He vomits. He stops to shiver uncontrollably. After a very long time, he reaches the top of the headland. A fox emerges from the tundra. Patches of its white winter coat glimmer among the remnants of the dark. It trots over to sniff the blood that has drawn it there.

"I'm sorry," Arkady wheezes. "I'm sorry I drowned you and ate you and left your bones in a heap."

With red-brown eyes, the animal looks Arkady up and down and steps delicately toward him, baring its teeth.

"Walk with me," Arkady begs. "Tell me, have you struck your tail like flint against these mountains, like Nikolai always said? Have you sent sparks up to light the sky? If I don't make it back to the izba, I will never see your lights again, White One. But never mind, never mind," Arkady mumbles, returning to his only task. Everything else slips from his mind.

The fox dips his head to Arkady's wound and nips at the mangled foot.

Arkady swings his arm toward the creature. "I am sorry, brother. I can't let you do that. Not yet."

The fox swerves away. Sensation in Arkady's claw-hands fades, and he senses the boundary between his earthly form and the elements growing as transparent as the air.

The pauses between his efforts lengthen to half-dreams and fixed stares across the sea or upon the inland crags. He has been struggling for hours. The izba must have moved, he realizes, and then, finally, he thinks this might not be a bad resting place, and by that he means *I'm ready to die.*

Some time after that, the izba appears in the dusky space ahead. The crags sigh from the landward side, and the sea urges him forward. While his teeth chatter, he drags his filthy, soaked body up and over the last rise and slowly across the tundra behind the cabin. He looks up, toward the sudden sound of cascading rocks. On the scree slope, the Dog is making its way down from the heights. Arkady tries to move faster, but pain and fear take away his breath. His was a mistake worthy of the Dog. Now, he will get what is coming to him.

He drags himself up the seven steps. The Dog is coming closer. There are only explosions of pain where his foot had been. He squeezes his eyes shut and lifts himself again, but he can't reach the door handle. The Dog trots onto the tundra and pauses, panting.

Suddenly, a figure unfurls itself from a shadow and kneels close to Arkady. This face is gray and cracked like driftwood, with black eyes glittering like pebbles in a stream. It is a man with a beard striped with seaweed, braided with gold thread, and hung with metal beads.

"Nothing in this place is what it seems. Not even you," the man murmurs. "There is a great force at work here, the same force as created the world. This place uses us all for its own purposes. I could let him have you," Starostin nods to the Dog. "But your work in your current form is not yet done."

Starostin opens the door, and Arkady drags himself inside.

CHAPTER 30

After the world stops spinning, Arkady crawls to one of Starostin's cupboards and barely manages to pull himself up to open it. Lucky for him, the bottle of vodka is near the edge. Arkady pulls the cork out with his teeth and pours the liquid down his throat before slipping back to the floor. The liquor's heat shoots through him with enough force that he shudders, and the bottle falls from his hand, and the rest of the vodka spills and is wasted.

In the brief episodes of wakefulness that follow, Arkady's wound terrifies him so much that he prays for oblivion. He is inexperienced in matters of the body, and his hands will not stop shaking as he struggles with the split boot still attached to his mangled foot. Mostly with his eyes closed, he manages to peel the leather away. His sock, however, is fused to the wound by dried blood and flaps of skin. Bones protrude, and bits of meat stick to his fingers as he feels for his toes. He can't think of what to do.

It takes almost all his strength to pull himself to a crouch near the bucket of stream water that he keeps for tea on the table. Once there, teetering at the table edge, he reaches for the bucket, but instead knocks it over, sending a small cascade off the opposite side of the table. He scoots over so that the waning stream of water falls into his wound. He tries to clean the mess of tattered skin, torn flesh, and broken bone, but there is so much dirt inside it that all he succeeds in doing is creating mud.

I gave myself to you, Mother Damp Earth, and now you've entered me. Can your mineral essence do its work?

He lies on the floor and looks out the window, where it has been dark for a very long time and snow falls in earnest. His need to urinate is profound. Again, he struggles to sit up and fumbles with his trouser buttons. He raises himself to a kind of kneel with his injured leg splayed in front of him. Arkady pisses into his wound. As he does it, he spies the thread and needle on the table. He grabs them and pulls himself over to the hearth. He opens the firebox and holds the needle over one of the tiny flames that still licks the embers. He lies down on his back and spends an eternity trying to thread the needle, but he can't. He turns onto his side and caresses the stove with one hand. Flashing stars whiz across the room from the Wonderworker's icon, leaving long, curving trails. More and more of them appear, filling the air before his eyelids snap shut.

Faintly, he hears the tapping of the window ornament. The wooden bobbins weave up and down by their own volition, hovering above a pair of folded skeletal hands.

Ah, it's all right, he tells himself. *I was never good with the details of living. Mostly I was a piece of fluff adrift on winds beyond my control. I wanted to be the northernmost holy man in the world.* He wheezes: a laugh. *But instead, what a farce! Covered in my own piss. Alone, as always. Well, maybe not quite alone.* Arkady folds his hands on his chest. From the wall, the Wonderworker leans out of his gilt frame to look at him.

For a long time, Arkady floats on his back with his arms folded across his chest aboard a narrow, open boat. He recognizes the mossy smell of old stones; he drifts along one of Solovetsky's canals. He hears the *swish, swish* of leaves rustling in the wind. Awash in happiness and relief, he watches the bent and graceful forms of Solovetsky's running trees pass above his head, their boughs laden with flickering candles. He drifts gently along, listening. *Swish, swish.*

Swish, swish. The wind ruffles his hair, but then it dawns on him that the sound actually is too regular to be the wind. He returns from a very great distance. *Swish, swish.* Pause. *Swish, swish.* He snaps back to Starostin's cabin. It is lighter outside. He is shivering.

Abruptly, he vomits a thin stream of alcoholic bile onto the floor. He is sweat-soaked and hollowed out. Like a woodland snail, he slowly slides across the room using his hands, leaving a slick trail behind him. Using every fiber of his remaining strength, he pulls himself up to look out the inland-facing window. By this time, he recognizes the sound of skis sliding across the snow.

Like an apparition, a figure glides toward the izba. Arkady has never seen anything more beautiful than this form, moving in long strides, each arm and leg swinging in harmony, keeping itself warm while achieving admirable speed. The figure arrives outside the cabin and unwinds long strips of hide to free himself from the skis. He tosses down his poles and hurries up the stairs. Arkady manages to keep himself upright as the door opens and the looming creature comes in and looks around.

"What a stench! How could you foul Starostin's own izba?"

Arkady strains to see inside the stranger's fur-lined hood. There are rosy, freckled cheeks. A copperish braid.

"I just came from the dwelling place of a demon." Saskia draws the hood away to reveal her face blackened by bruises and what appears to be a series of narrow burns on her neck.

"Oh—" Arkady yelps, raising his hand toward her.

She ignores him, pulling a rucksack off her back. An ice-bear pelt is strapped to the top. "Damn that wrong-in-the-head Swede. I waited for the snow for so long. I hacked his other pair of skis apart when he was asleep, so he couldn't follow, and now here I am. It was the only way I could outrun him. He won't be after me now. Why would he? And you found Starostin's hut. I didn't think you'd make it this far."

Arkady slides down the wall to sitting. He is wracked from the ribcage with shrieks he can't control, and then sobs, as if his body is purging all human feeling before leaving this earth. She is here. Then, he wants to pummel the Swede to mush, even as he remembers how quickly he hurried away from Kol's cabin. How thoughtlessly. He wants to embrace Saskia, though she seems so much bigger than before. As she takes off her backpack and overcoat, he sees that she is bigger, indeed. Her dress pulls tight around her middle. When she rises from the firebox, a flaming piece of kindling in her hand, she sees him looking.

"It will be born during the long night. Kuzma is the father."

Arkady has never seen a woman with child before. Saskia lights the oil lamp then grabs the ladder where it lies on its side against the woodpile. She props it against the loft and then looks around.

"When Kol realized I carried a child, he changed. He started in on me." She gestured to her face. "No matter. There is food here. Where?"

Arkady points to the cupboards. And then to the floor. "There's more down there."

Saskia flings open the cupboards. She opens baskets and jars and fills a wooden bowl with a few dried cranberries, a drizzle of honey, and a thin strip of dried reindeer meat. She climbs to the loft and places the bowl there. She comes down and asks for water. Arkady shrugs toward the toppled bucket, so the woman stomps outside and fills the mug with snow. She holds the mug near the firebox for a few minutes then sets it beside the bowl in the loft. When she returns, she opens the front door and looks out.

"This silly man doesn't know the proper greeting, but I know it, and we've laid a place for you. You may return. Come on, don't be shy." Saskia looks across the tundra and toward the stream. "That's good. Come on."

Looking down, she backs away from the door as if to let an animal inside. A breeze riffles the folds of her skirt.

"You leave the ladder propped here, you understand?" Saskia barks to Arkady. "This room is an anchor in the middle world. You see the table here, and the chairs. And the beautiful stove."

Saskia walks to the stove and lifts off the biggest iron pot. She leaves the izba, and Arkady listens to her heavy steps as she descends the stairs. Soon, she returns with a potful of stream water.

"But that's not all it is, little priest." She points down to the trapdoor. She points up to the tiny loft. "We are not here to disrupt this harmony; do you understand?"

She wipes her hands on her apron, apparently not looking around to see whether Arkady understands.

"So, you're hurt again. Let's have a look."

Saskia examines Arkady's foot and fetches a bottle from her backpack, uncorks it, and gestures for Arkady to drink.

"Small sips, but many."

Arkady drinks vodka more fiery than Starostin's. Thankfully, it warms and numbs him. He sips, swallows, and watches Saskia, who examines the stove, roughly brushing away tears with her fist.

"Little mother, thank the gods you're here. I battled so long in that damn Swede's house. I will tend you, I promise. I will roast fresh meat in your oven. I hear that stream outside, giving us water. Tea and soups we'll make. All will be well." She cocks her head, listening. "He still waits."

She's not referring to Arkady.

"I'd heard of his vigil, but so much is carried away on the wind, it's hard to know which stories are true." She stares at the stove a bit longer. "Now, then. Let's keep some for later, priest."

Arkady shakes his head, gripping the bottle tightly and swirling among the stars.

Saskia narrows her eyes. "You did this with an ax. I don't see an ax here, and it wasn't on the porch. Where is it?"

"I couldn't bring it back," he whispers faintly.

"Where is it, you fool? Starostin's own ax? We need it. It must live here."

"I think I'm going to die," Arkady wheezes. "My foot."

"Tell me where the ax is."

"Down the beach. Where I was chopping." Arkady points to the door. "There's a path. And a fox. And … maybe others."

Saskia looks again at Arkady's foot, scrunches her face, thinking. Then she is across the room feeding more wood to the fire and putting her coat back on.

"Don't leave," Arkady whispers, but Saskia slips away.

CHAPTER 31

ut the Dog could not be convinced, so he and the Sisters left their usual territories in the west and re-treated away across the backs of the inland glaciers to the great ice fields."

Saskia's voice reaches Arkady from a great distance.

"Away from all humans and all animals, too, except migrating ice bears, who they say brought messages to the Sisters telling where the Pomor hunting camps lay, so when winter came, the Sisters could easily find the men.

"They came upon a huge cave made from ice as blue and an-cient as the earth itself. The Dog walked through the cave's ante-chamber with the Sisters on his back and found that it continued on and on, through hall after glowing hall, lit by high crevasses and starlight trapped in ice. Deeper and deeper they walked, even the Sisters hushed by the strange, beckoning cave. After some time—maybe much, maybe little—they found streaks of earth mixed with the ice, then the Dog felt stones underfoot, and water trickled through the ice walls surrounding them. Warmth inside this great, cold palace caressed their faces, and the Sisters peeled off their layers. Soon, they rode naked on the back of the panting Dog. Well, they came to a great, high-ceilinged cavern where old, old stone encircled a steaming pool of clear water. The women slid down from the Dog's back and entered the hot water, gasping with plea-sure and splashing one another. At first the Dog was tentative. He sniffed the water of the hot spring and paced across the rocks. From deep within his primal being, he smelled something new, something that his ancestors had smelled but that he never had in his centuries of roaming the north."

Arkady opens his eyes. More than anything, he wants her to continue, but her voice has trailed off. He lies on his back, on top of a bed of hides by the hearth. He's flushed and nauseated. His head hurts but not nearly as much as his leg. Saskia stands at the window on the inland side of the izba, cupping her face near the pane.

"What is it? What's out there?"

She turns toward him. "You're awake. That's a pity."

"Why?"

"Because your foot's ruined and must come off."

Arkady tries to sit up. The lower half of his body is alien meat. Saskia has cut his tattered woolen leggings, so that one of his legs is neatly socked and covered, and the other leg lies bare. Some of the bones of his left foot are sticking out of the graying flesh. He recoils, scrabbling uselessly with his hands to get away from the abomination. His foot is cloven almost to his ankle bone. The edges of the wound are white and oozing. He tries to scream but vomits instead. Saskia sits down at the table with her back to him. He hears a familiar sound.

"This can't be. I'll die."

"You'll die if I don't act now."

"No!" His breath is quick and audible.

"Arkady, calm yourself."

"How can I do that? A madwoman wants to cut off my foot!"

Saskia shakes her head. "Think about it, little priest."

"I am not a priest. Stop calling me that! And stop sharpening my knife. I need to think."

"That's the last thing you need to do. The situation is simple."

Saskia's thick braids twitch against her broad back as she moves the knife across the whetstone.

"In Schoonhoven, Kuzma and I did much worse than this to the Pomors," she says. "We saw all manner of hunting injuries, not to mention the damage men do to each other in fights. You saw a bit of that. And ice bears, don't forget them." She whistles through her teeth, shaking her head.

In the firebox, a pretty little flame annihilates the wood of a hundred-year-old fir tree. Rivergoing after it was felled, and seagoing after it escaped its boom, the tree drifted in a great spiral of currents across three oceans and, ten years ago, rode the northward gyre to Spitsbergen where it came to rest near Starostin's izba. Arkady always felt something of the forest when he sat at the hearth of Solovetsky's great kitchen, of the taiga that surrounded Nikolai's cabin like a warm cloak in winter and a great cage of light in summertime. Arkady reaches out and touches the stove's warm masonry.

"She's a good little mother," Saskia says admiringly. "She is." She turns to him. "The flesh is dead. So many bones are crushed and broken in your foot that even if the flesh could heal, you'd never walk for the splintering. This is the only way." Saskia kneels next to him and grasps his hand. She pats it and clucks. "You didn't expect this place to be what it is, did you?"

"I am a fool," Arkady admits.

Saskia nods. "But you're not dead yet." She laughs. "Many others would have died on the way across Bell Sound. In the fog or the waves. But you may yet live to see the great bird way after all. Soon, soon now, it will appear."

Arkady motions for the vodka, and Saskia helps him. Over the bottle, his panic-stricken eyes seek her calm ones. He drinks deeply. Saskia resumes sharpening the knife.

"Starostin lived alone in this izba for thirty-two years," she says. "The Pomors brought him supplies, but he hunted reindeer and seal, and he faced the long night on his own. He loved Spitsbergen more than a human ever has; that's what all the Pomors say, anyway. They say that every spring the snow buntings would line up on his porch rail. When he came out, one by one they'd flutter up to pull hair from his beard and use it to build their nests. Foxes followed him when he went hunting, and ice bears circled this hut every year, but they never broke down the door. They say his bones do not lie in that grave up the rise. The Pomors say that one like him—who has banished himself to the farthest reaches out of love for the hunting grounds—does not die but shape-shifts."

"Have you been here before?"

Saskia gestured vaguely eastward. "Before, my sisters and I came near here to collect eider eggs after our colonies were raided by foreigners. I walked past this place. We paid our respects in our way, but we never came inside. People were told not to meddle in Starostin's affairs. But no matter. We are here for better or for worse."

Arkady can't imagine anything worse than what is about to happen.

Saskia pulls a pot of scalding water off the stove and brings a wooden bucket of rags to his side. She leans over him with her great belly pressing against his thighs and sticks the blade of the knife over the flames in the firebox. Then she sits back on her heels.

"There's a fox nearby," Arkady whispers. "Give it the flesh you cut away."

Saskia settles beside him and closes her eyes. "This wound and blood, this useless foot: Go into the dark forest. Go into the dank swamp. Go now into the green moss and old stones, to the iron trough. *There* you can ache and hurt. But in this one, in Arkady, right here in this land, hurt no more."

She opens her eyes.

"Remember: You don't die when you're old but when you're ripe. You're still green. Remember that." She places a piece of kindling in his hand. "Put this between your teeth."

CHAPTER 32

he Twelve Sisters of Scurvy live deep in the Dog's cavern. When the northerlies rise in midwinter, they get in their lodja and ride the wind. Often, they sail down to the hunting camps, where the Pomors sit by their hearths, knotting and unknotting ropes, trying not to fall asleep. They say that if you sleep more than five hours a night during a Spitsbergen winter, a Sister will disembark at the door of your hut. Sleep deeply more than two nights in a row, and she will come smiling inside to kneel at your feet. If that happens, you're lost."

Arkady listens in a drowse on the hearth, returning slowly, lazily, to the world like a great, old pike rising from the silty river bottom. The flames in the stove dance lightly above their embers. Nikolai never spoke of the Sisters, but who would tell such things to a little boy? Sensation washes over his body in formidable waves; when pain rushes through, he relaxes every muscle in his legs and loosens his mind even further so that he doesn't lock onto the knives burrowing through him. He moves through these phases without uttering a word. Between these periods, he's wonderfully comfortable: warm, drifting nearer then farther away from Saskia's voice, lightheaded one moment and electrified by piercing clarity the next: *I want to stay in this silence. I don't ever want to speak again.*

Saskia stands above him at the stove, tending to something. She might be singing. He smells tea, which makes him utterly happy. The whole scene is something out of a fairy tale, and he smiles when the outer hem of her apron brushes his shoulder. He easily refrains from considering his future; it's no small feat to control one's fears even in an everyday circumstance, not to mention one such as this. He feels the peace of one who has surrendered. Tears spring to his eyes. Someone is taking care of him.

Here are no hymns and no ringing of bells. Above, the roadless road stretches onward, carrying the parade of the dead. You haven't seen the moon through the snow and the wind. You haven't seen the stars wheeling around the pole of the great tree. No hymns to sing, no bells to ring: Here all is ours.

Sometime later, the oil lamp glows on the table, emitting its familiar ocean scent. Saskia sits beside him, dribbling broth between his lips with a wooden spoon. The peaceful feeling is gone, and, as soon as he can, Arkady covers his face under the hides. He cries in pain for all he's lost.

"But you must be wondering about that cavern," Saskia says. This is her offering.

Under the covers, he's angry that he doesn't possess the strength to strangle this madwoman. His left leg pulses with blood that has nowhere to flow. *No! Leave me in peace. Leave me to die.*

"No one knows for sure how the Dog came to Spitsbergen. Histories float across this land like eiderdown; some of them are caught here, where traces are still known by men, and some are completely lost out over the sea. My sisters told me the Dog has been here forever. They said that, when the sun and the moon were released to the sky, each had a great wolf chasing it so that neither the sun nor the moon would slow down in their course and meet the other. But after a while, the moon wolf came into heat. And you know how dogs are! That sun wolf couldn't ignore her. He galloped off course to mate with her, and all the people down below saw the sun cover the moon in the sky. My sisters said the Spitsbergen Dog was their pup. Both wolves wanted to keep him, and they fought bitterly over it. They couldn't agree what to do, so they put him in Spitsbergen. For half the year, the sun wolf has him, and for the other half, during the winter, the moon wolf. He's a lonely one, the Dog. Or at least he was."

Saskia pours tea for herself and settles down next to Arkady on the hearth.

"We know more about the Twelve Sisters. But I'm afraid it's not a happy tale."

Arkady feels no urge to speak one way or another.

"A Dutchman and his wife lived deep in Wijde Fjord up on the north coast. A harrowing place. They say he was a boiler at Smeerenburg, and when the time of whales ended, he stayed on with his wife and their small daughter, Isa. He hunted seals all summer and foxes all winter. Once every two years, he made an overland journey by sled and ski from the farthest reach of Wijde Fjord to the hunting stations at Advent Bay to sell furs and buy supplies.

The man was known as a skilled hunter. But when Isa was thirteen years old, they had a bad year, and her mother died of scurvy. Over the next twenty years, Isa bore twelve girl babies by her father. For a long time, she managed to keep her father away from the eldest girls, but when he took a particular fancy to one, Isa murdered him using her hunting knife. But before he died, he managed to stab her in the chest, and a few days later, Isa died, leaving her twelve sister-daughters alone.

"The Sisters chopped wood, kept up their fire, and rationed their food wisely. But none of them could hunt seals, and eider season was long past. Every day, they kept watch for any ship or sled that might appear, but none ever did. They were very brave, especially because, each night, after they built up the fire and lay down together next to the stove, they heard a great howling outside. The eldest sister, Maaike, told the littlest ones it was just the north wind singing. But the older ones knew it was no wind. Finally, Maaike grew angry at the disruption. One night, when she heard the howling, she put on her coat, lit a torch, and flung open the door.

"'I need my rest, you annoying beast! I've got eleven sisters to mind, and winter's almost here.' Maaike pointed the torch in the direction of a big black shadow on the snow, and the creature disappeared into the night. The sisters slept easy until morning, and when they opened the door to fetch snow for water, they found a freshly slain reindeer outside. Maaike rejoiced, and went to work skinning, gutting, and quartering the animal. The sisters brought the meat inside, spent the next two days roasting and drying it, and from then on, their nights were peaceful.

"Ten days later, when the girls opened the door, a slain ice bear lay on bloodstained snow. Rejoicing, they went to work skinning the great beast so that they could sew warm parkas for the coming winter. They spent the next five days processing the meat, and they knew they had enough food to survive. The sisters sang and played games on the hearth while the last light faded from the sky. Some time later, when the girls opened the door, a huge black wolf sat just outside.

"'I have a proposition for you,' said the Dog. 'I will provide meat, and seal oil for your lamps, if you come live with me. I am lonely. Come with me, to my camp in the south, before winter is upon us. Come with me, and you will live for centuries as I do.'

"The sisters brought out their father's oarboat and filled it with everything they had. They put on their fur parkas, draped hides over themselves, and hooked the Dog up as if the boat were a sled. The Dog carried them away with him.

"At first, they moved from place to place, so the Dog could hunt with the seasons. During those travels, they found the ice cavern, far across the inland glacier fields. Slowly over the centuries, the sisters grew into women, and they sought out the scant company they could find in Spitsbergen. They want progeny, you see. More than anything else, they seek human seed. Simple enough. And for each failed attempt to conceive a child, in vengeance they spread scurvy, the disease that ruined their family in the first place. Eventually, the Pomors named them the Sisters of Scurvy."

Arkady pulls the covers back from his face. The fire crackles in the stove. The izba overflows with food and firewood. The woman who cut off his foot sits cross-legged beside him, staring into the firebox. A deep, pulsing pain grows stronger and resounds from the place where his foot should be, pounds through his legs, abdomen, and chest. Where is his foot now? Dragged into some burrow? Floating in the shallows? He squeezes his eyes shut.

"You know this place teems with spirits."

By the quality of her voice, Arkady can tell Saskia is looking at him.

"You've encountered them; I can see that. You've even brought them here. Every bay and cove in Spitsbergen has one, and every mountain and stream is populated. Some are silent," she laughs, "and some certainly are not. Some roam, like the Dog. Some make themselves known to men, like the Sisters. But most of them remain quietly fused in one place."

Within the painful echo chamber of his body, Arkady listens while Saskia tells him about the spirits of places near the fjord where she grew up and near Schoonhoven, where the creatures apparently abound. She stops talking when he covers his ears. Safe in this muffled chamber, a trapdoor opens, and Arkady falls through into a silence as deep and obscure as the lakes of Solovetsky.

He drifts in and out of consciousness for six nights, then he sleeps deeply for another two weeks. From his bed on the hearth, he senses days passing, even though it's always night. His wound strikes knives against itself. He wonders if he will live, and often he wants to scream but, in the end, stays silent. He thinks perhaps, in addition to removing his foot, Saskia has stitched his mouth shut with some spell. But as time moves on, his silence deepens. He navigates his labyrinth of pain silently, and, little by little, as the pain subsides, his own silence opens into a clean, white room. In it, Arkady feels less loathsome to himself. He is not adding to the accumulation of lies that, up until now, he considered reality. Then, after a while, his sense of himself dissipates into this quiet room of his heart, and this is good. There is no need to speak. Also, Saskia talks enough for them both.

CHAPTER 33

atches of dusky gray reflect off the sea, paling Saskia's face where she stands at the seaward window. Arkady watches the room darken. Behind the izba, at a mystifying distance, the sun burns in unfathomable brightness. But here, along the scalloped edge of the coast, at the outer lip of Ice Fjord, this dwindling gray glaze is enough to silence them. Saskia presses her hands to the glass as if to make the ghostly light stay, but it disappears.

"And so it begins," Saskia says, fetching Arkady's knife and carving a mark into the wooden window frame. She stabs the knife into the tabletop, and it stands there, wavering. Without further elaboration, Saskia climbs up to the stove bench and pulls her bearskin over her head.

Blearily, he considers the new, abbreviated contour of the lower half of his body. He lifts away the blankets and discovers he is naked below the waist. What remains of his left leg is blotchy and bruised, but the bandages are clean. The space where his foot should be makes him dizzy. In the sudden certainty that he will live, he tosses the blanket back over himself and groans.

Later, Saskia comes into the izba holding a low, rectangular stool.

"For your leg," she announces. "It's time to move you up off the floor."

She drapes a blanket over one of the chairs and kneels beside him. She pulls one of his arms over her shoulder and heaves him up. Arkady gasps with the pain and tries to hop along with his good leg, but spasms rack his body, and the shock of sudden movement prevents him from helping much. Saskia sets him in the chair.

"Starostin's watching us. He noticed I am pregnant, and now he thinks we may be what he's been searching for."

Arkady frowns.

"When I first arrived here, he was sitting up on his Cross. Braiding rope and looking out to sea. He didn't notice me then, but he saw me, I think, when I went back for the ax. Now, he's standing over there, watching us."

Arkady says nothing. He knows his dealings with Starostin are not done, but he doesn't know more.

"Never mind for now. Let's get you settled. I've got work to do." Saskia arranges an old sheepskin on the stool and puts both his legs atop it. "Soon, you'll put just your wounded one here, but for now, both." She spreads another blanket across his lap. "You have a few books—prayers and that—I will fetch them."

Arkady shakes his head.

"Well. You must keep yourself busy."

Arkady doesn't move. He examines the tabletop's dappled grain. She stands there for a full minute with her hands on her hips. Then, she goes for her overcoat.

"Suit yourself. I'll be back in a few hours."

The cold is gathering force, and Saskia's parka doesn't seem adequate. Where is she going? *I am an invalid,* he thinks. *A cripple. A fool. Without her, I'd be lying dead on the floor. Stinking up Starostin's cabin. Attracting ice bears and foxes.*

After some time, he walks along the long-gone cave like the stone corridor of the boys' dormitory, following the lamplight held aloft by his starets. Father Ilya looks over his shoulder to make sure Arkady is still there. He's just a boy, and it's bedtime. When they reach the door, Ilya opens it and lights a candle on the table by Arkady's bed.

"Be sure to blow it out before you go to sleep."

"Yes, Father."

"Would you like one story before I go?"

"Ivan the Fool!"

Father Ilya shakes his head. Most little boys ask for stories of bogatyrs and knights, firebirds and quests for dragon-guarded treasure. Requests for stories of Moses, Jesus, or the adventures of the apostles abounded. But with confounding consistency, Arkady demands stories about the stupidest, laziest, poorest boy in the history of the Russian countryside. In times of hardship, Ivan the Fool could not be roused from the stove bench to help. When it was time for Ivan and his two (elder, strapping, intelligent, skillful) brothers to venture into the forest to seek their fortunes, Ivan hid in the cowshed. He was the youngest of the three sons. The puniest. The unluckiest. His terrible judgment cost his family endless hardship.

"I suppose we have time for one little story," Father Ilya sighs, pulling up a stool.

Usually cast out by his family within minutes of the story's beginning, Ivan bumbles into a world of wonders and magical allies, making all the wrong choices and accepting advice from the worst sort of characters. And every time, despite it all, and to Arkady's great comfort, in these stories, the weaker the hero (and there is none weaker than Ivan the Fool), the more luminous the magic that arises. Through pursuit of a firebird, or a kidnapped princess, or an enchanted ring, or even a holy life in the farthest reaches of the north, Ivan the eternal failure somehow, inevitably, remains the favorite of the fates.

CHAPTER 34

he place must have been known to the oldest spirits on the island, but the oldest are usually the quietest; that's what my sisters always said. The Dog stumbled upon the cavern by chance and felt that he alone had discovered it. Then, he fetched the Twelve Sisters of Scurvy and carried them up over the mountains to the ice fields and the cave. Inside, the ice was so ancient that even the steam from the hot springs couldn't melt it. The Sisters sank into the scalding water and vowed they would live there for the rest of time. The Dog himself didn't care to be wet, but he loved the feeling of warm stones under his feet. And when he sniffed the air, he smelled something unusual."

Every day, Saskia chops wood at the same beach where Arkady cleaved his foot. She has collected double what Arkady had before his injury, while carrying smaller loads due to the awkwardness of her protruding belly. She stacks it up to the loft along the south wall, then throws the rest in a pile on the porch, to stack later, she says. She tells Arkady she'll go out again tomorrow for two more loads, and then again in a few days. Then they'll have enough to last until the light returns.

Saskia pours tea and sits across from him at the table. She appears to rest only for a moment before pulling a ball of thick, gray yarn from one of her pockets and two wooden knitting needles. She casts on and begins working the yarn across the needles, creating fabric from row after row of interlocking loops. Saskia, and the whole izba, emits a subtle, golden glow.

"Following this scent, the Dog stepped daintily across the wet rocks. The Sisters' laughter faded in the distance, and as he walked, all he heard was the drip of meltwater. Deeper and deeper he went, until he reached the far side of the great cave. Strange curving shapes emerged from the shadows that he thought at first were the dwellings of humans. But as he crept closer, they turned into up-sweeping buttresses that flowed into a massive central column that disappeared in the heights. The Dog sniffed around the perimeter of the column's fluted base, intoxicated by the scent of something he'd never encountered before. The fragrance lifted his spirit so much that he rolled over and swiveled on his back, joyfully rubbing against the stones. Then, he jumped up like a great puppy, his front legs in a bow, ready to play. He rubbed his head and shoulders against the column, and he felt a long-forgotten part of himself awakening. It was not until later, when some of the Sisters came to see why he was barking, that he learned the scent was that of living wood. Deep in the ice cave, the Dog had discovered a single, gigantic tree. The only one in this polar land. An oak, as it happened. Leafless, yes, yet alive."

Saskia looks up from her knitting into Arkady's face. What does she see?

"That's enough," she says. "Let's get you back to the hearth now. I'm going to bed."

The next day, Saskia feeds him stew and fresh bread. She prepares an extra bowl and covers it in a cloth. She puts that aside for him to eat later. She binds her feet in strips of hide, thick socks, and her sturdy boots. She arranges him at the table before she goes out for more wood.

"Ah! I almost forgot." Saskia comes back with a long, slender round of wood in her arms. She places it on the table in front of Arkady. Then, she looks through Starostin's cabinets and along the shelves. "I'm sure he's got them. Where did you leave them, then?"

She ascends partway up the ladder and looks around the loft, then uses the ladder to go down to the cellar, where she opens and closes baskets and bins.

"Here! I knew it. Look at these beauties."

Saskia emerges with something wrapped in canvas. She sets it next to the wood.

"You need to keep busy. When you fret, you put both of us in danger. You're a Pomor; you know this. But don't misunderstand me. We can't have you trying to go anywhere, except to piss in that bucket by your chair."

After she bustles out the door, Arkady makes no move to open the bundle. The izba fills with silence.

For most of the day, Arkady alternates between observing the barely shifting darkness outside, and praying, although this kind of prayer is not made of questions. It's more like conjuring a doorway and moving through it into a space where all that matters is the continuation of that space.

He realizes that prayer is a breakage of time, an introduction of a separate space within the ordinary hours of life. As he steps forward, following only the temporary thread of his breath, he experiences a small freedom from the familiar cage of his memories. The scent of wood smoke comforts him, yet for the first time, memories of his grandfather's cabin do not overwhelm him. He hears the wooden ornament knocking against the window, but his mother's face, angling away from him, does not quicken his heart. He dangles at the edge of everything familiar and then drifts into the unknown. In this new place, his psyche hovers just apart from its accustomed cycle of fearful reaction to life's travails, in a gracious light. Could it be the Uncreated Light that Father Vasily wrote to him about? After some time, his eyes flutter shut into sleep.

Hours later, Arkady unwraps the canvas bundle and finds an old set of woodcarving knives. *So, I will be a Pomor after all,* he thinks. Somewhere on the roadless road, his grandfather Nikolai pauses in an open place, his head cocked as if listening to a faint call, wind lifting the coarse ends of his white-gray hair. Arkady turns one of the small-bladed knives over in his hands. *You will smile, Grandfather, until you see how inept I am at everything you mastered.*

Arkady cuts off a piece of wood the size of his hand from the round, and strips away the rough, seaworn outer layer. The grain is dense, denser than he's seen before. It's not a type of wood that grows near Arkhangelsk. Slowly, he shaves away the upper edge of the cylinder to form a head, then rough shoulders. He was never much good at it; the monastery presented few opportunities to carve, but winters were long in Nikolai's cabin on the Laya tributary, and there had been plenty of hours for his grandfather to teach him. Carefully keeping track of the proportions, he marks where the tips of the figure's fingers would be, and the waist. Then, working up from the feet, he ekes out a primitive doll. Surely Saskia will appreciate the gift for her baby. Even though the wood is difficult to chisel and cut, he is not entirely displeased with it until he tries to carve a face.

Saskia returns. Rubbing her belly, she goes straight to the stove to stoke the fire and heat the kettle for tea. Arkady frowns and looks at the table. She is doing everything, and in her state. He couldn't even carve a doll for her baby. When Saskia settles across from him with her cup and a piece of salted bread, she eyes the misshapen carved figure and then looks at him with eyebrows raised. He shrugs.

"We've enough wood for now," Saskia says, still frowning. "We have five reindeer grazing on the plain, just off your track to the beach, quarter of an hour from here. I'd better shoot them before they travel farther from us. One is just a calf; he must have been born very late. A bad sign … he will die, anyway, out there. I'll shoot them in the morning. And I'll need your help."

Arkady nods. His leg itches maddeningly, but he tries not to rub near the wound so that Saskia will rest and not feel she must tend to him. But she sees him twitching and clenching his fists, and she comes.

"Let's see to the wrappings, then. You're due for a fresh bandage."

Arkady still doesn't speak, but when Saskia reaches down to pull his chair back from the table, he grasps her hand gently in both of his. But her hand is raw from chopping. She quickly pulls it back.

"Don't get my blood on you. You just sit still for now. That's the only thing you can do. I've seen men with injuries who cannot keep still long enough to heal. They either die, or they're left with terrible pain for the rest of their days. So, you just sit tight, little priest. Keep your mind busy."

CHAPTER 35

he Dog made his true home there at the base of the oak, curled between two spiraling roots. He lay for many hours staring into the heights. Maaike, the eldest Sister, joined him there, and for a while shared his fascination. They whispered together, she becoming more and more curious and anxious about the tree. The massive roots and trunk indicated the tree had been there for centuries. They speculated about the amount and quality of light filtering through the ice, whether the tree were simply magical, or dying or sleeping in dormancy. They peered up into the gloom; they could barely see the tree's lowest branch, far above their heads.

"Finally, after many weeks, Maaike became so curious that she decided she would climb the tree. The Dog initially dissuaded her, but she gathered all the rope they had, and braided more using the tendons of ice bears. To one end of her great rope, she tied a stone. The Dog circled the tree excitedly as the girl coiled the rope at her feet and threw the rock up with all her might. The rock tumbled back to the ground, gouging a tree root when it hit. The Dog knelt at the root, smelling the rich, piney fragrance of forests he would never know.

"Maaike threw again, and again the rock crashed back to earth, this time narrowly missing the Dog's skull. He leapt to the side, huffing with frustration. The Dog could do nothing to help, but he growled appreciatively and nudged the girl to continue. On the third try, the rock flew over the ash's lowest branch. Maaike let the rope slide through her hands, up up up, until the rock descended on its tether, and the ladder was secure. She tied one end around a boulder and ran back to her Sisters for an oil lamp while the Dog held tight to the other end of the rope. Then, off she went, shimmying up to see what she could see.

"After a long time, the girl's voice came echoing back, telling the Dog to tie the rock back to the rope, untie the other end, and let her pull it up. The Dog watched the rope disappear into the cavern's heights. The whole night passed, and then the morning, with no sound coming from above, and no flicker of lamplight. The Dog listened to the eleven Sisters laughing and talking in the hot springs and dozed with his head on his front paws. He slept all day and half the night, and then awoke to a caress between his ears. He hopped up; Maaike stood before him, her hair wild and strewn with twigs, and her body covered with bits of bark and sap.

"'I threw the rope up to higher branches seven times,' she said. 'I climbed through the air and across the tree's limbs. I saw the remnants of great old nests filled with fox skeletons. Shields draped over higher branches, engraved with symbols I didn't recognize. Up higher were walrus tusks embedded in the living tree. I heard whisperings as I neared the top, like a thousand voices telling me something. I climbed and climbed, thinking that I'd understand their words as I got closer, but instead, blood covered my hands, as if it seeped from the tree itself. Then I reached the tree's crown. The whisperings faded to silence, and suddenly, I felt so dizzy, I clung to the tree with all my strength—I felt it tilting, even though it couldn't have been, could it? At the very top of the pillar, stuck deep into the crown of the oak, was a great iron nail pointing straight up. Constellations wheeled around it, and straight above us was the polar star.'"

Arkady claps his bloody hands. If he'd had both feet, he would have stomped. He grins and drums his fingers on the table, and then pounds the butt of his knife, all the while shaking his body enthusiastically. Across the table, above piles of reindeer meat, Saskia grins back.

"You recognize this tree, do you? I'm glad. I'm glad to see you weren't entirely deprived of stories. What Maaike said she saw was the world pillar holding our earth on its axis by that great iron nail. Deep in the ice caves of Spitsbergen. Away from the hands of men, safely hidden for all time. Or that's what the Dog hoped. Because as you know, if that pillar falls, so will the world."

They work for a while in silence, slicing strips of reindeer meat to dry, chunks to brine in seawater, slabs of fat to render and marrow-bones for broth. They drink a mug of fresh reindeer milk. Saskia had not yet killed the doe and calf; they are tethered outside, eating lichen.

"After Maaike came down from the tree, her Sisters noticed she laughed less often and kept apart from them. She plotted for the first time to raid the Pomors, for their company and for their seed. She never returned to the tree, but the Dog devoted his life to protecting it from harm.

"To this day, he patrols South Cape and Horn Sound, doing his best to scare men away from Spitsbergen by conjuring storms, planting fear in their hearts, and filtering the bounty of this land so that in the places men are, all their prey leaves. They say it was the Dog who persuaded the whales to migrate away from these coasts once and for all. He urged walruses to come instead. Walruses are the most difficult beasts to kill, you see, and the most dangerous to approach. And whenever a man dies on Spitsbergen, through care-lessness, stupidity, or error, the Dog takes his soul for his army. So that if ever a time comes that he must do battle to save this place— to save the tree—he can."

But what about the men who die honorably on Spitsbergen? What about Nikolai, my grandfather? And what does the Dog want with me? The questions burn at the back of Arkady's throat. A desire to speak chokes him until he sputters.

Saskia rises, then. Her bloodied apron stretches tight over her middle.

Arkady doesn't know why, but he knows: now is not the time for questions.

CHAPTER 36

rkady wakes into flickering light. He is comfortable on the floor by the hearth, though he longs to sleep on the stove bench again. He blinks drowsily. Firewood lines the seaward wall, and reindeer hides are stretched by nails on the others. He feels like a child, except that part of his body has been cut away.

What woke him? Over by the ladder to the loft, he hears a soft splash and trickle. He struggles to sit up. An ice bear crouches in the space under the loft. Then, in the shifting light and shadows, the great, white body becomes Saskia's. She kneels beside a pot of steaming water, scrubbing her face and then her neck. Her shoulders and arms, her chest, and her hugely distended middle. As she washes herself, she encircles her belly with one arm and sings to the baby. It is a sight for the iconostasis, and Arkady notes a golden light that seems now to fill that part of the izba, just like the gold-leaf tempera in the icon-makers' studio. Without all the drapery of Mother Mary. With the baby, but so differently. Her body holds a promise. It contains all the world. But soon …? For now, the sight of the woman bathing fills him with wonder.

"When you consider this wood," she says, "think about what might serve us the most. Before you start carving, give it some thought."

Saskia, now dressed for the outdoors, places two slender rounds of wood on the table in front of him. She'd just sat him up for the morning at his usual place at the table. She was going out on yet another task, though she hadn't told him what it was. She lays out the woodcarving knives. Then, she fetches two long pieces of driftwood from the porch.

"These can be your crutches. We'll try them out tomorrow." She leans them against the wall near the front door and eyes him curiously. "Let your mind get used to the idea before you try. I'll be back for lunch."

Arkady is left with a strange feeling. Before he could even consider what might be useful for him to carve, frustration overwhelms his mind. *Should I carve sled runners, so that she may pull me across the snow? Shall I carve the Cross for my grave and then slit my neck to fill it?* In no time, he dismisses his own usefulness in the world and curses his bad luck. The complaints of an angry child pour from and then empty him. Then, he eyes the crutches.

Arkady manages to lift himself out of the chair and use the table for balance for his initial small hops as an upright man. The skin of his wound is taut and sore, but more itchy than painful for now. He considers that his leg bone has been sawed off and he gags, gripping the table, feeling as if he will tumble and lose himself in the twirling, empty space below his knee.

Each hop jolts his head and feels completely wrong—he wonders that he doesn't tip over. He slowly hops once, and then again, in the open space of the room, his arms at his side. The floor pushes up against his foot. Through his socks he feels the edges of the floorboards. He will make it. Soon, he props himself with the two whittled branches. Proper crutches need a crossbar—why didn't she make them more comfortable? He turns and faces the stove, gripping the sticks. Because she doesn't want him to get too comfortable with crutches, he realizes. But why? He will need them for the rest of his days. That will be his penance for his many sins. Arrogance. Selfishness. Vanity. Stupidity. His heart sinks. Surely not. *I am truly not as bad as that, am I?* He looks at the uncarved wood on the table and the rest dawns on him: *I must carve a new foot.*

He scrabbles back to the table and picks up the wood. Yes, the piece is big enough. He turns the piece over in his hands. Yes.

He spends the next two hours carving the dense, finely grained wood, and then sees that the dimensions of the wooden calf are all wrong and he must start over, with the other piece. He carves until his fingers cramp and blisters form, and then he discovers that there is not enough room to turn an ankle. He throws the piece across the room just as Saskia stomps up the steps, shaking mud and a few stray snowflakes off her coat.

"What's wrong with you now?" Saskia's voice is weary; she moves stiffly to the stove. "It's not that bad, whatever it is."

He lifts his head and shrugs. He stands.

"What's this? Didn't I tell you to wait?" But her eyes twinkle; there's a smile in them. "Don't be foolish," she chides, eyeing the thrown piece on the floor. She picks it up and places it among the firewood. "Practice is the most important thing. And thinking." She taps her temple. "The first thing we do is measure your good leg. Measure everything, so you know what to carve. I cut many pieces for you. They are outside on the porch. You must practice, is all. It's good for the mind."

Arkady hobbles to the door. Outside, the cold rushes into his pores, stinging and burning his skin. The stump of his leg throbs. Only patches of snow cover the plain; the mossy tussocks glimmer in their mossy way. Far off, the mountains appear poised, mid-undulation, as if somewhere inland, a giant is airing out the great blanket of the land.

Beside the door lies a tidy pile of logs. He searches its rounds and salt-scoured edges, and hope licks at the edge of his mind. *Which one will become part of me?*

"They all came from the same tree. Who knows how long it has lain on the beach, waiting for you? Now come back inside. I have some string here. Let's measure."

Once Saskia pulls off Arkady's sock and rolls up his trouser leg, he cringes and squeezes his eyes shut. The skin of his foot has yellowed and his toenails curled. Saskia clucks and trims them with her sewing scissors and then massages his foot a little. As she kneads, sensation unexpectedly shoots through his body, and he clutches at the sides of the chair. His cheeks flush.

"There. Good. You look much better. Now, let's measure."

Along with the string, Saskia produces an old ruler, and by the end of the evening, they'd measured every angle and length of Arkady's remaining foot and calf, and he'd made copious notes on the tabletop with an old pencil. Now, Saskia dozes across from him, and Arkady looks over their work wonderingly.

It has really come to this, he thinks. *I lost my foot because I am stupid and unlucky. And now, because of her, I will become some new creature.*

Arkady hops as gently as he can manage around the table and pats Saskia on the shoulder. She starts awake.

"I thought I was back in our old cabin," she says, cradling her belly with one arm. "All of us were singing at the stove while the bears circled outside." Saskia yawns. "Let's get you back to the hearth. I'm as tired as a migrating bird."

Arkady shakes his head and points to the table.

"Still thinking, eh? Well, I'm off, then."

Saskia grunts as she climbs up to the stove bench and settles under her bear pelt. In a few minutes, she's snoring.

CHAPTER 37

askia returns from her mysterious work outside, wet with filthy hands and a new tear in her dress. Arkady offers her kasha with reconstituted reindeer meat, but she refuses everything except the frothing fresh milk. They had decided to keep the reindeer doe and calf for as long as they could—once they'd tasted the milk, they couldn't give it up. While Arkady and Saskia were awake, they tied the reindeer outside to the porch rail with enough rope for them to forage. They brought the animals inside the izba when they slept, tying them in the corner under the loft. After she drinks two cups of milk, Saskia climbs to the stove bench and sleeps.

Many weeks have passed since Saskia arrived at the izba. Months? *Surely the calendar approaches Theophany by now,* Arkady thinks. How can he drift unanchored through time? At first, he feels peace—there is so much less to worry about this way. But he soon hears an entire almanac of saints rustling toward him.

You need us, they chant from between the pages of his neglected prayer book. *You need us to animate your spirit! Without us, you are nothing but a dead husk.*

He glances at the Wonderworker on the wall, dozing in his frame. Arkady's lips crack when he smiles. *So be it,* he tells his chorus of martyrs. *This husk must carve.*

He fetches a new round of wood from the porch. Back at the table, which has become the center of his world, he measures the round. Stripping the outer layer off the whole thing, he examines it for cracks or knots that might have spots of dry rot in their centers. He measures it again. He marks in pencil where the calf will narrow to the shin, and the place where he will turn the ankle. In no hurry, he shaves away the first delicate curls, letting them fall to the floor and gather around him like feathers. By the time Saskia rises in the morning, Arkady's asleep on the hearth and several inches of exposed calf jut out of the log on the table.

Arkady wakes from a dream that he was back in his little garden at Solovetsky, transplanting mosses and arranging pebbles in spiral shapes. He taps the floorboards, so Saskia knows he's awake, and she turns toward the stove, shivering. He raises his hands in a question.

"Oh, don't you worry. You just carve that leg. Ready for tea?"

They eat kasha cooked in reindeer broth and tea with a drizzle of honey. Arkady is pleased that Saskia eats two helpings and then scrapes the cook pot and eats those leavings, too. When she puts on her thick sweater, scarf, boots, and overcoat, Arkady hops clumsily to the front door, frowning and blocking her way.

"I need to do something," she says brusquely. "It's none of your business." She pushes him aside, and he almost falls over. "Your work is there," she points to the table, "and only there."

She grabs a small pouch of tools and the ax from where it leans against the wall.

He watches her trundle down the steps and walk south along a new path made by her own crossings. She stops some way inland, near the stream. He tries to make out what she's doing, what has occupied her for so many days now, but pain in his leg doubles him over, and he falls to the floor.

She gathered the wood. She shot and butchered reindeer. She even managed to kill a seal somehow and render its oil. She made bowls out of clay from the stream bank and baked them in the oven. She made the bowls into oil lamps, to light their way through winter. The bowls line the shelves, and the oil fills two buckets down below. Now she's off again, and he has a bad feeling.

She does too much. I do too little.

All day, he carves and silently talks with Nikolai. Not about any of the big questions the old man left him with, like why he gave Arkady to the monks and not to the Pomors, or why Nikolai needed to die on Spitsbergen. Arkady talks with him mostly about foxes, about the one Arkady killed and the one that came to him on the path, just after he'd hacked his own foot in half. He mentions the way the falling rain made perfect droplets on the fox's coat and wonders: if a person could see the lines in the tundra where every fox has walked, perhaps he could read a new language of the world. Wonders if somewhere in their bones, foxes on the mainland know about Spitsbergen.

Arkady works carefully, cross-checking the measurements of his remaining leg that are scribbled in pencil on the tabletop. As he carves the heel and the shallow arch of his wooden foot, he silently discusses the project with Nikolai, admitting with a smile his ineptitude with Starostin's own woodcarving knives.

Yes, yes. You can't believe I'm using the knives of your beloved chief. Arkady shrugs. *I need a new foot, Grandfather. You should have seen the ax blow! Cleaved my flesh in two. But I clawed my way back, with some help from the fox. You always did love foxes. He got his reward.*

Finally, he hears Saskia stomping up the stairs, so he lays down his work and brushes the shavings from the table and his lap. He rises and props himself with the crutches. Saskia comes through the door stooped and limping. Alarmed, Arkady hops to her as quickly as he can. He drops the crutches to take her by the shoulders. At first, she jerks away, but she's not quite willing to let him fall, so she catches him by the arms, and they end up in an awkward embrace. He smooths her hair and lets his hand linger at her nape, hopping a little in place to stay upright, and she encircles him, either to keep him up or for comfort.

"You did it," Saskia whispers to him, looking over his shoulder at the carved foot.

Arkady nods.

"Let me see."

She leads him back to the table and turns the foot over in her hands. Arkady can't help but feel proud of his work; he knows it will fit, and this foot will serve him well. In the following years, though, he'll realize that a bare human foot isn't the best appendage in Spitsbergen, even for a man. Eventually, he'll stop putting a boot over it, and it will function as well as expected, but when it wears out, he'll carve a smooth wooden boot to replace it, hinged at the base of the toes with the old steel springs of a fox trap. When that one wears out, a decade from now, he'll fit himself with the whorled butt end of a narwhal tusk and find it works just as well.

Saskia sets the freshly carved foot down and kneels over her small rucksack. "You never go anywhere in Spitsbergen without a piece of this," she says, pulling out a folded length of something brown, thick, and wrinkled.

She sets the piece of walrus hide on the table and motions for him to sit down. She brings him her sharp scissors, tendon thread, thick needle, hammer, and a handful of iron tacks. Working in a small pool of lamplight, with occasional input from Saskia, Arkady attaches the walrus hide to the top of the wooden limb. Then, Saskia disappears into the cellar. Arkady hears her grunting, cursing, and the muted crash of birch buckets and baskets tipping over. She returns carrying a curved metal stave ripped from a barrel. Arkady raises his eyebrows.

"It won't stay on your body unless we harness it to you."

Saskia stokes the fire in Starostin's oven, feeding the flame and spreading the coals, until the cabin is sweltering and their sweat flows freely. Arkady bends the stave as much as he can, and then they heat the middle in the oven. The fire is not as hot as the forges of Solovetsky, but they work at it for a long time, heating the stave and then removing it to bend it back and forth between their two sets of hands, until finally, they break it in half. Then, Arkady pierces each red-hot metal end with an iron nail. After dunking the pieces in the water bucket, together they file the rough edges and straighten the stave pieces as best as they can. Saskia measures them against Arkady's body and heats them up again to break off the extra. Finally, after all the edges are filed and Saskia has fussed with the whole contraption for a long time, they nail the staves to either side of the wooden foot. Arkady attaches more strips of walrus hide to tie around his thigh, and then pulls off his belt. More strips of hide run from the belt to the staves, until the whole thing can almost stand up on its own.

"Well, try it on, then!" Saskia yelps, wiping her hands on her apron.

Somehow, Arkady has become accustomed to the tilt and grasping of being a one-legged creature. As soon as he puts on the new foot, he realizes how quickly a human can change. The floor suddenly rises up and crashes against his body. He's repulsed by the impact of the earth, and the stump-end of his leg itches madly in its walrus-hide socket and then burns. The metal brace and belt combination entraps and insults him. Crouched over himself, he limps.

Saskia laughs, already moving on to her next task at the stove. "Give it time. Just time. That is all it takes."

He hobbles around and around the izba. Gradually, he uncurls from the uncomfortable crouch and straightens up. He clears his throat. He walks over to where Saskia chops reindeer meat for a stew. He rests his arm on her shoulder. He has an urge to pull her close.

Saskia shrugs. "Oh, you're welcome. I wasn't going to just let you die, was I? How was I to know you'd be here in Starostin's cabin? Have some soup."

Arkady walks to the window and looks into the darkness. Buckled securely to his body, the carved driftwood echoes softly with ancient birdsong.

CHAPTER 38

After several days practicing inside, Arkady walks outside the izba wearing Father Ilya's old coat and his carved foot. Fog has settled over the land and sea. But it is not the light-infused fog of Schoonhoven. This is a dark lid on the world. It settles on his shoulders as an unshakable burden. The cold creeps up his sleeves and stings the stump of his leg. Starostin watches him from the yardarm of the Cross. Arkady limps with purpose away from the cabin.

After all his time watching Saskia come and go, seeing her hands become more callused as her belly grows, he is going to help her. He has been thinking about her wooden bear cub, and all the time she spends staring out the windows and muttering to no one. He has been wondering what she's doing out on the tundra plain and if she's all right.

His body aches. One of the metal staves digs into his thigh, and the uneven ground tweaks his leg every so often. But even at night, the moss still glows incandescent as if lit from below, and the sound of trickling water pleases him. It's good to be outside. He hears hammering and follows Saskia's path south of the izba. When he reaches the little stream where Saskia collects water, the path veers east, inland. He follows it toward the sounds of her hammer, and soon he sees her.

She is building a shed out of logs she can carry in her arms. She placed it right at the edge of the stream, with one side built into a small rise. Arkady's heart breaks to see it; she has worked so hard, alone, making such a primitive shelter. She leveled the ground using only Starostin's shovel, which is lying nearby. Now, three walls rise up to her shoulders, each one comprising many rows of short logs placed end to end, with moss packed between them.

He stumbles toward her. The shed is roofless, though somehow she's placed beams across the top, each one as long as a man. The stream babbles incomprehensibly beside him, getting louder and softer at random. She turns, puts down her bucket, and wipes her hands on her belly. Crossing her arms over her chest, she waits for him to reach her.

He takes her arm and points her toward the izba, gesturing that he will work on the building for a while.

"Don't worry," she says. "You must listen to me now. Since you can walk, and you're ready to help, take this bucket and pack in the moss. I must fetch the reindeer hides. They'll serve well enough for a roof."

He must have looked confused.

"I had to put it here, by the stream; don't you see?"

She strides away, and he ducks inside. She's made a mosaic floor of the round ends of logs, with stones packed between them. She built a wooden bench into the earthen wall and left a shallow hole in the middle of the floor. A fire ring. She's stacked firewood just outside the door, along with a pile of large rocks. For steam, of course.

He sits on the bench and lays his head in his hands. This banya, once filled with steam, is where she'll birth her baby. What kind of women's ways does she know? She and her sisters could not have been the only women in Spitsbergen, could they?

When he hears her footsteps returning, he forces himself up and picks a clump of moss out of the bucket.

"We've definitely caught his attention now," Saskia says as she pushes her way into the unroofed banya. She shakes her head and sits on the bench, breathing heavily. "I thought we were safe, but he's come down from his perch again. He better not interfere when the baby comes, or he'll be sorry. I don't care if he's Starostin or not. In all the stories I ever heard about Starostin—about after he died, that is—he was up on his Cross, never coming down. Just continuing his vigil to eternity. Starostin wants Spitsbergen peopled, you see. He wants this land loved by man, lived in, and honored. That's what my sisters always said, and they should know. Starostin cast himself from civilization out of love for this place." She paused. "Or else for love of hardship, loneliness, and cold. Who's to say? A Pomor is a Pomor, after all. Starostin wants people to come here. The Dog wants to keep them away. It's all part of the balance, same as your Russian holy men."

Saskia gives a strange laugh and ducks outside. Arkady continues with the moss. Her voice still reaches him, just a little muffled.

"Starostin. Most beloved of the Pomors. No one can get enough of the legends. Oh, at Schoonhoven, he's all they talk about. I grew so tired of hearing about Starostin, Starostin, Starostin! He was just a hired hand, like the rest of them. He worked for the Muscovy Company. A great pilot of lodjas. Brother of the Sea, they called him. As he grew older, he brought the supplies to build this izba up from the mainland—some say the wood came from Saint Petersburg, where his family was. He wasn't even a real Pomor; did you know that? Some say he was a student at the university in Saint Petersburg! Can you imagine? But he built this place and stayed here for twenty-eight years, winters and all. The Pomors brought supplies every year, but still.

"He was a great hunter; no one argues with that. And when it came time for him to die, he set off on the roadless road without looking back. But instead of leading to heaven, or to a great feasting hall like the Norsemen sang of, his road led around in a great circle of ice and rock, right back to Spitsbergen. They say he walked past his izba once, twice, and even a third time, laughing the whole way. Finally, he stepped off the long road to examine the Cross that his men had made in his honor, and he couldn't find his way back. He remains here by the will of the place, invited or tricked into becoming part of the land. To call people here or maybe just to watch for them. They say he's responsible for the warming of these waters. All the Pomors talk about it. Since Starostin died, different fish started coming here. And blooms of sea grass. Even bees in Ice Fjord during the summer. Who knows but the ravens will return? All I know is that he wants a new village here, a civilization of new northerners. Especially now that the days of the Pomor are coming to an end."

Suddenly, Saskia comes crashing back into the banya, wide-eyed.

"That's it! Starostin sees me about to drop a babe. He sees a man and a woman. Oh fuck, little priest. That's why he's interested in us. He thinks we're the ones to do it. He's been gazing out to sea looking for ships full of pilgrims. Now he sees a limping priest chasing a pregnant woman across the tundra. He need look no more. We are Spitsbergen's perfect Adam and Eve!"

Arkady touches her arm and then gently guides her outside the banya. He walks her all the way back to Starostin's izba. She is trembling, cold, hugging herself. He leads her inside the cabin and helps get her coat and shoes off. He guides her to her bed on top of the stove. Once she's in, Arkady follows her up the ladder and pulls her bearskin under her chin. She drifts to sleep, and he watches her for a while before returning to the banya. He finishes caulking the logs with moss. He stretches reindeer hide across the roof and nails it down. He works until the pain in his leg sends him inside the banya, where he lies down on the rough wooden bench and listens to the stream. After a while, the laughter of the water abruptly stops. In the quiet, terror rises in his heart. Then, he hears the human breath of a swimmer heaving herself out of the water. But the stream is only ankle deep, isn't it? Water drips off a body, and a shape hovers in the doorway. He sits up, the bench creaks, and swiftly the creature returns to the water with a splash.

CHAPTER 39

askia crouches, vomiting. Her bare head bobs above the bucket, and her great body heaves. When Arkady appears in the doorway, she gestures wildly. She wants him to leave. He shakes his head.

"No," she gasps, wiping her mouth and sitting back on her haunches. "You must light a fire in the banya. Now! Take my bag with you. Take the buckets, and that cut-up hide by the door."

He nods, and dread shoots out to clench his throat. He puts on his coat and fingers the monastery's flint and striker in his pocket. He loads himself up with all the things she's asked for.

"When the banya is ready—when it's full of steam and hot hot hot—then come back for me. It will take two hours to heat. I will be fine until then. But you must do as I ask, Arkady. We both know you are not the strongest man. But you are strong enough for this."

He teeters out the door and down the steps. His wooden foot slips on the last one, and he falls on his face. Saskia's things scatter. He scrambles up and looks around. The ghost of old Starostin leans against the corner of the izba, watching. Arkady shakes his head at him, takes up the bucket, and limps to the banya. He lays a good fire for her.

Once the fire burns hot and strong, he puts the first three stones in. *The Father, the Son, and the Holy Ghost*, he thinks. *Lying atop Mother Damp Earth.*

He feeds the fire and prepares the banya, even though he lacks the knowledge of what makes a birthing place right. He smooths the cold ground and spreads reindeer hides across it. After some time, the fire is hot enough to make coals, and he knows he can tend it well over time and that it will serve Saskia for as long as she needs. He wipes his hands on his pants and stands up.

As he hobbles back along the dirt path, a scream tears the air. He trips on a clump of moss, and his wooden foot jolts into the stump of his leg. He gasps, his vision blurred by a galaxy of stars, and for a moment he fears he will lose consciousness. He drops to all fours but continues toward the izba. He crawls up the steps, stands, and walks in.

Saskia sits on a chair, her spine rigid and face solemn. She looks out the seaward window. "I thought I heard Kol's voice just now."

After some time, he puts her coat over her and helps her across the tundra.

CHAPTER 40

fter five hours in the steamy banya, Saskia squats in the corner. Arkady wonders at this; though he hasn't ever considered what birthing entails until recently, he imagines women would want to be lying down. But Saskia first had been sitting on the edge of the wooden bench, going through her pains in that position. Between the surges, she paced. Now she's gone through a bad one squatting. She'd groaned and gripped the log wall for support, refusing help when he came near. Now, her head rests on her folded arms, which in turn rest on her knees.

Arkady prays for Saskia and her baby. He asks how he can possibly help her in this, the one thing for which there is no help? He tends the fire, heats and moves the rocks, and brings a bucketful of water in from the stream to make more steam to warm and cleanse them, and finally, after all of that, after Saskia sits naked with her head on her arms for a long time, the answer arrives.

He inhales deeply and walks out of the silent white room of the heart.

"Everyone in my village on the Laya tributary said that they'd never met anyone like my father, especially when he was a boy." He pauses to consider the shape of the story.

Saskia doesn't move.

"Neighbors said he fished at a certain spot on the tributary every day for a whole summer, trying different lures, different times of day, different positions on the boulders. He missed his chores on the farm, but my grandfather didn't scold him because hunters must cultivate patience and powers of observation. And then, finally, he caught such a fish as no one in the village had ever seen before! Its scales shone as emeralds, and its eyes glinted silver with the secrets of deep, cold water. It was a very old pike. 'No, not just anyone could have caught it,' they said. 'Only a special kind of person like Boris Nikolayevich Afanasyev, may his bones lay peacefully.'"

With a barely discernible movement across the banya, Saskia raises her head to listen.

"They say that when he was only seven years old, he carved and strung his own bow and a quiver full of arrows and then disappeared for two days in the woods. My grandfather set out with a group of villagers, and they finally found him, curled up asleep next to the most beautiful stag anyone had ever seen. He'd felled it with one arrow straight to the heart. They always described him as if he'd lived in an epic poem. The stories were all I ever knew of him, and there were many more: Boris foraging the most delicious mushrooms, the biggest, juiciest berries. What little boy would not tell the stories over and over to himself and use them to know the world and seek a place in it?

"Every time I went fishing or roamed in the forest, I felt my father gliding along right beside me but not as a guiding light or an inspiration. It was Boris who caught all the fish and found all the mushrooms, and none were ever left for me. And so instead of knowing myself to be Boris' son, I always came up empty-handed, and in the end, I was too lazy even to try."

Saskia contorts in another surge. She growls and, after some time, tips over onto her side and labors from there.

"My grandfather left the room when anyone talked about his son. I pestered him all the time to tell me about my father, and he always swatted me away. It was strange, because Nikolai, my grandfather, told stories unceasingly. He told Pomor stories, mostly, of the great bird way and how to pass the long night in Spitsbergen.

He told of geese hatching out of barnacles and great herds of reindeer stampeding across the sky with bells woven through their antlers. But he would never tell me anything about Boris. As I grew, I bothered him about it more. Almost every night I'd ask him, and he'd shake his head and launch into some other kind of tale. But one day, he snapped. I remember it was right after Saint George's Day, when all the villages' cattle were let out of their winter quarters to pasture. I was complaining in front of the stove, and finally, Nikolai threw down his mending and leapt to his feet.

"'You will destroy me with your whining, boy!' he said.

"'But you're his father. You know everything about him,' I remember saying.

"'No one can know everything about someone, especially his own child.'

"'Just tell me a story of my father. Of Boris.'

"'You've heard enough from all the flapping mouths in the village,' he said. But afterward, the old man jerked his head up and looked out the window; the sun had just dipped below the treeline, and darkness was rising. It was as if he'd heard someone call out.

"'What is it?' I asked.

"'There's only one story you haven't yet heard,' the old man said, still staring out the window. 'But once you hear, you cannot unhear. You will carry it with you always. That's the only problem with stories.'

"'Tell me.'

"'So be it,' said my grandfather, and I knew once he said it that this was the story I'd been waiting for my whole life. 'As you've heard plenty by now, your father possessed a natural skill for hunting and foraging,' Nikolai went on. 'He had patience enough for fishing in the tributary, and more besides. He ran fast. He worked hard in the field and in town, too. He didn't mind caring for the babes if that was what was needed, or he could marlinspike for the old Pomors. But strangely enough, despite all these gifts, Boris Afanasyev had no sense of the sea.'

"When my grandfather turned to me, tears welled in his eyes. Part of me wanted him to stop, but I was too mesmerized to speak.

"'None of that mattered for a long time,' my grandfather said. 'Boris roamed the forests and fields and grew into a man. He provided game for those in the village too old to hunt or who had no children of their own. Everyone thought he'd be a woodsman until the end of his days since that's what he was, and there's no harm in that. He had no desire to leave, and no one expected him to.'

"Well, one day in the spring, he went way out north of the village, stripping and hauling trees that he'd use to build his own cabin. He'd borrowed a cart and two horses to carry it all back. About dusk, he was driving through the village when he saw a crowd of people—mostly women—gathered outside Marya Pomelova's shop. Why did he stop there? He wasn't given to socializing; he didn't drink vodka or even much tea, for that matter. We'll never know what made him stop that day, but he did. He pulled up the cart and walked over to see what all the fuss was about, and that's when he first laid eyes on my mother."

"Ah," Saskia says.

"No one in the village ever told me stories of my mother," Arkady says. "Not one person. But her name was Oksana. She had black hair, curly like mine, which she loved to wear loose, though it would have been bound when Boris first saw her. She had gray eyes, and she was stubborn, like a girl from a fairy tale always doing what was forbidden. She was there, in town, peddling her lace at Marya Pomelova's. I don't know where she came from or where she planned to go after Arkhangelsk. There wasn't much ahead of her except the sea. She was a little older than my father. Who can imagine a young woman alone on that road? She was a wanderer. It was as if she materialized from some other world, with her trunk full of lace. With her bobbins and pins. Maybe that's what attracted Boris.

"But that part is neither here nor there. The point is that Boris fell in love with her right away, and she with him. 'Much too quickly'—that's what my grandfather said. 'Courting's how you plumb the depths of another, to see what lies beneath the starry-eyed surface.' That's what he said. But according to Nikolai, they had no time for that, and oh, they loved each other. No one could deny it. He said that when you saw them, you could feel the force that drew them together. People stayed away from them because that kind of love has a whiff of sorcery about it. It holds danger. It's no kind of love for the North. In a fancy house with servants and stables? Fine. In Novgorod? Fine. But here, where families fight to survive in the dark and snow? Where struggle is part of what we love, with our chapped hands and mewling goats, hand-furrowed gardens, and weeks at sea, hunting great, mysterious creatures who can easily kill us? No. Boris and Oksana inhabited an enchantment, and people stayed away."

Arkady goes outside the banya for more water, and for the first time since he arrived in Starostin's cabin, a clear night sky stretches out above him. Seas of stars glimmer into the far reaches, and the great bird way itself unfurls its milky path in a celestial diagonal, leading all the world's birds northward, along with the souls of the dead.

He pours the stream water over the stones, and the steam is so hot now that it scalds his nose.

"What happened to Boris and Oksana, then?" Saskia asks.

"They were married in midsummer, and Boris built Oksana a little cottage. But both of them could have been forest spirits for all the time they spent there. During that first summer, no one saw them at all. They'd be gone for days, leaving the door of their cottage open to the mice and the crows. She used lichen, mushrooms, and berries for her dyes. And her laces were extraordinary; that's what Nikolai told me. They were as sheer as mists, with tiny patterns all through them. Wedding gloves, collars, veils, yards and yards of trimmings—she worked like a spider, day and night when she wasn't in the woods. Instead of sleep, she only made lace. Nikolai would go to visit them before I was born, and Boris would sit across from her, watching her hands move back and forth across her work as if he were mesmerized. And soon he was talking about the sea.

"They had plenty of money from selling Oksana's lace. They sold it in Marya's shop, and once every few months, they went to Novgorod, and even shipped some to Moscow. They had more money than almost anyone in the village. And still, Boris signed on to fish and hunt in the White Sea for one of the fur and tallow companies. He hired onto a lodja that worked the coastline and offshore islands near Arkhangelsk, so he could be home most nights with his wife and, when I arrived, his baby son. I asked my grandfather why Boris went on the sea, and Nikolai only shook his head. Maybe he couldn't abide his wife providing for him. Maybe she wanted him to seafare. No one ever knew for sure.

"And so it happened that in his second year hunting, when I was just one year old, Boris signed on with a ship bound for Spitsbergen. His plan was to spend half the season hunting walrus and reindeer and then return to the mainland early so as not to be away for the whole summer. So, he hired onto the first lodja heading north in the spring.

"Well, as anyone will tell you, no one can foretell the weather, no matter how attuned one is to the length of icicles, whether thunder follows lightning, or if the crows repair their nests or not. Especially on the White Sea, and especially in the early spring. Just a few hours after Boris set sail, a southeasterly wind—not terribly cold but strong—blew the little ship far out on the waters. This could have been a boon since its course was to the northwest anyway, but after some time, an opposing blast from the north shot back through the straits. This second storm froze the water in the tributary, and the livestock had to be put back in winter quarters, even though it was a few days past Easter. Hail broke windows, and then snow came, enough to freeze the ground! At farms where winter supplies ran out and the new grass was killed by the cold, livestock was lost. Temperatures dropped low enough for some to board their windows again, as if it were November instead of April.

"During this time, my grandfather spent long hours at the village's public house, accepting vodka and cup after cup of tea from Marya Pomelova, whose shop was mercantile, restaurant, and tavern in one. He discussed the storm's personality with the men from the village: the direction and quality of the wind, its layers and patterns as they could be discerned from the senses and its tracks on the sea. The inquiry lasted hours, and then days, as the men compared it to the storms of previous springs, the resulting hunting seasons, and briefly in regard to Boris' voyage, which was on everyone's mind, though no one wanted to dwell on this so as not to attract even more ill fortune. Nikolai himself was still a captain then, so the Pomors speculated about the sea and the air for the coming weeks, partially to gain knowledge to take with them on voyages but mostly to keep Nikolai's mind trained on something other than his son.

"On the first day the sun returned, a stranger knocked on the door of Boris' cottage. Inside, Oksana lay in bed. I must have been there, too.

"This man, a fisherman from thirty miles up the coast, told Oksana that a lodja had washed ashore near his cabin. Without changing expressions, Oksana pointed down the path with a trembling hand and said only, 'Fetch Nikolai.' Then, she closed the door and went back to bed.

"Nikolai rode on a cart with the fisherman, and other men followed on horseback all the way to the coast, to Nyonoksa, to the fisherman's cabin. From there, they walked silently through the bladelike grasses of the frozen salt marsh. Nikolai craned forward, and soon enough saw the lodja keeled over on the beach, demasted and wrecked. He scanned the ship as he moved toward it, though he'd already recognized it as the one. When they got close, the fisherman dropped to his knees and crossed himself. And when Nikolai walked around to the deck side, he knew why: even at the ship's impossible angle, all twenty-three men held their places at the oars, as if they would row themselves right up over the marsh into the forest.

"Boris was slumped against the rail. His hands lay folded in his lap. His eyes were open but glassed over with ice. He was frozen solid, you see. All twenty-three of them were. As solid as chessmen."

"What a fate," Saskia whispers from the birthing corner.

"My only memories are the patchwork stories, and the stories are beautiful, even that one, in its way. How could I grieve for something I can't even remember?"

"But you have the story, and the story breaks your heart."

"I'm only sad about what happened next."

Suddenly, Saskia lets loose such a roar that Arkady jumps up. He goes to her, even though she'd insisted that he stay away. She squats again, and the muscles in her neck bulge. Her legs spread far apart, and she's bearing down, trying to push the baby out. When she reaches out to him, he clasps her hands.

Her cries ring out across the land, and Arkady wonders if Starostin will appear at the doorway. Saskia's fingernails bite the skin of Arkady's hand, but he doesn't let go. Finally, she does.

"The next surge will come soon, Arkady. Hurry, tell me what has you sorrowing, if not your father's fate?"

So, Arkady finally lets his mind turn fully toward his mother, and right away the feeling of the forest—warm and dappled by sunlight—washes through him. The filtered light illuminates fir needles and soil, and he smells tree resin mixed with the duff's undertone of sweet rot. These are the things he associates with Oksana.

She is just ahead of him with twigs in her hair, wearing a birch basket on her back, gathering nettles and searching for mushrooms, holding her carved wooden knife in her hand. Arkady tries to keep up with her. When she turns, she smiles and urges him on, but she doesn't slow down. This is their life together. They are together.

"At first, my mother and I stayed in the little cabin that Boris built. Actually, we lived mostly in the woods while the weather was warm. Nikolai was away hunting in Spitsbergen. Not even his son's death could keep him away. Oksana foraged: first nettles and last year's rose hips, new fir tips for tea, and then flowers and roots for her dyes. She trapped rabbits and found beehives. Later, she harvested berries and tiny wild apples. I toddled along behind her, and I remember sometimes she'd leave me tied to a tree so that she could climb up bluffs or walk up streambeds to catch trout. At night, we either walked back to the cabin or else Oksana would cover me with her shawl and spread leaves and duff over us both, and we'd just sleep in the forest."

Arkady's memories of this time are both vivid and fragmented: Oksana approaching with three dead rabbits held by their ears; Oksana bending down with a handful of wild blackberries and Arkady dipping his mouth directly into them; riding in her bark pack, on top of a load of birch leaves, drowsy and happy. Oksana spoke little—Arkady holds no memory of her voice—but she played silly games with him among the trees, and she showed him bird nests and fawn skeletons in the woods. At home, she fed him porridge and cloudberries, and he played at her feet while she worked at her bobbins.

"She'd be all night at her stool with the clinking of the bobbins and her unfurling patterns. I would fall asleep to that sound, and half the time, when I woke up, she was gone. Gathering plants. Hunting game. But she came back.

"I remember when my grandfather came to the cabin. It must have been August, when he returned from Spitsbergen. He was drunk and reeked of sweat and walrus oil, his hair bleached completely white by the sun. He staggered up to the cabin, shouting for his grandson. I remember being inside that hug, suffocating and pounding my fists against Nikolai with joy.

"'You're filthy! Where is Oksana?' Nikolai boomed, and all I could do was point to the forest. 'She left you alone?' Nikolai stopped moving suddenly and put me down. He marched into the cabin. 'Starostin's balls! It's terrible in here. What a mess! What are these piles of leaves? And rabbit meat drying on the bedframe? Oksana!' Nikolai shouted.

"With me under his arm, he walked swiftly back to his own cabin by the Laya tributary. When Oksana arrived there at nightfall, tear-stained but calm, she reached for me, but Nikolai held me aloft, so Oksana threw a bale of fox furs at the old man. I don't know what they said or how long they fought, but she left without me. The next day, she returned with her lacemaking stool and frame, and her birch basket full of thread and wool, and from then on, we lived with Nikolai."

"That doesn't sound terrible," Saskia says.

"At first, it wasn't. Oksana spent most of her time indoors. She carded wool, brewed dye, and spun new threads for her lace. She tended Nikolai's stove and helped with his few cows, goats, chickens, and ducks. But mostly, she sat at her lace-working stool while the light faded. Oksana told stories of cranes teaching their hatchlings to fly. Soon, we had summer in the morning and autumn in the afternoon. I followed Oksana into the orchard as she tested the breeze: a light wind brought a dry autumn, while a strong, gusty wind was a sure sign of bad weather to come.

"September arrived, and the days grew ever shorter. On Saint Simeon the Stylite's Day, the villagers stopped tilling the land, and Oksana helped the women dry grains and store root vegetables. Nikolai spent most days out hunting geese with the other Pomors. Oksana and I collected cranberries and currants in the forest, and in the evenings, we fed bits of gooseflesh to the rusalkas in our tributary, in the hopes of good fishing before the freeze.

"Michael's Day came, and the rains. Nikolai built a tiny lodja to be my bed and spread it with fox skins. He carved toy men and animals, and ships and carts for me to play with. As winter approached, the three of us entertained one another with stories that

Nikolai made up and Oksana embellished with colorful details of aristocratic families or gargantuan bears that made me scream in terror. Then, it was autumn in the mornings and winter in the afternoons. We filled our beds with fresh straw, stored up firewood, and sealed the joints between the logs in the wall of our cabin with moss. And shortly after Pokrov, just as Oksana predicted, came the first snow. For some time, autumn battled winter as the light faded. Nikolai and Oksana also fought during this time, but once winter settled in for good, we lived as amicably as could be expected because people in Arkhangelsk know the troubles and hardships of a good winter, and there's no need for adding strife to an already-delicate balance.

"Nikolai repaired and polished his weapons and tools, then braided rope and carved chessmen to sell. Oksana spun threads and wove them into fractal patterns. Only occasionally I awoke in my little ship to hear Oksana whispering fiercely to Nikolai, and Nikolai's angry voice telling her no, no, no.

"Shrovetide eventually arrived, with its epic battle between the darkness and the light. Winter died in the end, of course, but the holiday always brought thrills and terror to the children of the village. Every evening of the festivities, the three of us went down to the riverside where the big bonfire blazed through the snow as a call to the sun. Oksana carried a plate stacked high with blini, and Nikolai carried sweet cheese, butter, honey, and jam to share. I remember I stayed close to Nikolai, eating as many blini as I could, each golden circle a crisp, tart homage to the sun. After the quiet winter, the flames stunned me, and I was frightened by the mock battles, races, other games, and so many voices that all blended together. From across the fire, I saw my mother with ribbons braided through her hair and streaming out behind her, dancing with friends from the village, and then later, dancing with people I'd never seen before."

Silence and steam filled the banya.

"Saskia?"

"I am here. The surge has not come yet."

"Well, soon after that, before spring could fully take hold, a coughing sickness swept through the village. Brought by outsiders, people said, who had joined in the festivities and then disappeared. The sickness began with sore throat and headaches and then turned into deep, phlegmy coughing that lasted for weeks, draining the body of vitality and bruising the ribs. Then, the coughing turned dry and hacking and finally produced blood. One old woman in town died of it and also a baby. The sickness spread quickly, and everyone was shut up at home, tending to themselves or loved ones. Some people lost cattle in the woods, and others were too sick to go out to feed their livestock. So, Nikolai went to the village to speak with Marya Pomelova, who agreed that something must be done.

"Marya Pomelova kept the stove burning, the front door unlocked, and the samovar full all through the day and night, so that if someone needed shelter or ran into trouble, she'd scoop them up and tend to them. Marya Pomelova was born somewhere very far away, in the Altay Mountains, people said. It was not known how she came to live in Arkhangelsk, only that she'd married a Pomor who'd died in Spitsbergen, and after that, she stayed on. Well, Marya Pomelova was not just a tavern keep but also a znaharka, a healer. People came from other towns for her spells and herbs, and they all left comforted.

"'The earth itself must release its powers of healing here,' Marya told Nikolai as she wiped down the long tables. 'To fight this sickness, we need nine maidens and three widows. Tonight, they must plough furrows around every house in the village to release the earth's forces. They must howl and scream as they go but meet no adversaries.'

"By the time Nikolai returned to his cabin on the Laya, he'd called on all the women needed for the ritual but one. When he came in the door, he heard me coughing in bed. He ran to the bed-side and found his grandson red and moist with fever, while Oksana worked at her lace, as if in a trance.

"'Your boy needs you!' Nikolai shouted.

"Oksana turned to him stonily. 'He is just dreaming,' she said.

"'He is sick,' Nikolai whispered. 'Didn't you hear him coughing?'

"Oksana rose from her stool and strode over to the bed. 'I was working.'

"'What kind of mother doesn't notice when her child is sick?' Nikolai pushed past her and picked me up. 'We need you tonight, Oksana. There will be a healing circle of women. You are the third widow.'

"That night, I stood at the window and watched lantern light bob between trees at the edge of the forest. Among the flitting shapes of women who streamed into the back meadow and used old farm tools to cut a furrow around our house, I saw my mother like a forest spirit, laughing and dirt-smeared, holding a light above herself, attracting moths to the flame. She ran up to the window where I was and pressed her hand against it, and I pressed on the same place. Then she whirled away.

"I fell into a fever after that. Nikolai told me I almost died. Wouldn't that have been strange, if things had gone that way?"

"But they didn't," whispers Saskia.

"No. But when I woke up, Oksana was gone."

Saskia's breath shortens; Arkady hears the effort start up.

"Nikolai told me she waited until she knew I'd live. I don't know if that's true or if that was simply the only thing he could bear to tell me. She packed up her lacemaking tools and rode a peddler's cart out of town. She'd spent time in Novgorod, Saint Petersburg, even Moscow before she came to us. How could she stay in Ark-hangelsk? Nikolai didn't let me go with her. Deep down, I think he must have sent her away. I never asked, but every now and then, I'd catch him looking at me with a strange, guilty expression. There are some things that shape us that we never get to understand.

"Oh, but I missed her, Saskia. I was inconsolable. Nikolai tried everything to comfort me. Everything! When I first arrived at Solovetsky, the monks tried to find her. They wrote letters to monasteries far away, in different cities, for them to put out the word. But she never came back."

"Some people must be free," says Saskia. "They don't belong to any place, like your grandfather and I belong to Spitsbergen. Some people can only be alive if they are utterly free. Like you, Arkady."

"But I am not free," he whines.

"Aren't you? If that is what you think, not even God can help you."

"My father turned to a block of ice, and my mother floated away like eiderdown on the wind. I have never been able to reconcile the heaviness of the one and the lightness of the other."

Saskia's breath is the same as the whooshing exhale of a walrus at the water's surface. Then, Arkady hears her first cries of real pain. He stokes the fire, fills the bucket, and dumps water on the stones, fills the bucket again and sets it gently down for later. As he works, he soothes his own rising fear, and when he realizes that nothing in the world will curb the horror of it, he gently calls out.

"I'm coming to help now."

In a few steps, he is with her. Saskia lies on her side, with her higher leg bent up. Her body drips with steam. She's gripping the little bench, and her face is puckered like an old woman's.

"Can you see the head?" she gasps. "The force of the earth is upon me, and I can do nothing but push."

"Then push," Arkady says. He knows he must not let her know how frightened he is. *I walked through starvation and an ice bear chasing me*, he thinks. *I lived. I lost my foot and lived. I can help her.*

Kneeling before her, he touches her upward knee and peers at the swollen crux of her body. Her vulva is wide open, and a different, pale flesh pushes against it from the inside.

"I see the baby!" Arkady yelps.

Saskia's groan turns to a scream, and Arkady startles back.

"I will burst!" Saskia shrieks.

As she convulses into the next wave, Arkady holds out his trembling fingertips and touches the mucus-slicked skin of the baby. It's not the head, he realizes. He feels around more intently. The spine? He can't quite see.

"It's a shoulder poking out, I think. Not a head."

Saskia doesn't say anything right away. She squeezes her eyes shut. When the contraction ends, Arkady moves up; she has one arm over her face. He touches her hair.

"It's going to be all right. The baby will come."

She brushes his touch away. "No more steam now. I was foolish to build this banya. Always making things more difficult than they need to be, that's Saskia! See if you can get dry air in here. We need another lantern. Go, get one. Get the knife, and bring me my good scissors, and my fur so I don't freeze."

"Shall I help you back into the izba? The fire's still going in the stove."

"No!" Her sharpness surprises him.

While Arkady hobbles to the izba, Saskia screams through another set of contractions. When he returns, the steam has all escaped from the banya. The walls are dripping, and the place quickly turns very cold. He drapes the bearskin around Saskia and chops into kindling some of the wood she's stacked outside the banya. It's the first time he's used the ax since his injury. Soon, he builds up the fire, not for coals but flames. He's not sure it will burn in the damp, but it catches. He cuts a hole in the hide roof for the smoke. He doesn't want to go against Saskia's wishes, but he may have to drag her back to the izba. He wonders if he could even do that; she is so much stronger than he is, even now.

He sets the lantern down next to her. Another surge begins.

"Wait. Wait!" she whispers and bears down yet again.

Arkady clasps her hand, and she crushes it in hers. Afterward, she props herself up to look him in the eye.

"You see him, he's turned the wrong way. You're going to have to cut me, to get him out. We'll stitch it up after he's born."

"What?"

"With the scissors. You're going to have to do it now, before the next wave comes on. Arkady. Now! I need you. Do you hear me? We are bound together in this. That is why you are here."

"Yes." A wave of nausea ripples through his body and out through his head. For a moment, he sees the whole scene from the ceiling, and then he's back, crouching into an impossible position on the damp earth. He sets the lantern on the bench just above him and sits between Saskia's legs, leaning in. "Try to breathe," he says. "Do I cut upward, or down from the—"

"Down. A cut only half the length of your little finger."

Impossibly, Arkady inserts the scissor blade under the powerful membrane keeping the baby in, and snips. Immediately, the cut widens, and Saskia screams as it opens. The baby's arm slips out, and its hand opens and closes in the air of the world. Saskia howls, and the baby spills into Arkady's lap, unfolding from the interior like the unearthly traveler it is. Its body is grayish and slick with blood and mucus.

Saskia feels around for the baby. Arkady gives it to her and then tries to staunch the blood.

"Here he is!" Saskia wipes the baby's face and dips a hooked finger into its mouth. She turns it over and lays it across one forearm and thumps its back: once, twice, and the baby gives a thin wail. "Good boy," she growls.

She flips it upright and holds the tiny creature in her arms. Yes, a boy. He curls and uncurls his legs and shakes his head, eyes slitted to let the raw world in just slowly. Arkady still sits between Saskia's splayed legs, plugging her with the bear hide.

"We'll wait for the afterbirth, and then stitch up the cut," Saskia gasps. She's smiling at the baby but wincing.

"Is he hurt?"

"I don't think so. Let's wipe him off. Then we can wrap him in the blanket that's in my bag." She smiles.

Arkady is so relieved, and yet his hands shake uncontrollably and his teeth chatter. He shuffles over to Saskia's pack and pulls out a gray blanket knitted in interlocking patterns of thick wool. She wraps the baby, who raises his crumpled face. She takes him to her breast. She holds him there, and he nuzzles into her forcefully.

"Ouch! You rascal," Saskia says gently. "Good. That's the way."

For a few minutes, the only sounds are his slurping and the fire crackling.

"I will call him Mattis."

Arkady catches a movement at the door of the banya. When he looks, a girl with a badly scarred face is there. She's partly obscured by shadow and wears a band of leather adorned with the tips of reindeer antlers, like a crown. She pivots out of sight.

"I feel a surge," Saskia says. "Take him, Arkady. The afterbirth." Saskia throws back her head. She bears down, but the contraction is fruitless.

She nurses the baby again. Again, she smiles. But another mild contraction comes and goes, and the afterbirth does not come out.

"I should sew up the cut," Arkady says. "You're still bleeding."

"If you sew it up, the afterbirth will only rip out the stitches. Wait a bit longer."

They wait for some time—maybe much, maybe little. The baby nurses and nurses. Blood seeps from Saskia, and Arkady does not know what to do.

At first, she brushes away his worry. "Be patient," she says. "The afterbirth will come when it comes."

But the blood still flows into the bearskin. Then Saskia is quiet for a long time. No longer smiling.

"You have to reach inside me and pull it out."

He bows his head.

"Just follow the cord. Don't pull until you have the organ itself. Don't pull the cord because if it breaks, the afterbirth will rot inside me."

Breathing shallowly, he bows again before her. A roaring in his head prevents him from formulating clear thoughts as he slides his hand along the slick cord and beyond, into the softest antechamber of the body, then into its deeper cave. The roaring heightens but not enough to muffle her screams. He feels around, eyes squeezed shut, until her body tightens around his arm, and, terrified, he pulls.

"Did you get it?"

"No, I'm sorry."

Saskia covers the lower part of her body with the bear hide. For a few minutes, they stare at each other. The baby nurses with one arm stretched out upon his mother's chest. Then, Saskia grimaces and bites her lip.

"What's happening?" Arkady asks.

She shakes her head and tries to hold down the hide, but Arkady, panicking, lifts it. She bats his hand away, but not before he sees the hide black with a flood of new blood.

"Let me get the needle and thread. Or let me try again to free the afterbirth." How could he have not noticed how pale she has become?

"Just help him keep nursing."

And in this, like all the rest that he'll never forget, he helps. She leans back, her arms loosening from around the baby. Arkady holds him in place while she watches, eyes glazing.

"No matter what happens, he nurses for as long as he can," she whispers. "Do you understand me, little priest? Then, you feed him the reindeer's milk. You milk her twice a day. Keep the calf away from her now. Kill it. But you *must* milk her to keep her full. Bring her in the cabin when the long night comes; do whatever you have to do. When he's older, you blend kasha gruel with ground dried reindeer meat. You feed him all the fats you can and meat. Chew it for him, Arkady. It's going to be like that. Chew for him."

"I understand. Let me tend to you now."

He lays the baby next to Saskia and forces her to let go of the bearskin that covers her. She's gray. Finally, Arkady can overpower her. Until that moment, he had no idea how much blood a human body could hold, but now it was all right there in front of him, a crimson-black flood that not even the pelt of a full-grown ice bear can absorb.

"Make sure he stays warm," she whispers. "Sew him a carrying pack out of hide and fur. Take him with you everywhere. Everywhere. Even when you go out to fetch water from the stream. Don't leave him alone in this place. Don't leave him alone. They will be trying to take him. Chúdo-Yúda on the beach and the rusalka near the stream. Starostin on the Cross, and who knows how many others? This place wants people. Feed him reindeer milk, reindeer blood. Feed him eider eggs, Arkady. You've got to use your head now; do you understand? Understand me, Arkady." Saskia clasps his hand tightly.

"I understand."

"You must be smarter now."

Arkady nods. He listens to her ragged breaths and the sleeping baby's tiny ones. He holds Saskia close, reeling from the shock of blood and creation and the inner realms of women suddenly laid bare. He embraces her.

"I will take care of him," he whispers.

Soon, her lifeblood seeps away through the bearskin and down to a place where it melts a bit of frozen ground.

CHAPTER 41

rkady wraps Saskia's body in the bearskin and puts cooled stones around the edge of the shroud. He wraps Mattis in his mother-knit blanket and nests the baby inside his coat.

She saved my life, and I couldn't save hers, he thinks.

That is the nature of life itself, a firm voice within him—maybe hers?—rebukes. *Endlessly, people are entwined, and there is no one keeping a tally of what is fair or right. Best to keep your eyes open and move forward. That is the only way of things.*

Arkady hobbles away from the banya.

Starostin stands in front of the izba with his arms folded across his chest, following Arkady with his eyes. Arkady hides the baby.

"She is dead!" Arkady screams. "Do you understand? Saskia's dead. We're not what you're searching for! Leave me alone! Get back!"

He picks up a stone and hurls it at the creature. He misses. Starostin doesn't move or speak. Arkady hurries past him.

The rosy-skinned baby sleeps with one fist curled tight to his chest and the other hand outstretched. Arkady keeps him inside his coat while he restarts the fire in the stove. He'll have to fashion a cradle, he thinks. And clothes. Saskia's work apron hangs on a nail by the door, and he carefully lifts it down and spreads it on the table. Wiping the blood from her scissors, Arkady cuts the apron into small rectangular pieces and stacks them. That will have to do for diapers.

For hours, Arkady paces the cabin, replaying the horrible scene in the banya. He catalogs everything he knows about Saskia to write down later, for the baby's sake. How was it that he'd never asked her exactly how she came to be in Spitsbergen? Had she ever been to the mainland? He'd just assumed she had, but now he wasn't so sure. She said she came from farther north, Wijde Fjord, and that she had many sisters. How had he never asked for more? He will tell Mattis everything he knows when the time comes. He brings the reindeer into the izba, milks the doe, and feeds the milk to Mattis by soaking a piece of cloth and nuzzling the baby's mouth with the corner of it until he sucks.

Exhausted, Arkady settles onto his bed on the hearth with the little one still tucked in his coat. He drifts off to sleep but jerks awake again with his heart racing: Saskia is dead.

In the stove, logs burn down to embers and turn to ash while new ones alight. Mattis whimpers. Arkady warms more milk and feeds him. The baby sleeps with all his fingers wrapped tightly around one of Arkady's. Arkady stares out the window toward the banya.

I will use my head. I will be smarter. You'll see.

Arkady sings to the little one, making up meandering songs about the tundra plain, lodjas, and sailors who turn to blocks of ice in a storm and then melt back to life.

Five nights into the baby's life, Arkady wakes with a start. The child also is awake; Arkady can see the stove flame reflected in Mattis' eyes. The reindeer scuffles nervously. Arkady struggles to his feet. He has no idea what time of day or night it is; a disconcerting light shines through the window, and Arkady thinks he might be dreaming. But it is the full moon, bigger than any Arkady has ever seen, hanging just above the tops of the crags, sending a brilliant silver beam over the snow. Gray textures like faces dapple the surface of the moon; it is too close!

He wants to close shutters against it, but there aren't any shutters. He looks to the mountains, but they are still sleeping under the snow and in no position to help. The baby cries, but Arkady is unable to turn away from the window. Starostin is back up on his Cross, staring out to sea. Arkady leans his forehead onto the glass and shuts his eyes.

All at once, a roar unlike anything he's ever heard fills the air. Arkady jerks up. The sound emanates across the tundra: low, hoarse, but so loud that the windowpanes rattle. The baby stops crying. The sound comes from the south, and in the distance, Arkady sees a huge, white shape burst out from Saskia's birthing banya, sending the loosely built walls crumbling and the hides of the roof sailing off.

An ice bear bounds into view, shaking itself. The bear sniffs the air, then runs toward the izba. In just a few seconds, the bear paces at the foot of the steps. It lets loose another deafening roar.

Mattis lies quietly on the hearth. Arkady retreats from the window and coos softly, hoping to reassure him, even though his own body trembles uncontrollably. The baby makes a sound like a laugh. The bear circles the cabin; the great hump of its back appears in the seaward window then disappears. It growls and half-roars. Soon enough, it passes the window again; this time it pauses to look inside. The baby reaches toward it.

The moonlight fades, and the bear paces around the cabin for many hours. Whether it is Matins or Vespers or the middle of the night, Arkady has no idea. The reindeer is panicking, and Arkady tries his best to calm her.

The bear is still there the next day when Arkady runs out of water. He waits another full day, soothing the baby and forcing smiles at him. Arkady checks the window compulsively every minute or two; the great bear is still there, sniffing and pacing with its head down. It no longer roars or makes any sound. Finally, Arkady fetches the old rifle and loads it as he'd seen Saskia do. He agonizes over whether to leave the baby in the izba, but finally does as Saskia instructed and swaddles Mattis in the gray blanket and wraps a long strip of hide around his shoulder, making a sling across his chest, and secures the baby in it. He buttons his coat over this cargo, hooks one of the wooden buckets onto his left arm, and waits until the bear passes the front of the house. Shaking with fear, Arkady steps onto the porch.

The bear wheels around, nostrils flaring. It looks past him into the cabin. Arkady raises the rifle, and with each heartbeat, the sight pulses upward. Mattis cries out, and the bear swerves to look where the sound came from. Somehow, Mattis gets a tiny arm free and reaches toward the bear. At this, the bear leans forward to look at the baby. Then, she turns and lopes away.

CHAPTER 42

ime passes differently in the long night. The north wind lifts what would usually be called a day and stretches it over the tundra into an endless banner of darkness, with only the faintest outlines of snow-smoothed mountains in its folds. Hours unspool, freed of any notion of beginning or ending, and in this space, the rhythms of Arkady's life shift and elongate. During that first winter, he almost never leaves the izba, partly because, each time curiosity leads him to the edge of his small pool of light, he grips the sill with both hands against teetering sideways, triggered by a vertigo so powerful that it's as if the top of the world has split in half like an eggshell, and the night flowing in is so ethereal as to set him adrift. During all his years at Solovetsky, he'd never felt the dark like this, even though the monastery is almost as far north as any human ever dwelt. The hewn stones of those islands kept winter at a distance, he decides. Those stones built into walls and towers, bridges and walkways, sheltered the busyness of man. That, and also faith, kept the dark at arm's length. But here in Spitsbergen, only Maaike's iron nail holds the sky on its axis, and the force of other elements—wind, mostly, and the cold—makes a person question whether that nail will hold.

The other reason Arkady stays inside is Mattis. Arkady cares for the baby with a baffling ease. Qualities he never associated with himself spring forward: gentleness, affection, patience. *It is some kind of alchemy*, he thinks, *the way this baby alters my way in the world.*

Mattis takes to food as well as can be. He drinks reindeer milk and then milk mixed with a little bit of the doe's blood. After a time, it's clear he will live, even with such a beginning as his, and with such a guardian as Arkady. So, they sleep for most of the dark time under hides and blankets on Starostin's hearth, the baby stretched out and snoring like his mother did and both of them riding the hours next to a fire that records everything and sends their story up the chimney and adrift across Spitsbergen and into the ears of listening creatures.

While they sleep, frost feathers in under the door and creates films of ice in the kettle. These filaments show Arkady the narrow ledge where their survival rests. He tends to the fire with more care than he ever gave his prayers. He sits by the hearth with the fire iron across his lap, massaging his leg, or what is left of it, gazing at the fire, then Mattis, and then out the window at the stars.

Arkady has time to contemplate the usual winter occupations of Northmen: braiding rope; carving chessmen, dolls, even wooden shoes; working leather; and inventing games. But most of the time he doesn't do any of these. Instead, he thinks about how they will survive. Their stores of reindeer meat and firewood will last through the winter, but then he must hunt, and this is the problem. He never learned how to shoot, and certainly he will waste most of the izba's tiny barrel of gunpowder. He puzzles over this until he panics, and then he banishes it from his mind by sewing clothes for Mattis and preparing his food.

For two weeks out of every month, the waxing moon rises from the sea horizon and drifts around the izba. Sometimes clouds or snowfall obscure it, but when the air is clear, the moon disturbs Arkady deeply. As it reaches fullness, it is too close to the earth and shatters the night with an alarming lantern beam. This is the only time Arkady paces through the night, and when he can finally sleep, he dreams only of his long journey by foot—hunger, cold, a fox's eyes bulging under icy water, the feeling that someone is standing just behind him on the bare, vast beach. During these times, his missing foot itches, and desperation overtakes him. He cries for himself, Saskia, for his grandfather, for anyone at all.

When the wind finally rises and snow blows into the air, Arkady feels better because storms obscure the moon. And when the strong but waning ball of rock and dust disappears behind the crags, he thanks the mountains for their heights, and soon the stars return and with them the great bird way. Its milky path across the sky, woven among the stars and leading to the southern horizon, guides birds from their northern nesting grounds to their wintering places in the south. The birds' way leads the eye toward the world of men, but to Arkady that is more mythical than the Spitsbergen Dog.

More than the internal vicissitudes, and more even than the shrieking winds and snow-padded silences, the winter is one great outward sigh into which Arkady releases all that's left of who he was before the Pomors lashed him to their lodja's mast. He accepts the dark as an enveloping blanket under which he lies still and lets the season transmute him into something new. Time and Mattis himself are the catalysts for this change because an infant keeps one bound to the present moment and nothing else. And so, Arkady sews tiny shirts, bathes the boy in fire-warmed water, and, like Nikolai before him, soon Arkady is both father and mother.

CHAPTER 43

Arkady sings a lighthearted song to Mattis on the way to the beach, even though, with every step on this path, he's reminded of his own crazed crawling through the mud, his mind flickering against obliterating pain, and the swift, stupid mistake that cost him his foot.

The baby sleeps, completely buttoned into Arkady's coat. It is still far too cold for Mattis to be in the open air, and Arkady hurries over the snow, using as a cane the ax that maimed him.

At first, the light is a pale and fleeting dawn that has time only to interlace the land in delicate filaments before slipping back below the horizon. But soon, the balance shifts and sunlight beats back the darkness with thin but persistent beams, for first one hour, and then for two, then three at a time. Now, they take their first trip to the beach. Arkady doesn't need firewood, not yet. This is a new kind of search.

The lagoon is a solid crescent of snow-covered pack ice that echoes and pings. He had hoped the snow would have melted near the sea edge, like it did at the monastery in very early spring. But the snow is deep everywhere. He walks slowly among the driftwood, looking under the pieces that he can lift. The large, whole trunks don't interest him, nor do the forked branches. He walks half-bent over, pushing snow away and prodding with the ax handle. The cold nips his toes and fingertips.

"No matter, little one," Arkady whispers to Mattis. "We have all the time in the world."

As the light fades, Arkady spots an old plank wedged under a pile of driftwood. Its exposed corner is weathered and waterlogged and won't pull free. Arkady digs into the snow around it, kneeling and using one hand to steady the baby. When he still can't pull it free, he works from above, loosening the wood on top of the plank and pulling pieces off the pile one at a time. Soon, he's sweating. The baby rustles awake and whimpers.

"Patience, Mattis. I must find out if this is our treasure."

Arkady continues to move driftwood away from the plank. He even takes off his reindeer-skin mittens to pry more pieces away. He loses his footing and slides sideways against a big log, and Mattis cries in earnest.

"Hold on a little longer. We're almost there."

Arkady again pulls the edge of the plank, and this time it slides out of the pile. He brushes it off. Then he laughs and pats Mattis inside his coat.

"You see? Look, you see?"

Embedded in the plank are two long, bent nails. Arkady chops the nail-end into a piece he can carry and hurries back up the embankment with it. In the izba, he pries out the nails and sets them in a bowl on the table. Two weeks pass before he finds another one, but in that time, he fashions tongs from old reindeer antlers and lugs a heavy beach cobble into the izba for an anvil. He builds as hot of a fire as the stove will hold, heats each nail, and pounds its point into a flat, sharp edge.

Over the course of that early spring, Arkady finds a slender curved fir root on the beach that he whittles into a bow. Straight sticks become arrows. And when the sun finally rises above the horizon, Arkady leads the reindeer doe outside. Weakened by not enough food, bloodletting, and giving milk, she can barely walk. Arkady pets her as she eats a palmful of lichen, and then he encircles her neck with his arms, places a bucket on the ground below her, and kills her swiftly with a cut to the throat. He catches the blood and then lays her down gently on the snow. He dresses her meat and uses her tendon for a bowstring.

As Arkady predicted, he wastes shot after shot of gunpowder, missing every reindeer he aims for and scaring the rest away. He fashions a fish net out of strips of reindeer hide and places it at the mouth of the stream. The net yields nothing and soon disintegrates. They eat well from Starostin's larder; they have what they will need for now, but Arkady sees the future beyond Starostin's food, and in that future, Mattis only lives if Arkady can hunt. He collects ptarmigan feathers to fletch his arrows. Mattis spends hours each day strapped to Arkady, buttoned into his coat with just his face peeking out. Mattis watches Arkady shoot arrow after arrow at a target made from a hide draped over stacked firewood.

The pack ice breaks up in May, and Arkady spends more time at the beach, collecting firewood as always, and searching for nails. The greatest treasure he finds that season is an iron bolt that Arkady imagines once held a mast to a hull. He forges it into a point and lashes it to a long, straight stick. This spear provides a great deal of comfort; now if an ice bear attacks, he'll have more than the rifle and his unsteady aim.

Around then, Arkady finally hits a reindeer with an arrow. Struck in the flank and trapped near the sea cliff by Arkady on the other side, the wounded creature panics and tumbles down the bluff to the beach. By the time Arkady reaches it, the reindeer has almost bled to death. Ashamed and imagining the Pomors shaking their heads over the terrible shot, he kills it with the knife.

He pounds some of the meat into bits that he mixes into gruel for Mattis, who, as usual, eats eagerly. He dries and cures the rest. Near midsummer, they discover an eider colony two versts south of the izba. Arkady is able to shoot a few eider ducks, but he loses two precious arrows in the sea. They eat eggs all summer.

CHAPTER 44

uring the second winter, more structure shapes their days and nights: Mondays are for mending and working on hides; on Tuesdays, if it's clear and moonlit, Arkady walks or skis in one or the other direction from the cabin with Mattis strapped to his chest; Wednesday, he inventories the larder and inspects the wood pile; Thursday, he carves toys or puzzles for Mattis and reads to him from the Gospels or recounts the story of Maaike and the World Tree; Friday, they bake bread and eat pickled eider eggs; Saturday, they wash themselves and their clothes and air out their hide blankets; and Sunday, Arkady reads again to Mattis and tells the boy everything he knows about Saskia: how she saved Arkady's life more than once; her great physical strength and fortitude; her beloved ice-bear skin; her thick, red braids; and her skill as a storyteller.

Mattis' own hair grows into fiery curls, and by the time he is one year old, he is walking comfortably. For him, the izba is full of wonders: the cupboards, the ladder to the stove bench, and especially the woodpile. He pulls a round from the center and sends an avalanche of firewood down on himself. During this winter, he also burns his fingers on the stove, slips down the icy front stairs, falls into the cellar, cuts his finger with the knife blade, and scalds himself with kettle water. He does each of these things just once and not again. He's a strong, curious, and good-natured child. One day, Mattis climbs the ladder up to the loft by himself. By the time

Arkady notices, the boy sits laughing with his legs dangling, gnawing on the rock-hard bread that his mother had left up there for the house spirit. Arkady marvels that Mattis is sure-footed and happy. At night, he pulls the boy onto his lap and holds him for hours, stroking his hair and recognizing new worlds in his sleeping face.

When the light returns, Mattis cannot yet walk through the deep snow on his own, so Arkady carries him strapped to his back while he travels on skis across the tundra. The child is large for his age, so it's a blessing when the snow melts.

This spring, Mattis toddles away every time Arkady turns his back. Arkady can still catch the child easily, but it is the last season that's true, and Mattis is happiest when he's running. Soon the running away becomes a game, and Arkady spends all his time chasing after the boy. Arkady's hunting is sporadic; the reindeer keep away from the izba. He manages to shoot ptarmigan with his arrows, and he finds a place to catch fish in the lagoon. But mostly he runs after Mattis. Arkady usually doesn't mind—he'd entirely forgotten about the joy of play—but often, fog moves in quickly and obscures the running boy, and panic seizes Arkady so fiercely that when he catches Mattis, all he can do is hug the boy too tightly.

Toward the end of summer, Arkady hasn't collected enough firewood for the coming season, so Mattis and he spend their days making trips to the beach and hauling wood.

Arkady even rigs a tiny harness for Mattis so that the little one can drag one or two sticks at a time on his own, which the child loves. They haul and haul, and at night they sleep deeply, exhausted and happy.

CHAPTER 45

t the threshold of their third winter, Arkady welcomes the dark with open joy. Mattis speaks now and spends most of his time setting up carved dolls in different scenarios and babbling to himself in a half-decipherable language. Incessantly, he asks for more dolls, and Arkady carves them eagerly: at first monks and soldiers, then eight Pomors in an ornate lodja, and then, a woman with the face of an ice bear wearing long skirts and braids. He carves the great black Dog, a one-legged man with the head of a grizzled fox, and on and on across the hours and snowstorms, in beams of lantern light and moonlight, under great starry skies and in the midst of the aurora's strange figures, which trace a luminous script across the world and adorn Arkady and Mattis' lives with spiraling tendrils, with fierce and unearthly beauty.

Ice bears occasionally investigate the izba on their way north to the wintering grounds on the pack ice. But none ever stays more than a day or does more than circle the cabin a few times or half-heartedly shoulder the door. For no reason he can explain, Arkady doesn't fear them, and so neither does Mattis. The izba is a human home, and by the third winter, it is decidedly Arkady's. They are there; if anything were to challenge them, Arkady would defend the den, just like any other creature would.

Just once during those first years does Arkady fear for his life. In the deepest night of the third winter, still months away from the sun's reappearance, he sits at the table facing the hearth, carving beads for an abacus. Now that Mattis is three, the little boy sleeps up on the stove bench. Arkady has been working on the abacus for hours, but all at once, he stops, his knife hovering over the wood. The density of the silence in the cabin shifts and intensifies. He wouldn't be able to explain it, but it is as if a great hand laid a thick felt damper over the room. Later, he'd wonder if it were simply a wind dying or perhaps fog over the fjord lifting. He sets down his knife. Slowly, he turns around in his chair. Only lantern light flickers in the landward window. He walks slowly across the room toward it. Some shadowy movement outside draws him. He squints, at first seeing nothing but reflections. But as he draws closer, a circle of condensation appears on the glass. It fades, and then another one blooms. Rhythmically, it happens again. Something is standing just outside the window, looking in. Its breath is there on the glass.

Arkady covers his face with his hands. His terror grips him like a fox trap. Then he lunges for his rifle, even though he knows, somehow, it would be useless against whatever stands outside.

"Get back!" he hisses.

The circles of breath continue to appear, evenly spaced, for another minute, as he trembles there in his home with his rifle raised to the glass. Then, they disappear.

Mattis loves the izba and everything to do with Pomors, especially Starostin. During the third winter, and again during the fourth, the child rushes to the porch first thing every morning to see the old ghost up on his Cross. Arkady teaches Mattis to sew, which the child manages well, even as young as he is. While Mattis sews new boot linings, Arkady recounts as many of the saints' lives as he can remember.

Arkady tells Mattis that Kuzma the Pomor is his father because, by the time Mattis is three, there's a strong resemblance. "He kept all the Pomors at Schoonhoven well fed and happy, and he was a spectacular hunter," Arkady says, embellishing the tale to give the boy happiness. "And once Kuzma worked all night trying to save a

Pomor called Vitka, who'd been mauled by an ice bear! By God, he did. He pulled the man's artery back down from where it had sprung and mended it with stitches that would impress the Tsaritsa's own seamstresses! Soon, Vitka could walk again, and hunt again, all because of your father's skill."

The little boy beams up at Arkady, and Arkady smiles back. Love for Mattis clutches his throat, stopping his breath. The inner closet of his heart is a full, light-filled room.

CHAPTER 46

rkady spends all morning at the north end of the lagoon, while Mattis throws stones into the sea. In his years at the izba, Arkady has overturned almost all the driftwood there, and soon his search for nails and other ship-wrecked metal will take him into the next cove. By now, this pastime has grown beyond necessity; after all, he could have taken nails from Starostin's izba—from the porch boards, where they wouldn't be missed. But it would be wrong to disassemble the izba, like prying nails out of a ship while sailing in it.

The pack ice has broken up. Spring melt is only a few weeks away. A bearded seal swims near shore, gliding along the coastline, casting its opaque eyes toward land. Arkady rises to stretch his back and scans the water, looking for ice bears swimming toward the beach. He watches Mattis, who, at five and a half years old, stands tall in his reindeer-skin tunic, thick vest, and long curls. Suddenly, the boy stops what he's doing and pivots to face Arkady. Arkady smiles and waves, but Mattis doesn't respond. Instead, he picks up a stone and hurls it in Arkady's direction. It whirs past Arkady's left ear and knocks a ptarmigan off a log ten paces from where he stands.

Mattis hoots with joy and sprints over. Shocked, Arkady kneels with him over the speckled bird.

"Look, father! We'll roast ptarmigan tonight!" Mattis had hit the bird with such force that its skull was obviously crushed.

"It's a magnificent kill," Arkady says, uncertainly. "I couldn't have done it."

The boy is stronger than Arkady had realized. Mattis has his own knife and a small bow and arrow, and from the moment those tools were in his hands, he knew how to use them. Arkady could convince himself it was because Mattis had watched Arkady struggle to hunt since the boy was an infant strapped to Arkady's chest. Mattis knew how it felt in the body to shoot, to miss, and to try again. But the truth is there is something uncanny in Mattis' sure aim. He never misses, and it won't be long before the boy shoots a reindeer. He's even been eyeing the seals, which Arkady had never thought to try to kill.

Mattis quickly skins the bird, guts it, and carries it up the path toward the izba, whistling the tune of a hymn Arkady had sung to him as a baby.

CHAPTER 47

estled between two lichen-faced stones, a mound of interlaced sprigs emerges from an ice-ringed hole in the melting snow. The plant resembles a culinary herb that Arkady remembers vaguely from Solovetsky, but he can't recall its name. His life at the monastery slips ever backward, its spires and rocky shores disappearing off the horizon of his mind, replaced by bright and dark seasons away from other men.

Already on this walk, Arkady has seen other plants that will soon send out tissue-thin petals and strange, veined orbs or sturdy blossoms strung along spiked ladders. Lichens already catch sunlight on their tiny, pocked hides. He feels the sun's powerful force just as much now as he did the first time he'd opened the izba doors to greet it, when Mattis was still a baby; Arkady is turned inside out. His faith no longer resides in his head or his heart; it is painted on the land. And he puzzles, as he did that first spring, over the perfection of these seasons and cycles, in this place that seems to Arkady to sing out more clearly than Revelations: *I am the alpha and the omega. I have existed since the beginning of time and will exist beyond all that is human.*

Arkady and Mattis stand together at the sentinel rocks and look out to sea, where a thin ray of sunlight glimmers on the whitecaps. They are off to the eider colony to see if any outliers have arrived early. They both carry bows and arrows, and each has a knife at his belt.

On the path, Mattis runs ahead, leaping across stones and pausing often to throw rocks over the bluff. He moves across the tundra easily, without any of the hesitation that Arkady still feels. Mattis wears walrus-skin moccasins lined with fox fur, and knitted socks. His shirt is made from pieces of Arkady's old wool overcoat, which originally belonged to Father Ilya, whose name has never been uttered to Mattis. Over the winter, Arkady unraveled Mattis' baby blanket and reknit the yarn into the thick cap the child now wears. Arkady watches the red curls bob ahead of him and then disappear down the steep path to the colony.

Arkady stops on the bluff above the cove. He is reusing as much as he can, and so far, they are warm and relatively well fed, but Starostin's stores are finally dwindling: the gunpowder is long gone, as is their bushel of rye flour, and the cranberries lasted only through Mattis' first year. They have enough for the summer, and they both will hunt meat, but without grain and stores of dried fruit, they will lose vitality, and why should they? They have been eating dried seaweed, which makes a decent broth, and mixing pulverized scurvy grass into everything. But this summer, they must go northward to Advent Bay, deep in Ice Fjord, and see whether anyone's there and if they can buy supplies.

They haven't seen a single lodja enter the fjord in the years they've lived in Starostin's izba. But the Pomors may still have a camp in Advent Bay, like Saskia said. And the ships could have come and gone in fog or at night or simply when Arkady wasn't looking. He sometimes wonders if Starostin's cabin is invisible to other people. The old, gray-faced chieftain still sits on top of his Cross with lichen hanging from his clothes. Starostin no longer searches the sea but sleeps upright, supported by an unknown force. Even this strange creature now is part of Arkady's home. Would he even be able to leave the vicinity of the izba, or would he circle back like Starostin did so long ago? Either way, they must try.

"Mattis! Wait!"

Arkady starts down the embankment, leaning heavily on his rifle for support. The boy never waits for him, but he's still so young that Arkady is not certain how much real danger Mattis perceives. An ice bear could be lurking near the eider nests, although this trip was more a fancy than a real hunt—it is too early for eggs, and the chance of a duck for dinner is slim. No matter how early in the season it is, they're both exhilarated by the warmer air sweeping across the land: spring is coming.

Arkady scrambles down the bluff, slipping on pebbles and loose earth. His wooden foot is holding up well. He can't complain, but still the going is not easy. He must look at the ground before him, glancing up only occasionally to scan for Mattis' bright hair. Arkady finally sees him standing on the beach, near a great boulder in a cap of snow that is painted by last year's guano. The boy gestures with one hand. Arkady squints and slips down the last section of trail on his bottom. On the beach's uneven shale, he stumbles forward. Just as Mattis turns to look at him, Arkady discerns a figure outlined against the boulder.

Camouflaged in garments the same gray as the stone, a thin shape tilts out of the background. As Arkady comes closer, he can see that her hair is wreathed in twigs and eiderdown, and her face is strangely blurred. Even closer, he sees that her face is badly scarred. This is the same person who peeked into the banya on the night of Mattis' birth. She leans down and whispers something to the boy. He nods, and the girl meets Arkady's gaze. Arkady can't get there soon enough. The girl slips around the far side of the boulder. Arkady rushes to Mattis and limps around the rock but finds no one.

"Who was that?" Arkady kneels so he can look Mattis in the eye.

"Vasilissa."

"Vasilissa," Arkady repeats. He has seen enough in this place to know the girl probably isn't human. She could be Vasilissa the

Fair, wandering far from her place of honor as the most beloved heroine of the Russian countryside.

"She says she lives with the reindeer. Up there." Mattis nods toward the mountains. "She says where she lives there is a lake and a waterfall. She lives behind the waterfall with the reindeer. She says you still owe her for the life of the fox. What does she mean?"

Arkady's breath catches. The fox's eyes bulge in the waters of his memory. How is this girl holding the scales of justice? Doesn't she know he still cries over the fox? And if the loss of his foot wasn't enough to repay this debt, what about Saskia? No, this isn't Vasilissa the Fair, sprung from the story. This is Vasilissa the burned one, keeping a discerning eye out for human folly from her vantage point in the Orthodox calendar. Vasilissa of Nicomedia, somehow risen and walking among the living once again.

"She ... knows me," Arkady says. "Have you seen her before?"

"Once before. She says the first eiders will arrive in two weeks. This will be a good year for eggs, but the summer will be short, and many of the chicks will die. She says to tell you that no one is at Advent Bay. Does that mean we don't have to go?"

"We are going." Arkady kneels in front of the little boy, trying not to show fear over the creature's appearance and her message. "It's only a few days' journey north from the izba, so we've got to try."

"Is there really a waterfall up in the mountains? How would the reindeer get behind it?" Mattis' earnest expression breaks Arkady's heart.

"I don't know, little one. Come on, we can fish for salmon off the point there. Let me see how far you can cast."

Arkady extends his hand and envelops the smaller one, but Mattis shakes off Arkady's grip and bobs off ahead of him. Numerous times, both of them glance back over their shoulders to the boulder.

As the light returns, Arkady cannot stop Mattis from running. As soon as the ground dries out, Mattis is away across the tundra plain, climbing the sentinel rocks, scampering inland along the course of the stream, or chasing the mottled flash of a fox's tail. Even when Arkady calls for him, the boy never pauses. Mattis doesn't stay away long, and he usually returns with a handful of eider eggs, a ptarmigan, or a reindeer calf, but he goes where he fancies. The child builds elaborate towns out of mud and stones near the stream and populates them with his carved wooden dolls. Even when he accompanies Arkady on trips to restock the woodpile, Mattis wanders to the farthest edge of whatever beach they're on, and comes back with treasures: an old oar, fishing buoys, and once, even a cloudy, sea-eroded glass bottle trailing a kelp frond.

This spring, Mattis wears through the soles of two pairs of hide boots and then goes barefoot. Arkady rests in the tasks of daily life that have become their routine. With his hands busy and his heart engaged in the new rhythms of the child's life, for the first time, he is happy. Even the bare crags, which he once saw as threatening forces passing continuous judgment, form a protective shield over them.

At some point, Arkady leaves off trying to contain Mattis. Every sentient being deserves to be free, he tells himself in the years afterward, and in such a place as Spitsbergen, why shouldn't he let the boy's exuberance express itself? Mattis cannot be ruled by fear of ice bears. He's a boy without the company of other boys or anyone at all except Arkady. Why shouldn't he make friends with the foxes and the wind? Where others see a hostile plain, Mattis sees home.

Arkady sews two leather rucksacks: one large and one small. He sews a sleep sack of reindeer hide and bear fur. He repurposes all he can find into warm layers and assembles enough food and cooking utensils to see them through.

One sunny evening, Mattis races into the cabin holding a fish in each hand, both hooked by the gills through his fingers. He holds them out to Arkady. Their iridescent skin flashes fuchsia and green. Black spots dapple their sides, and their bellies shine pure silver.

"I haven't seen trout since I fished in the lakes of Solovetsky," Arkady whispers.

Beaming, Mattis gives Arkady the fish.

Arkady turns them over. "Where did you get these?"

Mattis shrugs.

"Where did you get them? Answer me."

"In the stream."

"How did you catch them? Your fishing pole is there, next to mine in the corner."

Mattis shrugs again.

"I've never seen trout in our stream," Arkady says. "Or heard of them living anywhere in Spitsbergen." He lays the fish carefully on the table.

"She gave them to me," the boy whispers. "Vasilissa."

Arkady just slits the fish bellies and prepares them for the pan. "Here, try this on." He points to the backpack he's made. He still must adjust the straps.

The boy shakes his head. "I'm not going to Advent Bay."

"It's only a short trip. Six- or seven-days' walk. We'll get provisions and then come back."

"I want to stay here."

Mattis climbs into Arkady's lap. Arkady will try with the backpack again later. He hugs the boy—feels Mattis' small body relax and lean into his chest—and they examine the fish together. Later, they fry the fish in reindeer fat and salt. After so many months of the same four or five foods, the flaky flesh overwhelms them with delight. Arkady declares he doesn't care where these fish came from; he just hopes there are more.

After dinner, Mattis falls asleep on Arkady's lap. Arkady strokes the boy's hair and covers his earth-stained feet in blankets. His love for the boy is a strange wonder: frightening one minute and peaceful the next. You can never unlove a little boy. After so many years of struggle and confusion, Arkady rests, finally, in that.

CHAPTER 48

he day of their journey rises bright and warm. Arkady bustles around the cabin with the door flung wide open while Mattis sits, legs swinging, on the edge of the loft. The boy sings to himself as he finishes his breakfast.

"Pomors have had camps at Advent Bay for longer than anyone can remember. They say Pomors built many small huts inside a great hall. When you walk through the doors of that hall, it's like an indoor village, and each hut has its own metal stovepipe snaking up through space through the high ceiling above. The great hall keeps out the wind and keeps snow off the roofs."

"Do children live there?"

"I don't know. We'll have to find out for ourselves."

Arkady works at the stove, packing cooked kasha and reindeer meat in a lidded pot for their first day of travel.

"Advent Bay used to be the main hunting station for all the Pomors. They gathered there at the beginning of the season and then set out for the hunting camps. My grandfather had stories of two hundred men living there. What a chaos that would have been! We'll have to count how many are there now, and what stories they have for us. They will have stores of flour and dried cranberries. Maybe even strawberries! Wouldn't you like to taste one, Mattis?"

Arkady turns around, smiling at the thought of that chewy burst of sweetness and the way that Mattis will leap in delight when he tastes it, but when he looks up at the loft, his eyes skitter across empty space.

He walks onto the porch. "Mattis!"

Bare-armed and without shoes, the boy is running across the tundra. He's still fairly close by; if Arkady had started off then, maybe he could have caught up, even without a real second foot to run on. But he pauses. The same thing that had caught Mattis' eye catches his: Two yellow butterflies. Butterflies! Bright jewels dropped by the sun. Here? Their colors blink on and off with each wingbeat. Mattis laughs as he runs after them, and for a moment, even Arkady smiles as they lead the boy away.

Arkady sets off after him, but he is not fast enough; Mattis soon reaches the base of the crags where the little stream pours out of its rocky channel. He climbs up the scree slope to the steeper face of the mountain. The butterflies still float before him.

Like lures, Arkady thinks suddenly, as if someone else put the thought in his head.

With goatlike agility, Mattis finds footing on the narrowest ledges, and he continues up and up. Arkady follows, sending tiny avalanches down behind him. The stream drops through its steep channel in slender waterfalls and tiny pools, and its causeway provides Arkady's surest footing, though his boots are soon soaked.

"Mattis!" he screams, but he is breathless, and his voice doesn't carry. *No, no, no, no*, he chants silently.

Halfway up the bluff, the slope softens, and a kind of footpath emerges. Arkady picks up speed and shouts again. But Mattis either cannot hear him or chooses not to heed. Arkady concentrates on his footing for a few paces, and when he looks ahead again, Mattis is holding the hand of the thin, camouflaged creature, Vasilissa. She walks smoothly, as if she's hovering just above the ground. Strangely, Mattis seems not to be struggling against the rugged terrain, either, but gliding through it. Arkady hears wisps of both their voices.

"Mattis! Wait," Arkady screams. He claws and climbs, gasping for breath and straining against his physical limits. *Oh God, bring the child back. Protect him from this hungry land.*

Tears blur the world, and suddenly, a familiar sensation washes over him: There is someone just behind his right shoulder. He whirls around, and Starostin looms there. His frightening smile reveals a row of gray teeth.

"The boy now belongs with us," Starostin says softly. "His fate is with Vasilissa. She has become part of these crags, of the heights and the inland places. She will protect him. They will be together. The island wants new life. We must be stronger, and peopled, for what lies ahead. You have played a part in it, too."

Starostin puts a hand on Arkady's shoulder and moves him aside. The old Pomor strides faster than any human could up the scree and out of sight. Trembling, Arkady goes after him but far too slowly ever to catch up.

By the time Arkady reaches the top of the escarpment, Mattis is nowhere, and Arkady can barely breathe. A wind much colder than at sea level lifts his hair, and fog is rolling in—strangely fast—from the sea.

"Mattis!" he yells until his voice is hoarse. The boy is not even wearing shoes.

From the bluff, Arkady looks southward along the coast, along his original path to Starostin's izba, and to Mattis. To the north, across several coves and lagoons farther into the fjord, he sees their journey to Advent Bay, their future, already disappearing. Which way did she take him? From his perch on the escarpment, he has a sense of the different stories of his life spinning in a spiral above him: his father carved out of ice; the resin-scented forest and his mother foraging for mushrooms always just ahead and out of reach; Nikolai with his back to him, humming as he looked out the window toward the Laya tributary; Father Ilya, smiling and gesturing toward the perpetual bewilderment of Ivan the Fool; Father Vasily in his twig hut, looking northward even then; Saskia with Mattis still unborn, leaning over him, saving his life. And radiating from these are the paths not chosen, other stories, swirling in eddies out of time: Maaike never climbing the tree; his mother, Oksana, still by his side; Saskia alive. Starostin embracing Natalya, his wife. What is ahead? What, if anything, is truly past?

The exposed bedrock of the mountains tells of the making of the world. Being in this place connects him to epochs of time: centuries of hunting, yes, but also the time before that, of storms and thawing, great migrations of ice bears and reindeer, and ancient secrets still hidden in glaciers that one day will reveal themselves. The wind riffles Arkady's hair and he turns slowly, pivoting on his wooden foot. He chooses a path. He follows two sets of footprints inland.

CHAPTER 49

 rkady walks for more than an hour, following prints that make lighter and lighter impressions in the damp soil of the streambank, as if Vasilissa and Mattis transform into something more ethereal as they go. He screams Mattis' name for as long as he can and wrecks his voice. Later, he learns to yell out at regular intervals timed to the rate he is moving. He follows their tracks all the way to a lake of clear water reflecting jewel green. On the far side is a waterfall, and Arkady calls and waves as he limps toward it, ignoring the pain in his legs. He comes to a field of boulders, and he steps carefully across one and then the next. They are wet with spray, and soon, Arkady's legs slip out from under him, and he slides, faster than an otter, into the glacier-fed lake.

The cold forces his breath out and clamps over him like the lid of the world. He struggles up to the surface and manages to pull himself onto shore.

He tries to reach the waterfall again, and this time makes it one boulder closer before again falling in. After it happens a third time, he pulls himself out and slumps over on his side. He'll die this way. He has no coat and not even the gun to convince Vasilissa to give Mattis back. So, he crawls along the boulders on his hands and knees, like a dog. He moves much more slowly than he thought he could bear. All he can think of is Mattis coming to harm.

Finally, the waterfall is before him, and he gasps as he crawls through its icy white curtain. He holds up his hands, shouting,

"Mattis! Mattis!" but behind the water is sheer rock. He crawls on, and across the boulders on the other side, to solid ground. He is freezing cold now, shivering and limping, his good leg cramping and his half-leg pinched in many places. But he climbs upslope to follow the stream, and at the top of the rise, he faces another lake at the inland end of a cirque, and at its far side, another waterfall. When he passes through it, the same rock wall faces him as before. Above the second lake is a third. Shivering, he realizes he's crawling as much toward his own death as toward Mattis. It takes him some time to decide what to do, and then he turns back toward the izba to gather supplies.

In the following weeks, amid terror and a grief that blurs his vision, Arkady finally becomes a passable hunter. While he searches, he shoots ptarmigan on the bluffs. On the thawing ground, he dresses, roasts, and eats them. He even hunts reindeer and consumes what meat he can before moving on. He works quickly, and as the days grow lighter, he has more and more time to search. He travels many miles inland. He walks in great circles out from the streambed to the north and south. He walks lightly across the roofs of glaciers, listening to the groans of ancient ice under his feet. His inauspicious love for Mattis narrows to a singularity that leaves no room for anything else. So, he walks on his one good leg and often uses two long walking sticks so that he becomes a four-legged creature who can move with more endurance on the land.

He searches and searches, sleeping on the bluffs or in shallow ice caves, covered by wool and hides. He returns to the izba occasionally to warm himself by the stove, but after several weeks outdoors, he is an alien inside, and no chair feels comfortable. When he is outside, searching for Mattis, he perceives with each step the land pushing back against his foot, reaching tendrils up into his sinews and muscle, supporting him. He is no longer separate from the place where he now belongs forever.

Arkady's hair grows into chaotic clumps, and his curly beard catches soil and lichen. He searches and searches through the summer, doggedly following a filament of hope that possesses the tensile strength of spider silk, until all at once, after months of constant motion, on a frosty day with a storm gathering in the north and a deep overcast suffocating what light there is, standing on Starostin's porch, he stops. There is movement in the distance. The Dog materializes out of the gray, running, then loping toward him, then slowing to a walk and finally stopping near the izba. He looks at Arkady and then back over his shoulder. He takes some time to examine the sea horizon and the crags on the other side. He turns, clearing a circle around himself once, twice, and on the third, he settles down, wrapping his tail around his body, and closes his eyes. A frigid gust of wind blows back Arkady's hair and, as quickly as that, the cold and the dark flow into his body; the silk filament snaps, and the north wind's stirring carries it away. He goes into Starostin's cabin and shuts the door behind him once and for all.

CHAPTER 50

attis' absence is a wound worse than the one issued by Starostin's ax. Without the boy's exuberant energy feeding his days, Arkady cannot bear the loneliness. At the same time, grief has ruined him: he can conjure no desire to move forward. He recalls the words of a Greek bishop he once read: *When the two beams of the Cross are joined, I adore the figure. But if the beams are separated, I burn them.*

He locks himself inside with neither enough wood nor meat for winter. He sits on the hearth with the fire iron across his lap. He keeps it there as an anchor; otherwise, his husk would drift up the chimney flue and dissolve in the air. With his mind and his heart dark, Arkady simply moves through time, watching the fire. Sometimes there are footsteps on the porch outside. At first, he leaps up and flings open the door, but no one is ever there, and after a while he does not heed the sound.

He burns the woodpile. Then he burns the porch bench. He burns the kitchen shelves, then Starostin's cupboards, and then one chair. As he eats a thin, scurvy-grass gruel, he hums under his breath: *Give me strength, give me courage, give me sustenance, or give me death. Give me strength, give me courage, give me sustenance or death.* He eats tiny portions of dried meat until halfway through winter when the meat runs out. For weeks, he survives on pickled eggs. Then, he sifts through barrels and baskets in the cellar, gleaning a few threads of dried meat here, a forgotten handful of beans there.

After the lamp oil runs out, he lives by firelight alone. He burns planks from the loft, the ladder, and finally Starostin's table and the remaining chair. Numb and starving, he sits cross-legged, staring at the fire when he still could have been out setting snares for ptarmigan at the foot of the snowy crags. He can find no reason to walk to the beach for more wood, so in the end, he burns his wooden foot, drinks the last of the water in the pail, and lies down on the hearth. *Give me death.* High up in his wooden frame, the Wonderworker averts his gaze.

As Arkady grows leaner, and his grief pours out of him as thick as Saskia's lifeblood, he is not afraid. For the second time in his life, he's starving, and this time he's not even hungry. He looks inward with glazed eyes, and he sees something new. A new feeling enters him. Not physical vigor because his physical form is wasting away. The thoughts that sometimes flit across his mind are that he has been selfish, small-hearted, cruel, and stupid. But the new feeling is a slowly growing clarity. Yes, he's been a fool. And what's done is done. And with that comes an unexpected acceptance of where he's headed, which appears to be that long road first described to him by his grandfather on the shores of the Laya tributary.

I will die, and that's as it should be.

Arkady unfolds the last letter he received from Father Vasily: *I exist in sacred light. I abide in sacred darkness. All around and through me resounds a divine hum—the very engine of life in our world. Up here, on this holy perch, high above the woes of civilization, all truth and folly are made visible. From this bedrock springs all of creation. Join me, novice. Join me in the sacred practices that make this world thrum and kick! Up here, all are nourished, even in deep winter. You will see. Come to me, Arkady. I must share this joy.*

After some time, the door of the izba opens. Arkady is very cold. He'd been sleeping without even a blanket, and his lips, arms, and neck are stiff when he moves. Footsteps approach. Arkady gazes at the ceiling, barely curious: Is it Saskia come back from the dead to save him once again? Mattis? This thought, once it catches hold, inspires him to turn his head. Standing above him is an ogre, its face wrapped in a scarf and a misshapen back looming above. The ogre leans down to look at him and then emits a gravelly roar.

"*Knulla mig! Det är den ryska!*" the ogre says before roaring again: laughter.

Familiar. The figure wrestles a huge backpack off his shoulders. Then, he turns around and goes back outside. Arkady looks at the ceiling, absorbing this turn of events. He hears the ax outside —slow strokes, weak strokes—and then the man returns with a few hacked-up porch planks. He's limping badly. Once he fills and lights the stove, he peels off his mittens and soon unwinds the scarf from his face and pulls off his hat. It is Kol. His face is covered in blood, and he's holding one arm close to his body.

"*En mamma isbjörn.*" He shrugs. An ice bear. Then, extending his shaking arm to make his index finger and thumb into a gun: "*Jag sköt på henne men missade.* I shot at her and missed," he repeats the words in Russian.

Once the stove is warm, Kol heats a can of beans. He pours the food into two cups, eats his first, and then brings the other over to where Arkady lies on the hearth. Kol kneels over Arkady and leans in until he's right above him. Arkady can smell the food, as well as tobacco and blood. He gags. Laughing, Kol dribbles soup onto Arkady's face.

"*Vill du ha den här, du lura?* Aren't you hungry?" Chuckling, he keeps the beans out of Arkady's reach.

Kol limps around the cabin, muttering in Swedish. Arkady has burned the shelves, the cupboards, the ladder to the cellar. Kol stomps back to Arkady.

"Where is the food?" Kol chokes over his own words and coughs, bent over, for a long time. Blood streaks down his neck from under his bandages, and there's more on his right hand, dripping off his sleeve.

Arkady doesn't answer. When Kol's recovered enough from coughing, he kicks Arkady in the ribs. Arkady turns away, facing the stove. Kol paces around the cabin some more and finally sits down against the wall since there are no more chairs and the Swede is too hurt to climb up to the stove bench.

Saskia must have taught him a bit of Russian. The thought of her makes him weirdly happy. Saskia, sitting across from Arkady at the table, both of them preparing reindeer meat. He thinks of her giving birth to Mattis and then crossing over to death. *I could live*, Arkady considers. *For her. But not tonight.*

When he wakes up, his legs are wet. He discovers a pool of blood has flowed from Kol's wounds across the floor to his own body. Arkady's good foot is sticky in his sock, and Kol still sits against the wall with his eyes on the seaward window.

"Kol!" Arkady whispers. "Kol. I could live."

Arkady scoots across the floor. He shakes Kol's thigh. The Swede's head lolls to the side; his eyes meet Arkady's but do not see. He shakes Kol a bit more, but it's clear the Swede has died.

Arkady eats the rest of the beans on the stove. This makes him even hungrier. He has no crutch and no foot, so he crawls across the room. He feeds the rest of Kol's chopped wood to the stove, caressing the plastered bricks fondly.

"Here you are, little mother. You will awaken one more time to warm this sack of bones."

He sits in front of the fire for hours. Finally, in the flickering light, Arkady pulls Kol's body into a prone position. He strips off all of the Swede's clothing and burns it. He washes the blood away and cleans the carcass the best that he can. As he sharpens the reindeer-antler knife that belonged to his grandfather, he gives thanks: *Here it is, here is it. I see how You are working in my life. Now I see: You did not give me strength. You did not give me courage. You did not give me death. But you sent sustenance.*

CHAPTER 51

The energy of the season infuses Arkady's body with each pull of the oar. Not only is the sea quiet today—a rare delight, these undulating curves instead of foam-laced peaks—but also overlapping shades of blue, lavender, and gold besmear the sky. He strokes through the dawn lightening from beneath several layers of wool. A seal pops up and watches him. Other creatures also watch.

He looks over his shoulder to gauge the distance to his destination. From the izba's seaward window, he's been looking out at these jutting rocks for almost seven years. At last, he can reach them. All across the jagged backs of the little islands, a breeze ruffles the feathers of nesting eiders, and their down floats in the air. Eggs again. Not to mix into sacred pigment but for simple food. The ducks are early this year, and he's here for the gleaning. He pulls the oarboat onto the rocks and walks slowly past a group of hauled-out seals, who flare their nostrils.

Arkady spent months of the past dark winter hunting ptarmigan and wondering about the oarboat that he'd last seen at Kol's hut. He brought down Saskia's skis and, by firelight, modified them to accommodate a new foot, which he'd carved in the shape of a boot. He made it to Kol's in six days, nearly half the time it had taken him to walk the same route so long ago. And there was the Pomor oarboat, upside down outside the hut, gray as a boulder blending into the land. He didn't take anything else—why would he? What did he need that he didn't already have?

It took Arkady five days of glorious rowing to return. For once, his legs didn't strain to move him. Muscles loosened that he didn't even know had been overworked. And he'd been lucky with the weather; there'd been nothing more bothersome than a little fog, so he stayed close to shore, and now that the fog has lifted, he stops off at the bird islands.

Arkady fills his pockets with eggs and eiderdown. *You who ignite and snuff out the sun, thank you for this abundance. A creature giving food and warmth is a treasure to keep, a treasure to keep. May the good sun warm the nestlings through the summer, so they may grow strong enough to return next year and multiply.*

He feels the land rise up to meet his prayer. This new feeling comes more and more often. The earth meeting his feet with every step. The stars blessing him with their light.

Tonight, I will fry eggs in seal fat. Tonight, I will look out on my good boat and sprinkle ocean salt on my food, and tomorrow, I'll catch meltwater flowing from the inland glaciers to the sea.

Standing at the crown of the islands' highest outcrop, Arkady turns to the north. He catches a flutter of sound on the wind. The air carries a different aspect. On land, beyond the sentinel rocks, a thin column of smoke crooks into the air. He can smell it. Someone is there.

Pockets bulging, he rows north. His mind is a curious blank as he rounds the sentinel rock headland and passes below Starostin's izba. He hears hammering. Voices. Sounds too loud to be Starostin himself or any of the others he's now accustomed to seeing among the boulders and plains of this place. Just before he'd left on the skis, in pale, predawn light, a group of ancient whalers had filed past the izba. They were faded Basque figments in woolen berets and kerchiefs, carrying their flensing tools, each one looking at the ground in front of him.

These new voices speak Russian. Arkady rows more vigorously, and by the time he sees the sail-furled lodja moored in his own little cove, he is smiling. He pulls up the oarboat, breaking two eggs in the process. He hurries past the place—always bloodied in his memory—where he cleaved his foot. Muttering to himself, Arkady cranes forward on the narrow path, willing his limping form to fly for once instead of stumble. From the rowing—and before that, skiing—Arkady is winded; he is newly awakened from the long night, after all. He pushes upward. At the top of the bluff, he picks up speed and rounds the final bend. There is a group of men at Starostin's izba. One is hammering a new plank into the porch steps. Another repairs the landward window. Two more stand in conversation. The door to the izba is wide open, and Starostin's ax leans against the doorframe.

"Who goes there?" someone shouts.

Arkady moves forward. A veil lifts between these others and himself, and a figure emerges from the group.

"Name yourself! Are you real, or have you sprung from the rocks?" The man moves toward him.

"I am real," croaks Arkady, uncertainly.

And suddenly, the world snaps into focus. The men smell of tobacco and ale. Their clothes are strikingly bright: red cord on their coats, shearling curling at their cuffs; silver beads around their necks, and luminous white fur trim in their caps. Beards of every hue and bright, sea-gazing eyes. Pomors.

"I am Arkady Borisovich Afanasyev. I know you, Evgeny. You brought me north from Solovetsky some years ago. I stole supplies from you at Schoonhoven, and I am sorry for it."

Evgeny leans down and narrows his eyes. "It can't be." The Pomor searches Arkady's face. He scans Arkady's ravaged and healed body. He sees a wooden boot instead of a foot. "What was the name of the Pomor killed at Schoonhoven while you were there?"

"Vitka. May he follow the long road to a peaceful waypoint."

"Starostin's great balls!" Evgeny roars. "You are Arkady! Kuzma! Kuzma! Did you hear this? That little priest is alive. Just look at him, though. Come here!"

And out of the izba runs Kuzma, as great as a giant. Arkady sucks in his breath. He sees Mattis grown into a man.

"Kuzma convinced me to come up here," Evgeny says, gripping Arkady by the shoulders. "We came from Arkhangelsk on the first southerlies, but we planned to stay in Schoonhoven to hunt the camps around there. But Kuzma drove me mad with his plans to visit Starostin's hut. He said there was a message that we must come. A message!" Evgeny roared. "As if someone delivers the mail in Spitsbergen! But in the end, even I couldn't ignore his prattling. We all love Starostin, don't we?"

And the Pomors all shouted that they did.

"He's not here anymore," Arkady says. "Starostin. He's left his Cross."

Evgeny's eyes stay on Arkady's while the other Pomors look toward the Cross. "So, it's been that kind of place for you. By God, Arkady. We all thought you'd died long ago."

"Come inside, come inside," whispers Kuzma, tugging Arkady's sleeve. "We see you burned everything that was his."

"Only to stay alive," Arkady says.

"We're building a new table," Kuzma continues. "We brought supplies for the cellar. Meat. Food. Rye. Honey. We do it every five years or so, in his honor. We fixed his rifle. It's good that you have another."

"I don't use it," Arkady says. "She isn't here, you know," he says softly to Kuzma alone. "She was, but she isn't here anymore."

"Saskia?" Kuzma whispers. He draws Arkady to the side, away from Evgeny, who wanders back to continue his work.

"She saved my life."

"Yes, I am looking for her. I don't know how many more times we'll sail up this coast; the hunting is bad."

"You won't find her."

"She is gone back to the Sisters?"

"She is dead."

"Are you sure?"

Arkady hesitates. "As sure as I can be of anything in this place."

Kuzma nods. "Either she is dead, or she went back to Wijde Fjord. It's all the same. Perhaps she'll be back someday. Maybe when I'm an old, old man." The Pomor chuckles and stares at the inland crags. "She'll burst into my cabin with her braids flying." He turns his pale eyes to Arkady. "And you?"

"I am alive."

"Are you wanting to go back to the mainland, then?"

"No."

The Pomors give him tea and stew. They prepare venison from the mainland that tastes of juniper berries. Arkady sits on a newly built bench and watches as the men go about their work repairing the izba. Sated and bewildered by the admiring way that Evgeny and the others now regard him, Arkady feels less at home in the izba than at any other time. As the Pomors fix the house, they erase the scars and the many dissolutions and renewals he has endured here. By evening, he is outside, staring at the lodja.

Makers of these heights, wanderers of these cliffs, see me now as I return to my original purpose. I am not the same man I was. Now, I am of lichen and stone. I see the land's many hearts. I've emptied myself of stories so I may know countless more. I will move deeper into Spitsbergen. The wide, open spaces will not frighten me. Take me to Magdalene Fjord at last.

CHAPTER 52

The ship turns east into the fjord after a smooth, foggy voyage up the coast. As they sail the gently narrowing finger of sea, the fog lifts, and the water turns from black to gray to fish-scale silver and finally brightens to green. Protected by the shoulders of mountains, this fjord, if not placid, maintains a hush. A glacier stoppers one end, and the adjacent bay, where the lodja moors, is round as a bowl. Tiny black-and-white seabirds fly together at great heights from one rocky colony to the next. They are little auks, Saskia's favorite bird. She told Arkady all about them during the winter they spent together in the izba, and he'd seen small colonies before. But there are thousands here, and the minerals from their droppings have cultivated brilliant-green patches of moss and lichen on the slopes below.

Jutting out from the beach is a low, rounded bolus of land covered in small cairns. Back behind that, just above the beach and built into the leeward side of a great boulder, Father Vasily's hut is almost completely camouflaged. But by this time, Arkady's eye is sharp and especially attuned to the distinct angles of a human-made thing. Unlike the howling wind and high bluffs of Starostin's place, this bay is a quiet haven set back from the outer coast.

Arkady takes the first oarboat to shore and walks across the pebble and quartz beach. He passes by the rusty outlines of two ancient oil-rendering stoves. He looks up and down the shoreline and then into the heights. No shadowy figures show themselves. No hunched and mossy creatures sit atop the boulders. Arkady smiles. Give them time.

Among the cairns, Arkady encounters the ancient graves of whalers and generations of Pomors. Each year's cycles of freezing and thaw have buckled the ground and spit up what is meant in most places to lie covered for eternity. Arkady steps over lichen-patched skulls still wearing ragged knit caps, and, in one place, three coffins lie at the surface of the earth, open to the elements with their skeletons exposed: two short, and one very tall. Sunlight sparkles across the bay; he feels at ease here among the bones. After traversing the beach like a hermit crab seeking a new shell, Arkady walks up to Father Vasily's cabin.

Nothing stirs inside the dim room. Along one wall are shelves from floor to ceiling filled with jars of pickled eider eggs. Like Starostin's, this cabin has a good, sturdy stove and stove bench, and wood stacked high. By the window overlooking the bay is a table and chair. On the table is a folded paper covered in familiar, spidery handwriting.

The Divine Light called me away. Its music is as clear as a monastery bell. No human has ever ventured this close to God, and I can almost see him from the top of the glacier. Even here in this bay, the voices from the graves obscure the light. Their stories blur that which is truly pure. I must go on, northward toward the creation of the world. Toward light that has not touched a soul, a heart, a story.

"That is not my path," Arkady says aloud. *I belong here.*

Arkady glances across the room. Up on the stove bench, there is a shape under the covers. Could Father Vasily be sleeping there? The brightness of the day and the warm feeling he already has for this place stops any fear from arising. Simply curious, he goes up a few rungs of the ladder to the bench. He nudges the shape gently and then more firmly. He turns back the blankets and finds not a man but a huge, folded animal hide tied carefully with leather cord. Thinking of Saskia, he strokes the coarse, transparent guard hairs of an ice-bear pelt.

He pulls the bundle down to the cabin floor and unties the bindings. He lifts up a sewn garment, and his grandfather Nikolai suddenly turns toward him, his pipe, walrus ivory carved in the shape of a fist, between his lips. Arkady's a boy again, seeing these famous trousers for the first time.

Arkady puts on the trousers and walks back outside. The Pomors stop what they're doing.

He looks inland, toward the great ice fields and an old, deep cavern hidden under the ice, where Maaike's oak tree holds up an iron nail. Somewhere to the south, Vasilissa and Mattis walk hand-in-hand, and Starostin watches over them. From high up on the scree, little auks scream and fly in a tight flock over the bay, startled by a great black creature running downslope. The Dog dances across the rocks and tundra. He comes at Arkady. The Pomors shout and gesture to warn him, but Arkady raises an arm to silence them. The Dog slows to a trot and then walks. He comes close enough for Arkady to see his tattered ear. The Dog nudges Arkady's hand with his nose, tongue lolling, and then continues on his eternal way. The Pomors raise a cheer.

Eventually, the Pomors leave, and Arkady lives on in Magdalene Fjord. He finds his grandfather's bones and rebuilds the cairn over them and restores other, older graves. The Dog's ancestors chase each other around the earth and through one season after the next. Years pass, and a lodja appears. He buries Evgeny, and years later, Kuzma. This is the Pomor burial ground, and he stewards it until the time of the Pomors passes.

His skin turns the same color as weatherbeaten wood, and bright moss weaves through his hair. He hears the whispered secrets of the glaciers and the groans of shifting bedrock. The ocean gyre bathes the coast and brings shoals of salmon and, with them, seals, walrus, and whales of many kinds. Over the decades, new stories drift across the horizon: Men in metal ships pass the entrance of the fjord; dark clouds blown from southern factories arrive on the winds, and soon after that, the prospectors themselves appear, picking at the rock for coal, gold, and marble. The Dog's army rises up to guard the land and then subsides for a time, like the tide, and the cycle continues in a great spiral. Across the years, ice bears pace from the northern pack ice to the southern cape and back again, while the wind carries little auks and eiders and all of our stories across the world.

ABOUT THE AUTHOR

Stacy Carlson is a novelist, naturalist, and educator. *Publishers Weekly* called her debut novel, *Among the Wonderful*, "Intelligent, engrossing, and utterly unique." Stacy's essays and fiction have appeared in *Tin House*, *Post Road*, *Inkwell,* and elsewhere, and she has received fellowships and residencies from the Mesa Refuge, The Arctic Circle, Djerassi Resident Artists Program, and Signal Fire. Her background includes work as a historical ecologist, fish cannery worker, hot springs caretaker, and hiking guide in Big Sur. She grew up between mountains and sea in the Pacific Northwest and has lived in New England, New York, Northern California, and the Upper Midwest.

AUTHOR THANKS

For inspiration, friendship, and feedback, I thank L. J. Moore, Zhanara Nauruzbayeva, Cedra Wood, and Paul Corman-Roberts. Special thanks to Oron Frenkel for walking me through the mechanics of near-fatal flesh wounds and to the late Kirill Ershov, who selected the Russian curses. To Kate Garrick, Toni Gentilli, and Elena Mills, thank you for the early support. For generously offering advance praise, eternal thanks to Lynn Coady, Kathryn Nuernberger, Joan Frank, and Colin Dickey.

The Arctic Circle residency offered a singular opportunity to visit Svalbard/Spitsbergen, and for that I send heartfelt gratitude to Aaron O'Connor; Arctic guides Theres Arulf, Sarah Gerats, and Åshild Rye; the captain and crew of the tallship *Antigua*; and the other artists aboard. Thanks also to the Djerassi Resident Artists Program and Signal Fire for two incredible opportunities to engage with wild places, creative practice, and communities of artists.

Thank you, Leah Angstman and Alternating Current Press, for believing in this book during a tumultuous time for independent publishing and the arts. To my parents, Stanley and Susan Carlson, I am profoundly grateful for a literary upbringing, our island cabin, and the freedom as a child to meander deep into the woods, getting lost and finding myself again and again in wild nature. To the love of my life, Jason, and our fierce daughter, Djuna: Your curiosity, bright imaginations, thought experiments, and adventurous spirits mean everything to me. Thank you for supporting my life as a writer.

COLOPHON

The edition you are holding is the First Edition of this publication.

The cursive cover font is set in Amarila, created by Balpirick Studio. The block font is set in Viper Nora, created by Popdog Fonts. The italic serif font is set in Amperzand, created by A. J. Paglia. The Alternating Current Press logo is set in Portmanteau, created by JLH Fonts. Headers and footers are set in Avenir Book, created by Adrian Frutiger in collaboration with Monotype Type director Akira Kobayashi. The drop capitals are set in Morris Jenson Initialen, created by Typo-Graf, and based on William Morris' famous initial letters of his Kelmscott Press, c. 1890s. All other text is set in Crimson Text, created by Sebastian Kosch. All fonts used with permission and full commercial license; all rights reserved.

The cover jacket was designed by Leah Angstman, with photography by Petra Pezibear. The Alternating Current lightbulb logo was created by Leah Angstman, © 2013, 2026 Alternating Current Press. The interior chapter headers were created by Gordon Dylan Johnson. Some artwork is governed under a Pixabay Content License. Author photo by Djuna Swecker. All images used with permission and full commercial license; all rights reserved.

Other Works from

ALTERNATING CURRENT PRESS

All of these books (and more) are available at the
Alternating Current Press website: altcurrentpress.com.

altcurrentpress.com